THE
SYMPHONY
HEIST

A TALE OF MUSIC
AND DESIRE

KAMEEL NASR

CURIOSITY
BOOKS

This book is fiction. The author tried hard not to represent real people. If any characters do resemble real people, it is pure coincidence. Orchestras and police departments may not function as depicted here. The musical opinions herein may differ from the opinions of the less enlightened.

ISBN 978-0-9961753-7-1

Nasr, Kameel
The Symphony Heist: A Tale of Music and Desire

Fiction. 1. Mystery--Cozy
Fiction. 2. Boston
Fiction. 3. Music—Classical
Fiction. 4. Music—Orchestral

Library of Congress Control Number: 2016903498

Printed in the United States of America

Curiosity Books is the imprint of the Curiosity Foundation which promotes tolerance, sustainability, and the arts. All proceeds from book sales go directly to the Curiosity Foundation. For more information visit

www.curiosityfoundation.com

It is cruel, you know, that music should be so beautiful. It has the beauty of loneliness of pain: of strength and freedom. The beauty of disappointment and never-satisfied love. The cruel beauty of nature and everlasting beauty of monotony.

Benjamin Britten

Counterpoint: Two or three melodies combined to create harmonies of thirds, fifths, and octaves. It is the most mathematical form of composing, common in early music.

Prelude

Twenty-two minutes before the heist, a lone woman waits in a stolen blue Toyota in front of the National Braille Press. Her two accomplices take their positions on St. Stephen Street.

Two Boston blocks away, a man in a black parka stands near the Christian Science Mother Church across from Symphony Hall. Two Peter Pan busses are parked outside its Mass. Ave. entrance, ready to take the musicians to Logan Airport for a concert in Rio de Janeiro.

Another two blocks away, forming an equilateral triangle with the Toyota, the Boston Symphony Orchestra principal cellist locks her apartment and walks down Westland Street, her white fiberglass cello case strapped to her back.

On this quiet Sunday morning in January, when the air should be still and empty, everything sounds staccato to her. A car accelerates sharply and brakes. A lone robin chirps up the scale and stops. A dog barks in short yelps.

She feels music like other people feel hot or cold. Her perfect pitch transposes every sound into notes. She converts people's voices into musical rhythms. She knows by resonance when the wind shifts directions. All she needs is a couple of bars, and she pins the composition. Long before she developed her revolutionary bowing and fingering technique, she could listen to a new piece of music and then go home and play it, as the fourteen-year-old Mozart had done when he had heard Allegri's *Miserere* in the Sistine Chapel, a work that was forbidden to be played outside the Chapel.

She pauses at the corner of Mass. Ave., where two dozen protesters are holding a banner that reads, "DON'T GO BSO." She inches up to them, her face covered against the cold—or so she thinks.

One month ago, the BSO shocked the musical world by announcing that the Rio concert would be connected to the signing of the Advancement of the Arts Agreement, an international treaty for copyright, royalties, and subsidies, an agreement she and almost all musicians had protested against, but it got rammed through Congress after mountains of campaign donations from Internet providers. Now the BSO will give it legitimacy.

She has to play for the signing of a treaty she had campaigned against. Conflict of interest—the interests of corporations versus artists. Guess who won?

"Melody Cavatina!" one of the protesters calls out to her in the high register of childish surprise.

How embarrassing. She recognizes the voice from when she helped with a banner drop on a Storrow Drive overpass.

"You want a royalty clearing house run by the entertainment giants?" he says.

So much for being incognito. What can she say? Your heart's in the right place, or some other banality?

She closes her eyes.

The protesters are from For Art's Sake (FAS), the coalition against the Advancement of the Arts Agreement. The government has a remarkable way with words, screwing artists and musicians and calling it advancement.

A woman from the middle of the protesters steps forward. "Mel has to play."

Tasa's mezzo voice, come to the rescue.

"She's doing something special for all of us," Tasa says. The guy backs off.

Tasa comes up to Mel, and the two women hug through their insulated coats.

"Go," Tasa says. "Look straight at the audience and play with your eyes wide open."

Mel isn't just going to play. She's the main act, sitting in front of the orchestra, her Carletti between her legs, playing before presidents and CEOs, the world watching. Even though she is principal of the country's leading orchestra, this will be her first ever solo, and all the musicians know that she's going to blow it, as she has blown every concert for the last six weeks.

The protesters start chanting couplets rhyming with BSO.

"Ho-ho, just say no!"

"Oh no, stop the show!"

The cold air keeps their chanting voices near the ground.

Although the protesters lost their cause, Mel hears the meter of their chant—long, long, short-short-short—as an up-beat cadence of victory. "Mambo Number Five" starts playing in her head: one, two, three-four-five.

Concentrate. The fingering.

Two hundred and thirty-two treacherous bars. The most difficult parts are totally exposed. She's going to blow it big time.

She turns to the sound of the busses idling. Musicians are converging one by one, their boots hitting the subway steps as they climb, car doors opening and closing as spouses drop them off. Those who live nearby sound a crisp rhythm as they walk toward the busses, heads down against the cold, or perhaps against the agreement they're helping to establish.

Walter, the BSO general manager, stands on the sidewalk looking at his watch, his middle-age baritone shouting out minutes like finishing times in a road race.

The assistant principal cellist also sees through Mel's scarf and says good morning, another staccato but very upbeat, a wide smile, anticipating another chance at the principal chair.

"I see you're nervous."

Melody hears the rising tones of joy and revenge.

When anyone screws up in an orchestra, others keep looking at their score—only the maestro corrects—but Mel's playing became so atrocious that people turned and stared open-mouthed at the offending sound coming from her cello. She is principal, in charge of the entire cello section for an orchestra whose patrons have a lengthy reputation of severity. Half the audience walked out on the premier of Brahms's *Third Symphony*.

The BSO gave her a warning. She is still in the orchestra's one-year probation period. Walter sat her down in his office and told her directly, "Pull yourself together, or you'll be fired." Walter, an imposing man who walks as if marching to a John Phillip Souza refrain, almost cried in front of her. Once darling of music directors and audiences, now she faces an abrupt end to her short, fiery career.

Walter pleaded, prodded, pried her for an explanation.

Stumm. Nobody there.

Most musicians feel sorry for her because they heard the power and beauty that made the entire cello section lush, but no one can help a broken musician except the musician herself.

Instead of checking in with Walter and going to the busses, Melody walks around to the loading area behind Symphony Hall, where crates of instruments are being packed onto a silver, thirty-foot truck. The other musicians turned in their instruments after last night's concert, but Milton, the BSO transport officer, allowed Mel one last night to psych up for what he called "the mother-in-law of all solos."

Milton is waiting for her inside the loading door, his hands on a hydraulic jack. The transport officer is a bear of a man with a full brown beard. He wears a rounded leather hat and a plaid wool jacket that makes him look like a cross between a 1920s race car driver and a lumberjack. He is a burly-faced guy, the type Melody sees sleeping in vacant doorways or in church when she gazes at the stained glass.

"Walter gave me one chance," she says. "I have to play this solo like the world depends on it."

"It does depend on it."

She takes two truncated steps forward and hangs her head. The BSO made her trim her bangs so they no longer cover her eyes, making her feel even more exposed.

Milton stands right in front of her, looking up from a bent position to catch her eye. "Once you're on stage in front of the orchestra, lights on you, and the audience falls silent, you'll be transposed into a goddess bestowing wonders on the multitude. You'll be great."

She appreciates Milton's words, but his constrained pitch, which rises up and down two or three half-tones, expresses trepidation.

The loading area is empty except for a large black crate in the middle stenciled with the BSO logo and marked "Cellos." The truck driver and his partner sit on a cement stoop in the back of the room waiting for Milton to finish loading the crates.

Melody unstraps her cello and hands it to him.

"My beautiful Carletti," he says, his red face animated, his voice filling the concrete room.

He opens the case and lifts out her cello.

"Start by tenderly putting your fingers around her neck," which he does. "Caress her shoulders," which he does. "Smooth her curves with the soft of your right palm," which he does. "Listen to her whine and blush. But if you take her by the hips." He grabs the Carletti. "She squeaks and squawks like a French Horn."

Mel jumps back. He almost made her smile.

Milton loves music, feels it in his chest, and he loves instruments. He's a *quark*. That's what Mel calls oddballs who relate to the world through sound. Less than half of the orchestra members are quarks, according to her. Some talented soloists aren't quarks, while others who can't even read music are.

Milton's face becomes as pensive as a Mahler slow movement. "Some people never get beyond the first movement of their lives," he says, putting his free hand on her arm. "They keep everything superficial, afraid to delve into the melancholy of the adagio. But you've been trapped by it. Break free with all your might, Mel, and you'll find your life's allegro."

"I'm going to do it!" She shakes her fingers to loosen them. "I've got to do it!" She breaks down in tears.

He takes the cello in both hands and digs into chest voice. "When you nest this Carletti between your legs and stoke her strings, up bow and down bow, you speak to me, dance with me. You tell me about myself. And then it all makes sense. Everything makes sense."

His speech generates a two-second silence between them.

"Mel, can you feel what your playing does to people? You're the type who plays from feeling. Whether the feeling is anger or fear, get in touch with it. Straighten your spine, and let it roar out of you."

She yanks her shoulders and stands Alexander Technique erect. She had even neglected posture.

"Handling your Carletti gets me all excited," he says, putting it back into its case. "When you let me oil her, I rub her belly delicately, then faster and faster until she vibrates through her f-holes." He winks at her. "Then I rosin up her bow hair."

She can't resist a smile, the first smile in two months. She adores this man. If she can't clear away the fear, she has to use it.

She hears the heat blower turn on, looks at the drivers listening from the back of the room, and lowers her voice. "I'll be alone in front of everyone."

Milton's voice turns *grave*. "You have a great future, so fresh and full of heart. You know how thin the thread is. You go there and give them hell."

Walter arrives and steps inside the loading door. Milton disses him with a tight jaw.

"Are you sure you haven't left anything out?" Walter asks.

Milton raises his gloved hands in front of Walter's chest. "Take a breath, Capo. You've been a bigger pain in the ass than a conceited soloist. What will the orchestra play next? Sonata for Coca Cola? Fanfare for Citi Corp?"

She hears Walter's voice shift to minor. "Put yourself in my shoes. I have those protesters on one side, the government on the other, and big donors all over the place. I've had fist-fights in front of the building, and even members of the orchestra scuffled."

"You caved in for money."

"No I did not," Walter says, returning to major, his hand raised as if taking an oath. "I never bent a knee for a cent. I will never give in to anyone's threats."

"Horseshit," Milton says. "Guys like you never change. You just get older and more hazardous."

Milton packs Mel's cello in the big crate. He raises his head as pianists do before pounding a declarative theme. "You're on dangerous territory, having a stranger handle my instruments. A bass has slumped shoulders, and a violin is flat-chested, able to deflect the punches of a brutal world, but a cello is all woman, delicate and sensitive. If you disrespect her by making her play for money, she'll turn melancholy, and she'll speak only in laments and requiems."

Walter checks his watch and snaps his fingers at the truck drivers. "It's six fifty-five. Let's get going."

Melody leaves for the busses, her boots hitting cold concrete in a mournful cadence, the door hinge creaking behind her, rising in pitch from middle G to high B-flat. Beyond the streets and buildings, a silent, vacant city, the slow roll of a kettle drum in the sky, sounding both the glory of the winter sun and the shiver of its cold.

The maestro's brother is waiting for her on the sidewalk. The hijackers on St. Stephen Street are waiting for their signal.

By the time Jules climbs into the red cab of his thirty-foot truck, a thin layer of ice has formed on his coffee under its plastic cover. He had set it on the dash while he and his partner waited in the back of the loading room. During those forty minutes, it formed a cone-shaped fog on his front windshield as it condensed from steam to miniature ice crystals without passing through liquid.

Jules is a dignified, churchgoing man, ebony black, who wears a charcoal suit too large for his fragile frame, a tie hanging loosely around the neck of his white shirt. He plans to drop off his Symphony Hall load at the cargo terminal, then hurry back and stand among the deacons in the front rows of the Roxbury Pillar of Fire Church shouting, "Amen!"

Milton hands him a shipping document through the open door.

"The BSO shouldn't go," Milton says. "Right is right. It's money that we have too much of."

"Their music does not speak to people anymore," Jules says, as if quoting scripture—or Fox News—his back straight, his first two fingers raised like an icon of Jesus exhorting piety. "A free market of entertainment."

"For the people here, music is not entertainment."

Jules' partner, Weber, climbs into the passenger side and puts his hands in his pockets, elbows and knees sticking out, eyelids uncomfortable with early Sunday morning.

"You know what a cello does to a woman's left tit?" Milton says. "It props it up and hardens the bottom where the cello sits, and eventually she walks around with a high left tit. Very provocative."

"I'll be praying for you when I get to church."

"You know why fundamentalists aren't allowed to have sex standing up?" Milton asks. "It might lead to dancing."

Jules tosses the shipping document next to his coffee and starts the engine.

Milton walks to St. Stephen Street and waves flamboyantly at the protesters. He turns and salutes Jules, who returns the gesture with an outstretched arm like a preacher giving a benediction. Jules looks to the right up the empty one-way street, blinded by the rising orange sun that is turning windows of tall buildings aglow.

Jules turns left. Within a block, they are surrounded by Northeastern University student housing, brick and brownstone residences, sturdy, denuded maples and elms along the sidewalk. He passes Symphony Road, stops at the flashing light on Gainsborough Street, and shifts into first.

"I like that," Jules says. "Music is not entertainment. What is it then?"

"He was talking about that dead music they play. Rich, old white men listening with their fingers on their chins. What do you think it would take to get them dancing in the aisles?" Weber guffaws at his own wit. "They'd have to rise up out of their walkers first."

Jules lets out the clutch.

"Isn't it amazing that white people think they

invented everything?" Weber says. "But even with eighty people sitting on a stage playing million-dollar instruments, they still can't make a beat, while some wild dude in the middle of the jungle bangs a zebra skin and has people moving."

Jules is concentrating on an old white Ford station wagon with faded plastic wood double-parked on one side of the street ahead, a blue Toyota double-parked on the opposite side.

"Look at how these kids park," he says tapping the steering wheel and pointing at the Ford sitting in front of the National Braille Press. There's barely room to squeeze through. Two bundled-up people are walking on opposite sides of the street. Jules maneuvers the truck around the Ford at five miles an hour, then swerves the other way around the Toyota. Halfway into the turn, the Toyota lurches forward. Jules jams his brakes, jolting the truck.

The two pedestrians rush the sides of the truck, their faces hidden by black ski masks. Each yanks open a door of the cab and points his gun at the men inside. Jules and Weber throw up their hands, even though the gunmen don't say anything.

"Easy," Jules says. "We don't want no trouble."

From each open door, a gloved hand reaches inside, unhooks a seat belt, and pulls a stunned man from the cab. Holding them from behind, the masked men force their hostages to each side of the Toyota. The woman sitting behind the wheel gets out and hops into the truck's driver's seat.

The gunmen snap plastic handcuffs onto their prisoners and silence their mouths with duct tape. Then they push them into the back seat of the Toyota.

The robbers leap into the front seat, and the driver moves the Toyota to the side, allowing the truck to pass.

The woman drives briskly, turning out of the

residential neighborhood, then out past the buildings of Northeastern University. The Toyota follows, its side windows hazed to look frosty.

Two blocks later, the truck makes a left turn while the Toyota continues past the Museum of Fine Arts and the Harvard School of Public Health. They pass Brookline Village and the reservoir in Chestnut Hill, turning right into an empty lot behind a train station and coming to a stop.

The robbers stuff paper bags over their captives' heads and shuffle them out onto the ground.

"Sit still for five minutes and contemplate how lucky you are," the masked driver says. It is the only phrase the robbers speak before driving off into the deserted suburban streets.

The bound men sit on the sidewalk ready to obey the driver's orders, but after a long minute, Jules shakes his head as if rousing himself from a trance. He gets on his knees and uses Weber's body to slide the paper bag off his head. Then he puts his face next to his partner's hands so Weber can take off the tape. As soon as Jules' mouth has voice, he begins shouting.

"Help, police!"

A second floor window opens, and a man with a shaved head wearing an orange terrycloth bathrobe looks out.

"What's the hassle?"

"Call the cops," Jules yells.

"Why? What happened?"

"Just call them," Jules pleads on his knees. "They got everything."

Other neighbors look out.

"Why are you in handcuffs?" the shaved head asks.

"Jesus," Jules says, but he isn't praying. "Just call the police. They robbed the BSO."

"The what?"

"The sym-pho-ny," he enunciates as if to a child. "They got all their instruments. That girl Melody ain't going to have nothing between her legs."

Romantic: A musical period from about 1820 to 1900 charac-
terized by emotion and individualism. This era, which pro-
duced more difficult music for performers, developed bigger
orchestras, a conductor, and a reliance on chromaticism.

Overture

Seventy-seven minutes before the discovery of the first body, Melody clears security.

It takes the eighty-two musicians twenty minutes to pass through the Terminal E scanners at Logan. From the ceiling speakers, Melody hears Massenet's "Meditations" played with intense melancholy on a blues harmonica. The din of background noise flips from middle A to B-flat. She hears a cash register beeping as they pass Starbucks, the solitary concession open early Sunday morning.

Concentrate on the solo.

Walter, walking as straight as a drum major, leads the musicians down the bare terminal to gate E2, where a charter awaits them.

Melody is trying to remember which of the three traumas happened first—receiving the score for the concerto she is to premiere in Rio, the BSO's announcement that put it on the side of the arts agreement, or when the sheriff arrived and told her point blank that her accusation against her father was wrong. She, who senses honesty by pitch, stress, and juncture, expended a decade of erroneous, hurtful blame.

Eduardo handed her the score. He had discovered her, gave her the name "Melody Cavatina," and then became her lover. She stared at the first page. Her head banged with dissonance. "Is this for cello?" One section had three-note cords. Cellists can bow two notes on adjacent strings, but what he wrote was impossible to finger. Thereafter, her hands tumbled and mumbled and refused to be tamed, and she bowed as if her biceps were in spasm. The more she tried to control them, the worse they got. She dislodged her muscle memory.

Her first time alone in front of the orchestra, the audience full of people who travel in entourages.

"You want to humiliate me," she said to Eduardo. "You built me up only to throw me down when I'm vulnerable. I never want to see you again."

Her friend China brings her back to the present. She takes Melody by the arm, as buddies do, and charges her down the terminal to the head of the group, her shoulder bouncing off Mel's.

"Walk up front. From now on, this is where you belong."

"I'm concentrating on the solo."

"Yeah, concentrating like your eyeballs aren't bulging out your head. You won't talk to Eduardo—won't talk to anyone. And, oh yeah, you've been playing like a dunce. You're totally distracted."

China speaks as swiftly as a Rossini scherzo. She's a quark.

Melody is, in fact, concentrating on the solo, finally, eleventh hour. She awoke fired up, running lines of the concerto in her head. All morning she's been picking off sounds and relating them to her solo. She heard the beauty in Eduardo's writing, a melody that never leaves your head. She was his melody. That's what he named her.

"Last night I started asking, what's that piece all about?" Mel says. "My life? The pain of shyness?" They continue walking. "I have to keep running the score until I get its meaning. That's what I've been missing, the meaning coming out of me."

Mel had focused on the mechanics, the quick runs and difficult passages, which includes playing disparate melodies simultaneously on adjacent strings while plucking bass notes with the same hand as she's fingering the two melodic lines. They don't teach that in conservatory. The orchestra would be silent during those frenzied bars. She would either sound amazing or atrocious. But only now has she started to understand the piece, and she can't express unless she understands any more than she can give directions to a place she doesn't know.

Milton is right, she thinks. *Quarks play by projection, not technique.*

She will engage the score more on the flight.

Melody whispers to China as quietly as a Chopin nocturne so Walter won't hear. "When I walk out on stage, before Borges raises his baton, I'm going to make a special announcement. Then I'll play my heart out."

"Are you kidding?"

"I got it. Last night. It all fit together. I'm going to ace it, not because it's curtains for me if I don't but because I'm playing for someone special."

"Who?"

"I've never played for anyone before. All I ever did was play alone and then play for the BSO."

"I never heard you like this." China says, "What's going on?"

Yes, that's it. China's brisk soprano voice pegs the four essential notes Eduardo uses. *Slow-slow, quick-quick.*

For the past month, the music in Mel's head bounced between Henryk Gorecki's *Symphony No. 3* and the *Cantus in Memory of Benjamin Britten* by Arvo Part, the two saddest pieces ever composed, which isn't the best way to psych up for her first solo. She has to jettison that diminished seventh blue note still haunting her and restore C-major. Right away.

"What's going on?" China repeats in a faster tempo. "You usually avoid exaggerated drama."

"Trust me, China."

Walter's phone rings. To Melody, it sounds like a fire alarm. Walking next to Walter, she overhears the voice of Louis, the big boss, and the way Louis says the general manager's name stops him mid-stride.

"The flight attendants are gesturing at me to board," Walter says into his phone.

"Wait," comes Louis's voice.

Everyone stops behind Walter, expectant, staring at him.

"The baggage truck has been compromised."

Walter stands transfixed.

"Hello?"

"Did you say 'compromise'?"

Melody holds her breath, leaning toward him.

"Compromised."

"Compromised?"

"Hijacked."

Walter raises his head above everyone. Mel doesn't hear his words. She hears an AH-AH-AH scream followed by a piercing shrill unleashed by several female musicians.

"I've been playing my violin for twenty years," one person cries out.

"Thirty," says the principal flutist.

"Forty," proclaims a cellist.

"My parents bought my viola when I auditioned at Eastman," an Asian woman says. "I've been playing it every day—three, four, six hours a day."

Musicians drop into seats and cradle their heads. Others pace.

After six minutes of anguished cries, Walter marches to

the dark carpeted center of the seating area and raises his shoulders. Everyone gathers around him. As soon as he begins speaking, the musicians fall silent.

"The police commissioner is mobilizing his crack team. Louis assured me that they will blanket the city with police and resolve this quickly. Let's not despair. Let's get the facts."

He is about to step aside when someone shrieks, "Our instruments!"

"They don't stand a chance of resolving this soon," another cries out.

Walter assumes his Teutonic stance, his eyes fixed, his large forehead creased, strands of brown hair combed straight back, the only man wearing a suit. "No one can do anything with the instruments. You know that. Imagine someone trying to sell Raphael's trumpet or Richard's viola, let alone the others. Whoever the robbers are, they will want to settle."

"Our instruments mean nothing to those FAS militants," a violist says.

"They know what they're doing," Walter declares. "They know they have to get the instruments back to us. We have money for a ransom."

"They don't want a ransom," another voice says. "They're saving the world with their righteousness. They'll smash our instruments to call attention to their cause."

"Corporations pushed this phony arts agreement through to swindle artists and musicians," a female violinist yells. "We helped them by agreeing to this concert. We got what we deserved."

"We have no time buffer," says a male violinist who often sits at the end of the second violin section near Mel's principal chair. "If they keep our instruments until tomorrow, it will be too late to play the ceremony."

"What do we do?" a percussionist asks.

All eyes turn to Walter.

"We won't go anywhere without our instruments." He

turns to the flight attendants. "Cancel."

Someone points to Tito the bassist. "Are you satisfied? Are you happy at what FAS did to us?"

"You're blaming the wrong people," Tito says. "Blame EMI and Time Warner for trying to shaft us."

Many agree.

"We all felt uneasy about this trip!" one shouts. "Most of us support FAS. We shouldn't have allowed the good name of the BSO on this."

"Let's wait for the police," Walter says, his ample voice spreading across the terminal.

The orchestra members fall silent again.

"They're sending their finest inspector. A man named Lowell."

Melody sees the Czechoslovakian violinist, his face puffed red, push his way in front of Walter. He is to solo the *Fantasia de Movimentos Mistos* for violin and orchestra by the Brazilian composer Villa Lobos, who was a cellist himself.

"My Strad belongs to loving and trusting patron," the Czech says. "What I supposed to do, call him and tell him I lose it?"

"I'm sorry."

Mel sees Walter's mouth trying to wrap around his name.

"We're all in this—"

"You know what my Strad worth?" the Czech says in the atonal discord of the 1960s. "Do you? You have any idea?"

He is a stout, disheveled man with short, fleshy fingers. Melody is amazed how he slides them up and down the Stradivarius's tight fingerboard—not a clean musician but a powerfully expressive one.

"The police are working for us—"

"You can't bargain with these people. My Strad is lost."

Walter tries to calm him with soothing arm gestures, but in simple time, the Czech puts his hand on his hip, grunts, and stalks off to the far side of the terminal.

Melody sees Maestro Borges having a mini fit in the corner, his big plan lost, but nobody can be as upset as Mel. She hardly thinks about her Carletti or the arts agreement. She understands immediately the consequences of not being able to play her solo. She knows she'll be fired if she doesn't play brilliantly and make up for her recent disasters. She didn't imagine that she would be denied the chance to play at all, which would end her career just as swiftly. But even her career is secondary.

"We have to go," she mutters to China. "I have to play for someone."

Lieutenant Lowell's bedside phone startles him awake at 8:08 a.m. Lowell is lying on his back in plaid flannel pajamas half-listening to a Rimsky-Korsakov *Chastushka* on his nightstand radio. He has it set to wake up to easy listening, but on Sunday morning it switches on the "Russian Hour."

"Three guys pulled off the heist of the decade," the commissioner says with an urgency that Lowell has heard only when the commissioner's overly protected daughter was busted for peddling Ecstasy.

Lowell sits up and switches off the radio. He hears his Irish Setter running upstairs, the ringing telephone signaling it is time to rouse the house.

"I just got off the phone with the vice president," the commissioner says. "Do you know what it's like to be buzzed awake and hear the vice president of the United States shouting at you?"

He recounts the robbery on St. Stephen Street. Telephone calls, he says, are bouncing between the halls of power, and Lowell is the final bounce.

"A line of dignitaries a mile long is meeting in Brazil the day after tomorrow, starting with our president and a whole lot of other presidents, to sign that Advancement of the Arts Agreement."

Lowell reads medical journals but rarely keeps up with the news. He hears the dog using his paws to twist the door handle and barge in.

"What's it matter whether they play or not, as long as the guys with meaty handshakes sign on the dotted line?"

"The ceremony revolves around the Pops. They built a stage for them at Copacabana facing that huge statue of Jesus on the mountain. The concert itself serves as a model of how money will be divided among artists in the future. Everybody will be watching. The VP claims the instruments were robbed to sabotage the ceremony."

The Setter jumps onto the bed, sticking his nose all over Lowell, turning to lick his wife, who pulls the covers over her head and holds them with tight fists.

"There's a lot riding on this deal," the commissioner says. "Not millions but billions. Smart money says that rich people are doing themselves a favor while leaving artists barefoot inside a cave of stalactites."

"Stalagmites."

Lowell sits on the side of the bed, his feet searching for his slippers, pushing away the dog.

The commissioner explains how the protesters organized under the FAS coalition, whose members range from Boston Brahmin to motorcycle militant. "Homeland Security kept track of them. When they drew up the Advancement of the Arts Agreement last month, every union in the country denounced it. Who would have thought that a thing like royalties could cause such outrage?"

"Copyright is mentioned in the constitution," Lowell says, squeezing his size-twelve feet into his size-eleven slippers and standing. His self-assigned experiment on digestive juices requires him to check and record his pee color and strength of stream first thing each morning.

"The VP says that if the Pops don't show up, the president won't humiliate himself on an empty stage. If you don't get their instruments in time, they'll scratch the ceremony. No one will dare to face Jesus on the mountain after that."

Lowell starts dressing while the commissioner continues. "The Pops had security up the caboose. We gave them a four-car escort to the airport. The feds took charge. They wouldn't leave it to us, and now they're bound to blame us!"

Lowell's wife is curled up on the edge of the bed as if trying not to let Lowell's conversation and the dog's howling wake her.

"You know what will happen if we don't get their instruments?" the commissioner says. "They'll chain us to the front row in that symphony building and make us listen to a bunch of flutes and violins."

It takes Lowell sixteen minutes to dress and drive his big blue Buick from his South Boston apartment to the scene of the hijacking, ignoring red lights *en route*. Cop cars are already on the street.

Getting out, Lowell hitches up his pants and walks over to Sergeant Rodrigo, who is standing near the double-parked Ford. They shake gloved hands.

"What've we got so far?" He speaks to the urgency of the moment with a broad Boston accent that interchanges the "a" and the "r."

Rodrigo looks at his notepad. "You won't find a thing here, Lieutenant. The robbers didn't leave no résumé or nothing. This was probably part of it." He points to the Ford. "Belongs to a guy in Allston. Not the kind of vehicle someone would steal but probably stolen for the job. There's nothing else."

Lowell looks up at the three-story apartment buildings

around him. "You mean nobody saw nothing?"

"They picked it right. Quiet street. Cold Sunday morning."

Lowell gazes at the National Braille Press, an imposing white stone building. "I guess we won't get too many eyewitnesses from there either."

A Northeastern University police car pulls up with flashing blue lights, and the head of campus security steps out, a large-boned, dark-haired woman whose generous breasts strain the buttons of her brown shirt inside her half-zipped parka.

"Almost all residents here are students," she informs them. "Private housing, but mostly students."

"Someone must have seen something," Lowell says, eyeing her stretched buttons.

"Students don't get up before noon on Sunday," she says.

"Maybe someone was out walking the dog." Lowell imitates his yanking Setter on a leash.

"College students leave their dogs at home."

Lowell knows this to be true. His daughter left her Setter with her parents. When Lowell tried to refuse, she started a litany of what a rough childhood she had suffered under him. He had to shut up and keep the dog.

Lowell looks half a block west, where the street ends at Opera Place. "Not even a singing fat lady?"

He glances at the woman cop to make sure she isn't offended. Lowell wears his belly proudly. He stopped physical exercise as soon as he didn't have to take phys ed in high school, reasoning that since the brain uses thirty percent of the body's blood, exercising the mind can oxidize the organs much better than subjecting them to all that jiggling of running and jumping.

"They had the good sense to tear down that opera house and build a dorm." She points to where it once stood.

"They performed ninety operas a year to full houses,"

Rodrigo says.

"Taxpayers paid for it," she says. "They stiff us so they can listen to their snooty music dressed up in their jewels and furs."

Lowell moves to the center of the street, gets down on one knee, and points east toward Mass. Ave. "They must have had a spotter near the symphony building," he says to no one in particular. "When they planned this, they would have stood where we're standing, looked down the street and thought about everything that could go wrong. They would have timed it, rehearsed at home, practiced every gesture, every word, so when they went into action, they were on automatic."

"Professional thugs," the head of campus security concludes.

"Or professional musicians," Rodrigo says. "Isn't this all about music?"

"Who subsidizes me when I go to a country music concert?" she says. "When regular people say *enough*, they resort to terrorism. Well, we're not backing down. Give into terrorists, and they'll keep terrorizing."

"How much do investors care about culture?" Rodrigo says. "After this agreement, all we'll have left will be Clear Channel and World Wrestling."

"They think their music is better than mine."

Lowell tells Rodrigo to have the drivers brought to the scene. "We've got to work systematically, and we've got to work fast."

Systematic was a word he stressed when he spoke at the annual police conference in the Hynes Center. Pulling out his ringing phone, he finds the anxious commissioner on the other end.

"I need walkers," Lowell says, "guys to ring doorbells. Better be guys with an attitude who thrive on verbal abuse."

"I'm giving you the entire force. Report directly to me."

"Today could be a bad bacteria day," Lowell predicts.

"Stress upsets the bacterial balance and causes bowel inflammation."

"Where do you want the guys?"

"We have four pounds of bacteria in our gut alone." Lowell sniffles into his gloves and hitches up his pants one hand at a time. "We'll start here at the scene of the hijack with the drivers, then go to the symphony building. Can we get this on the news? Maybe someone was walking around."

He sees two TV vans with satellite dishes on their roofs drive up the street. "I guess we don't have to worry about the news," Lowell says. "Bacterial imbalance shoots up to the brain and ruffles our judgment."

"I'll make a public appeal for information," the commissioner says. "The press will ask us why a few security guards can control a rowdy rock concert but we can't protect a truckload of flutes and violins."

"Send that woman spokesman," Lowell says. "She knows all about classical music. Every time I pass her office she's got 'Climb Every Mountain' and stuff like that playing on her stereo."

Dissonance: *Two notes whose wavelengths create an edgy sound. A dissonant chord remains unresolved until one note in the chord is changed up or down a half tone, bringing release.*

First Movement —*Presto Agitato*

When Melody's mother died, the cello cried for her, and those who heard the tears dripping off her bow cried with her. And when, earlier that same day, her cello triumphed at her first competition, they jumped up, cheering, "*Brava!*"

She got on her knees next to her mother's closed casket, turned and embraced her Carletti as her only remaining friend. She put her ear on the cello's belly and listened as it amplified the sonic vibrations bouncing around the cello's empty body.

The cello is in the range of the voice. When Melody plays, she hears a woman. At fourteen, long before she developed her radical bowing and fingering technique, she listened to her instrument as her ear penetrated beyond the sounds of the contemporary world and arrived at the wisdom of a vulnerable but sensible woman.

Sound never dies; it only weakens. The sounds made in the next room or the next state broadcast themselves in wave ripples, becoming ever fainter but continuing to agitate the air. A delicate ear can sense the radiant holler of a child in the next city, a gunshot in a distant country. An even more sensitive ear can perceive a sound vibration created a minute ago, a month ago. The standing waves in the air contain the war cries and death cries of centuries past, the dances of aboriginal peoples pounding the earth. Our history is engraved in sound.

Next to her lifeless mother, Melody heard a slow semitone in the middle register rising then falling like the "Lord Have Mercy" lamentation of the liturgy. She sat and played long, painful notes on the low string.

Now new tragedies are piling on, one after another, as if karma suddenly remembered several lifetimes of faults.

Mel sits next to China on the bus returning from Logan. She hears the discordant cries of other musicians conferring among themselves or on their phones, which contrasts with the bus's smooth E-flat hum.

She doesn't belong with them—she knew that from the day Eduardo tricked her into auditioning for the principal's chair. The other musicians grew up in comfortable homes, have musician parents. Many have advanced music degrees. Melody never went to conservatory, practiced at home, never had a teacher, which makes her technique so wild and exciting.

The musicians were so haunted by her audition that the music director stopped the process and hired her on the spot. Her first ten months were spectacular. Then shell shock.

She dials Eduardo's number. "Are you awake?" Her voice is quaking, her fingers re-tightening. "Have you heard?"

"I just heard on the radio, a special bulletin on WGBH. I never heard them do a special bulletin before."

"They got everything."

He transposes her dominant chords to a pondering adagio. "They got physical objects, but they didn't harm a soul. In the overall scheme, the rest is unimportant."

"Why am I surprised you're so aloof? This means so much to you. You haven't talked about anything else." She pauses, a reflective cadenza. "It means a lot to me, too."

"You, me, and the other composers, but it's out of our hands. What good does it do to curse the universe?"

"You can't just intellectualize this away. How can you, who, you know, has feelings, have no feelings? Do you know what it means if we don't go?"

"Of course I—."

She cuts him off. "Do you know what they'll do to me if I can't play? I've been practicing every night. Every night."

Eduardo is silent.

"It's the most beautiful thing you ever wrote."

Melody's eyes are wet. Her arms shiver as her mouth stumbles for words. She isn't sure what she wants to say, isn't sure why she called him. Does she want to apologize? The solo begins agitated and unsure, shifting tempo and rhythm, then flows like a Persian carpet: under-colored, rhythmic, magnificent. Could it be about believing in possibility?

That piece would inaugurate the New World Compositions, a series of musical works about the Americas written by dozens of composers.

"We're returning to Symphony Hall," Mel tells him.

"I'll be right over."

"How could FAS have broken through all that police security and stopped the trip just like that, after the millions that corporations spent to get that arts agreement passed? Last night I heard an activist say that if big business got its way, it would justify armed struggle to topple the entire greedy capitalist enterprise."

"Those types talk about armed struggle from their armchairs."

She hears musicians nearby weeping into their phones—grating keys, cacophonous chords. She looks down as her predicament sinks in.

"Maybe it's good that you didn't come with us. Everyone's really emotional now." She takes a full measure rest before a restatement. "I didn't mean that you're bad at handling emotions."

"The State Department wouldn't let me go with you," he reminds her. "I had to fly with the press and stage crew."

"When you came last night, was it to talk about my solo?"

"I came to talk to you."

"But you didn't say anything."

"There are more ways to talk than with words. You know that—you transform everything that moves into sound."

China strokes Melody's fingers to loosen them, and they keep holding fingers on the seat between them, *toccata.*

Lieutenant Lowell collapses his chest and locks his arms over his worn Eddie Bauer coat, a futile effort to protect his belly against a blast of January wind that is tearing through New England and bearing down St. Stephen Street, a short, narrow road named for the first Christian martyr. Other cops arrive and block the street. Lowell hands one a twenty and puts him in charge of caffeine and cholesterol.

"Get fluffy ones with cream. Call my wife and have someone bring a belt and a razor."

Lowell picks five guys with mean, square jaws. "Go around and knock on doors. Ask everyone if they saw or heard anything. Ask if they've noticed people hanging around the last couple of weeks."

The cops sneer at each other, thrilled to be rousing kids after a Saturday night of drinking.

"We have to work fast," Lowell says.

Rodrigo gets off his phone. "The guy who owns this car couldn't believe someone would want to steal it."

With his arms wrapped around his stomach, Lowell inspects the white Ford. It has a ticket, which the Northeastern security woman takes from under the windshield wiper.

"Non-resident parking," she says, "not double parking. They parked here overnight, then pulled out and double-parked right before the heist."

Lowell notices an Allston resident sticker on the rear window. He looks at the pavement and sees only the grit scattered by snowplows, salt and sand left after a liberal New

Year's Day snow, thaw, and harsh refreeze. Then he hears another cruiser arrive with the truck drivers in the back seat.

"They had guns," Jules says as soon as he steps out. "We couldn't do nothing."

Lowell makes a calming gesture. He separates them into two cars and has Sergeant Franck question Weber while Lowell and Sergeant Rodrigo put Jules in the back seat of Rodrigo's car. The two cops get in the front seat, Lowell relieved to be out of the cold. A cop passes him a box of Dunkin Donuts. With his large thumb and index finger, he squeezes several donuts on the top and sides like a plump grandmother at a vegetable stall, picking one that has cream oozing out the bottom. Rodrigo selects one without Lowell's digital imprints.

"To eat this fluff," Lowell says in his Yankee vernacular, "the small intestine secretes mucus to protect the duodenal lining."

Rodrigo nods heartily at Lowell's digestive discourse.

Lowell offers Jules a doughnut. "Let's go through every step. Where and when did you start this morning?"

Jules, his arms and shoulders shivering with a mixture of cold, fear, and regret, tells them the story in a few sentences. The robbery happened too fast. He didn't see faces, only ski masks, didn't have time to think, can't believe what happened, is trying to find someone else to blame. The robbers were neither tall nor short, neither fat nor thin. Lowell asks him a couple of times to repeat exactly what the robber said.

"So you got the consignment from the transport officer who came down especially for the day," Lowell says.

"He wheeled the crates onto the truck. It's refrigerated. When you flick it on reverse, it gives you heat in the back. At the airport, they roll the crates right into the plane. Milton, the transport officer, he did it all himself. All we was supposed to do is drive."

"We'll talk to him now."

"You can't. As we drove off, he was walking to Mass.

Ave., where his latest kitten was waiting. They're driving to New Hampshire."

"To go skiing?"

"He don't ski. Ever heard of someone going to New Hampshire in January who don't ski? He stood in the middle of the street and waved his arms at us."

"He waved his arms?"

Jules sees interest on Lowell's face. "Waved big time, because he was set on doing this woman. He ain't got no wife, just goes from one pair of thighs to another. You ever hear of a classical music guy getting it on? And he's over fifty—a middle-aged classical music guy!"

"For your information," Lowell says, "a man's prostate grows with age."

"So do a man's ears, but he don't hear no better."

Lowell bites a ninety-degree wedge from a second doughnut, but he doesn't talk with his mouth full. "You think this fifty-year-old stud had a finger on the heist?"

"His outlet ain't grounded. He's got this perverted thing with those big violins, like he takes them in a corner, plucks them, plays with their holes. You should have heard the sin coming out his mouth." He transforms Milton's metaphors into an X-rated litany. "Someone like that is capable of anything. His boss was there, too, and so was this pretty girl who was turning in her big violin. Milton was all over her. That place is a den of iniquity."

Lowell gets out of Rodrigo's car and asks Sergeant Franck what Jules' partner told him. "Identical stories," Lowell says. "Both said that the robbers asked them to 'contemplate'— not a word you expect from gunmen."

He gets the drivers to demonstrate where and how everything happened. They get into the reenactment as energetically as freshman drama students unleashing their suppressed natures, showing how they had no choice, did what anyone in that situation would do.

"I'll have the lab go over their clothes," Rodrigo says to Lowell.

"Do it right," Lowell says, even though his gut tells him that no one lost a hair in the operation. "Send a couple of guys to where this car was stolen and ask if anyone saw anything. Get the word out about the second car."

They walk down the middle of the street, retracing the truck's short drive. Even with all the commotion, the neighborhood is hardly awake. Approaching Symphony Hall, Lowell gazes at the loading area. It seems supernaturally still.

"I understand the hijackers," Rodrigo says. "I have musicians in my family. The money we give the arts is petty cash compared to the billions that Universal and Sony make off them. We have to protect creativity or we'll have the dullest, most purposeless world. FAS are organized and fired up. The last thing FAS wants is for us to solve the case today."

Lowell steps aside to phone his daughter Amy. He explains in a contrite voice why he can't pass by her house.

"I got a call straight from the commissioner," Lowell pleads. "We can take care of him next weekend, but I can't move from here today."

When she hangs up on him, Lowell turns to Rodrigo. "We take the kid so she can go out and meet people. Guys sense that she's desperate."

"She's young and bubbly," Rodrigo says. "I wouldn't worry about her."

"She has a guy now, but she also has a temper. When she explodes, the guy runs. Then she blames me. She said that I was responsible for her break-up. I mean, how was I supposed to know that the guy was squeamish about how much gas gets released when you're on the potty?"

Rodrigo is sympathetic. He's an efficient, clean-cut cop who walks straight and doesn't clutter his Mexican-accented speech with fancy words.

"Men are no match for women," Lowell says. "They're

taking over every field. Look at the schools—they're outdoing boys in all subjects."

"It would be better if women ruled," Rodrigo says.

"Bad for cops. There'd be less crime, and we wouldn't have jobs. Certainly no overtime. You think a woman boss would allow guys to stand around on a corner shooting bull?"

They enter the stage door and present themselves to the pale-faced security guard, whose wrinkles suggest that he has been stubbornly putting off retirement.

"I know who did it," the guard says.

"I knew you'd phone Eduardo," China says to Melody eighty-seven minutes after the heist.

The buses returning from the airport pass Huntington Avenue, Symphony Hall's original entrance, and turn on St. Stephen Street.

"I only called him because of his première," Melody protests. "The New World Compositions that he's been working on for the past two years," she explains, though it doesn't need explaining.

China winks with a quick squeeze of Mel's hand, then she straightens Mel's fluffy black turtleneck, which covers her hands to her knuckles.

"Maybe it's good that the trip is on hold," China says. She slows the usual quick pace of her speech for emphasis. "You're sure to foul up."

China's absolute declaration changes the sound in Melody's head to the piercing high notes on China's oboe. "I changed. Last night I changed. I have to play. I can't go back. I've practiced the piece to death. I got the fingering."

Their violinist friend Wisteria sits on the opposite seat listening to their conversation. "You've been a pressure cooker, my dear," she says. "Release the emotions trapped inside you instead of letting them simmer."

"You know what it was like to play when I knew I'd mess up?" Mel says. "In the last concerts, as soon as I touched the bow to a string, I knew it would be better if I didn't play at all. What can I do with myself if I'm fired? It would be like asking a bird who had tasted freedom if it wouldn't mind going back into its cage. I need one last chance. They even give that to prisoners before they're executed."

"Borges will be ecstatic if you're run out of the orchestra," Wisteria says, referring to the guest conductor. "He's had it in for you the moment he met you. Don't let him do that."

At over sixty, Wisteria has attractive, grey-streaked hair wound into a French twist. She always dresses in shades of bright purple and brilliant pink. Melody admires her colorful wardrobe, but Melody wears black even when she isn't performing.

"We shouldn't be talking about anything but the theft of our instruments." Addressing the air, Melody asks, "How do you talk without words?"

Melody practices. Some musicians get it right away, half an hour with the score before the performance, but quarks have to do each passage over and over until it comes out the way they hear it in their heads. Principals have the added anxiety of playing short solos within many orchestral works, and she has had an excess of them this past month.

She picks the hardest sections and keeps repeating them, sometimes two or three bars, repeating and repeating. Then she puts her cello on its side, retracts the end pin, and walks into the kitchen looking for a snack—not a meal, not anything fattening, but a taste in the mouth to break the anxiety. Sometimes she has to sleep on it, pick up her cello after waking and replay the piece until that one moment when the music flows through her head like an open spigot. She takes the score off her stand in both hands and announces to it that they are friends.

Before getting off the bus, Melody whispers to China, "I knew it couldn't last. The jinx would show up. One day the audience will stand hissing and booing me, or they'll fall into the aisles laughing."

The dejected musicians dash through the cold into the stage door. Following the transport officer's advice, they had left their coats in their basement lockers.

A long block away at the Gainsborough intersection, a police car blocks the street, the sun blunting its flashing blue lights. A bit farther, police are stringing yellow crime-scene tape, though they have no evidence to collect or protect.

Melody sees Raja, her Bengal cat, who looks like a small leopard, on the sidewalk near the stage door. He rolls on his back as soon as he sees Mel, and she kneels on the cold sidewalk to rub his belly.

"You knew we'd come back, didn't you?" Mel used to worry about him among people and traffic in that congested area, but he made such a high-pitched howl when locked inside that she gave up, installed a cat door, and let him go wherever he wanted. He jumps rooftops and strides, street savvy, the two blocks to Symphony Hall.

"Don't go inside," she tells him as she walks to the building. He flashes a Bengal grin. Once, he had two distressed security guards chasing him backstage during a concert.

While the musicians mill around the corridor, Lieutenant Lowell introduces himself to Walter.

"You see," the general manager announces to the musicians, "the police arrived before we did."

Walter instructs the musicians to go into the auditorium. Everyone follows Ms. Goldberg, the concert-master, to the beige metal door that leads into the main lobby adjacent to the auditorium.

Walter turns to Melody as everyone is leaving,

proclaiming like Aaron Copland's *Lincoln Portrait*. And this is what he says: "Do not worry about a thing."

But the notes Mel hears are alarm, not confidence. He sounds like her father when he preached hell and spit fire. He never meant it. His devil had been a mischievous fellow, never a hurtful one.

The guest conductor's brother, whom people call Guru, is waiting for Melody on the other side of the metal door.

"You're still here?" Mel says. "How did you know we were coming back?"

He rushes to her side, agitated, speaking quickly, running from one side of her to the other, then back again. "I taught Walter how to manage the orchestra," he says, his face and body animated.

Guru's small eyes dart about, his pug nose scrunched, a perpetual smile on his blemishless face, his hair hanging halfway down his short forehead, giving him an Emperor Nero look. Physically and mentally, he is the opposite of his brother, the famous Brazilian maestro scheduled to conduct the première of the New World Compositions. He's the kind of guy everyone lets wander anywhere.

Melody tries to hide the orchestra's distress from Guru. She walks him away from the group into the Hatch Lounge, the front salon where wine and coffee are sold during intermission.

"I know a secret," he says.

"Whisper it in my ear."

Although he is five years older than Melody, she speaks to him as if he is a child.

"I won't tell. Only I know. Guru knows everything."

His voice and his movements are manic, but his simplicity creates an Eric Satie delicateness in Mel's head.

"You're right. You know more about what goes on here than any of us."

She remains with him, walking distractedly among the tables and chairs of the vacant room. Eduardo's four notes haunt her, four notes that wind around each other like the four nucleic acids of DNA, complexity from simplicity.

"I taught soldiers how to keep a secret even if they're tortured."

"Whose secret is it?"

"I won't tell. Guru collects information. My brother lives for music. Guru stores information."

She hears him speaking as fast as Paganini bowed his violin.

"I'm playing an April Fools' joke."

"Guru, it's January."

"A real April Fools' joke won't be in April."

He laughs in random beats, and Melody forces a smile to appease him. He has become particularly attached to her during the past month.

"I collected information for the Secret Service," he says. "Milton left for New Hampshire. Walter has a daughter."

"Those aren't secrets. I told you that Milton was driving up to his camp. Walter has two daughters, and now he has to take care of all of us."

"My brother is building a special school in Brazil so I can train spies. I won't tell the secret even if I'm tortured. Schubert wrote five hundred works by the time he was twenty-three but couldn't get any published."

"He also composed dance music, but he didn't dance."

"My brother wrote a song for me," Guru says, chest puffed, "like Eduardo wrote for you. My brother talks to the vice president of the United States. I talk to people, too. I told him about FAS."

Melody stops. "He hates FAS. He hates me, too."

She shouldn't have said that to him. She puts her hands a few inches above Guru's shoulders. "I have to be inside with everyone else."

He becomes still and looks away. "You won't, you know, be told to go away, will you?"

"My fingers haven't been working the cello. Isn't that silly? My life revolves around my fingering. The orchestra isn't as harmonious as it sounds." She brings her hands down on his shoulders. "The world changed since we talked an hour ago."

At first, Guru freezes at her touch, but then he bends his head and snuggles to her side like a cat on a cozy sofa. He looks down bashfully. "Melody, you're really nice. Last night my brother played my favorite piece for me, the slow part of Chopin Two."

Melody nods kindly, struck by the analogy. Chopin had written the larghetto of his *Piano Concerto No. Two* in F minor, an exemplar of romantic trill, for a pupil he loved because the young composer couldn't muster the courage to confess his love in words—as Eduardo writes music for her, expressing what he has never voiced.

"It's my brother's secret. He's making a lot of money on this trip."

Lowell watches the musicians file into the auditorium. He stands opposite Walter in the unadorned corridor near the security station.

Outside Symphony Hall, news crews are chatting up the police and arranging their equipment. Two video crews are filming the silent scene along St. Stephen Street, one aiming at an underdressed newswoman holding a mike and facing the camera, shuffling her feet and covering her ears from the cold. When given her cue, she calls the robbery, ". . . the consequence of a divided America. Business demands free markets, including a free entertainment market. FAS, For Art's Sake, claims that without protection, art and creativity will be overwhelmed by commercialism. This brazen raid shows the emotions behind the issue. Anti-agreement activists have drawn the line here." She points to Symphony Hall.

"FAS did it," the security guard says to Lowell.

The guard had rushed to Symphony Hall as soon as he heard about the robbery, taking his place on a stool behind a windowless cubicle at the stage door entrance. "They think the crap Hollywood churns out will turn us into slugs. They hung outside this door with flyers trying to stop the orchestra from going, which gave them an excuse to stake out the place."

Lowell thanks him for his insight.

"We must recover the instruments today," Walter tells Lowell without shaking hands. "Our reputation is at stake."

"The wife and I went to see the Pops last year. Or was it two years ago?"

"What clues do we have?" the general manager asks.

"It was two years ago. I was worried that she might have stones in her gall bladder. Boston wouldn't be the same without the Pops."

"We are not the Pops," Walter says, as if he knows that he's been consigned to collaborate with a combination of Don Quixote, Falstaff, and Papageno. "We are the Boston Symphony Orchestra."

"The commissioner told me Boston Pops." Lowell pronounces it like "paps."

"The Pops and the BSO are the same orchestra, mostly. The BSO plays classical music. The Pops plays tunes."

Walter buries his tongue in his jaw and looks at his watch. Not only does he refuse all dealings with the Pops, if a piece that he considers too trite is suggested for an upcoming season's BSO schedule, he writes terse notes to each person on the programming committee, exhorting them to keep their standards, and they listen.

"I see, the Pops and the Symphony," Lowell says.

"Did you see how upset the musicians were? Did you? It's normal to see women crying, but it's absolutely not right to have fifty-year-old men in tears."

"What's the world coming to when musicians are

moved to tears?" Lowell says in knee-slapping geniality.

Walter looks at him mutely.

Lowell fumbles to explain. "Musicians in tears means that they're really into their music."

Not a muscle moves in Walter's face.

"Like they're real emotional," Lowell adds awkwardly, his expression losing its hilarity, and then he drops it. "Were all the instrument players on the buses?"

"All the *instrument players* plus the guest conductor." Walter speaks in distinct syllables. "Mrs. Schutz, my secretary, remained here. No spouses were allowed, because it was a high security trip."

"High security is advertising for trouble."

"The stagehands and press were taking a two o'clock flight via Washington." Walter's attitude is surly.

"You were in the loading area earlier."

"I wanted to make sure nothing was left out."

"You normally do that?"

"This trip is as normal as Beelzebub lounging on the sofa sipping a vanilla latte."

"And a young lady was there?"

"Melody, to drop off her cello. Maestro Borges' brother was there, too. He has Asperger's Syndrome, and he has a crush on Melody because she's kind to him. People call him Guru. He hangs around. He must have discovered that Melody would stop by the loading area this morning."

Walter observes that Lowell is a skilled listener. "The presidential liaison for the arts saw us off. Two of our people were late, so we didn't get rolling until ten after seven."

"Who was late?"

Walter hesitates, reluctant to give out information about his players to someone he does not yet trust. "Tito, the bassist, and Felix, the principal clarinetist."

"Ten minutes is enough to signal as the baggage truck left."

"The State Department arranged a heavy escort," Walter says. "I've organized many trips. This is the first time we've had police, and this is the first time we've been robbed."

"Significant."

"We plan every detail. It costs hundreds of thousands of dollars to put together an international trip."

"So the government knew the trip was risky enough to surround the buses with cops, but they left the baggage truck wide open for two guys and a broad to knock off in front of a blind folks home."

"We put our trust in their hands."

Lowell senses that Walter's trust isn't resilient. "I'd like to speak to everyone right away."

"They're waiting for you in the hall. I hope you'll be more serious to them about our loss."

Walter and Lowell walk down the wide corridor lined with bulletin boards and information sheets.

"Who do you think did this?" Lowell asks.

"You won't be hard up for suspects. The trip was planned last year to initiate an intense round of musical composition called the New World Compositions, involving composers and performers from the Americas. The government turned it into this political circus last month. Add to that any thief wanting to get rich fast."

"This isn't about hocking instruments at fifty bucks a shot," Lowell says. "They were high rollers—they wouldn't bother with musical instruments."

"Bother with musical instruments! Who do you think we are, a bunch of hucksters who play on paint cans and washboards? Bother with musical instruments at fifty bucks!"

Lowell realizes that he has offended Walter. "How much are the instruments worth? You got any idea?"

"I don't *got* any idea, I know exactly. I do insurance for them every year. Musician insure their own instruments, but the BSO also insures them as a group. And now we have that

Czech's Strad."

"Which Czech?"

"One of our two soloists. He plays the Iberian Strad. It's famous. So is he. Composers have written for him—sonatas for solo violin and concertos where he dominates the stage in front of an orchestra."

Walter hits his forehead with his hand. "Holy shit."

It isn't the language Lowell expects to hear in Symphony Hall.

"Holy shit," Walter repeats as he reels to the side and leans his head back on the wall. "We're insured in the building. We're insured in the airplane. We're insured in Rio, but I don't know if we're covered two blocks away."

He holds his head in his hands and inhales noisily. "With the Czech's violin, what the robbers took has a value of fourteen point five million."

The number bounces between Lowell's temporal lobe and his thalamus and is thrown into his forebrain, which tries to sort out amounts between thousands and millions. It should be thousands, perhaps tens of thousands, certainly not hundreds of thousands—or millions.

"Fourteen point five million," Lowell repeats mechanically. His cheek muscles lift, wrinkling his eyes. "What do you mean? How did you get a figure like that? Each instrument is worth a few hundred, a couple of grand."

"The bows the string players use are each more than a couple of grand. The concertmaster also has a Strad endowed by one of our patrons. The guest violinist's Strad alone—he was ready to spit the number in my face—is easily worth five million. The concertmaster's violin is valued at four and a quarter. The principal flutist has a white gold-plated instrument. Several violins and cellos from the early 1700s are a couple of hundred thousand each. We also have a Guarneri, a Maggini, a 1725 Albanais, a 1760 Gragnani, an 1831 Pressenda. The basses, the winds. It wasn't that big an orchestra this time—

imagine if we had to play Strauss—but it's worth fourteen point five million dollars."

"Fourteen point five million," Lowell repeats.

"There are tens of thousands of dollars in cases alone."

"You put million-dollar violins in a crate?"

"It's the safest way. Due to hand baggage restrictions, our rule is that even piccolos go in crates."

"If I had a million-dollar violin I wouldn't let it out of my sight."

"That's what people do the first year they play one, but gradually, it becomes routine."

"I thought this would be my first robbery where money wasn't the motive."

Maestro Borges stalks down the hall toward them, his face enraged. "I kept warning you!" he says to Walter in a controlled yell. "The State Department kept warning you, but no one did anything. You have terrorists right in the orchestra, like that Maoist bassist and that silly girl soloist who doesn't know the difference between a cello and a fire engine siren. They gave the robbers inside information."

Lowell watches Borges swagger back down the hall, a halo of flame around his head.

"The guest conductor," Walter says. "He's the most upset."

Walter answers his phone. He falls silent with tight eyebrows. "Who is this?"

Lowell perks up.

Walter listens, then pulls the phone off his ear. "It was them. They parked the truck with the luggage in front of the Malden police station, but they say they'll destroy the instruments if we go to Rio. He bragged that they used toy guns."

Scherzo: *a jest, a lighthearted upbeat section. Composers during Beethoven's time added a scherzo to replace the minuet.*

Fortissimo

At 9:32 a.m., seventeen minutes before the discovery of the first body, Melody says goodbye to Guru and enters the hall where the other musicians are gathered. She stands silently with China, though China's silence is never quiet. China's open eyes are always moving, engrossed in her surroundings, the smile of curiosity on her high cheek-boned face that makes people turn to her to spice up a conversation.

A fairly tall, frizzy blonde, China looks like anything but how a woman named China should look. In constant animation, as if Vermeer has crafted her soft face with perpetual light shining on it, she instills every activity with adventure, talking to old friends as well as meeting new ones, playing the standard composers as well as new music, her bright face expressing a spirit of discovery. While other musicians are distraught about the robbery, China's green eyes are those of an explorer looking through binoculars at uncharted land. She's won every music competition she's ever entered.

If more women than men are looking for dates, it is because men are holding out for a China. When she and Melody jog along the Charles River, up the Esplanade and across the bridge to Memorial Drive, men stop to gaze, turn to stare at their departing butts. Truckers honk, taxi drivers stick their heads out their windows, and one time an entire construction crew ran down a scaffold to cheer them on. China returned as much enthusiasm as she received, an alluring smile from Melody.

They had auditioned at the same time, playing on the Symphony Hall stage behind an opaque beige screen, which hid both gender and age from the judges. When the BSO announced in *International Musician* openings for violin, oboe, and principal cello, hundreds of résumés arrived for each position, coming from Germany, Seoul, Switzerland, Shanghai, Seattle, Detroit. Over sixty were invited to send CD samples. The forty invited to audition for each position walked on stage without shoes and played. A line of six to twelve BSO musicians judged from the other side of the screen. Candidates paid their own travel expenses.

Those auditioning for a violin chair played four pieces, including the *scherzo* of Schumann's *Second Symphony*, which terrorizes veteran violinists. At the end of the arduous process, no one was invited to fill the empty chair. The BSO would rely on subs. They spend $1.5 million a year on subs.

Blind auditions were introduced in the 1960s to improve the racial mix of orchestras. They didn't, but they changed the gender imbalance dramatically.

The oboists were assigned fairly plain pieces: Telemann's *Sonata in A-major*, written at the time of Bach and scored for continuo but now usually played with piano, which is far less interesting than his oboe concerto for small orchestra; the twentieth century Czech composer Bohuslav Martinů's *Concerto for Oboe*; the French composer Vincent D'Indy's *Danses for Wind Septet*, which has a long oboe line but isn't too interesting played by itself; a Hindemith sonata; and Strauss' tone poem *Don Juan*, which include treacherous parts for just about every instrument.

China played with a fervor that no one had heard in those works, generating a hushed silence among her judges after her eight minutes. She had a haunting *bisbigiando* technique, using her fingers to alternate rapidly between ground and harmonic on the same note, creating a subtle tremolo, and then she accented the sound by shifting her lower lip on the vibrating reed or touching it lightly with her upper teeth. Far and away the best in technique and projection, she was selected as a semifinalist, a finalist, and, unanimously, the winner. Her excited voice radiated off the walls.

An oboe can make as much sound as an entire string section. The slightest mistake blares and glares. Composers often run their melody lines through the oboe and violin played in unison. The oboe is heard frequently in movie music. China is able to play long passages on a comfortable diaphragm. Her lone vanity is not wanting to be seen with her cheeks puffed. She knows circular breathing but will use it only if no one is watching.

For the cello audition, Melody was asked to play Benjamin Britten's *Suite for Solo Cello*, part of Elliot Carter's *Remembering Mr. Ives*, and a John Harbison piece. The auditions were far more rigorous since it was a principal chair, and the process took longer, but when they heard the wild yet controlled sound that came from her cello, a sound no traditionally-trained musician was capable of making, the music director brought down the curtain to see who was producing that sound. Instead of seeing a skilled veteran, he looked down on a shy pretty girl, creating instant controversy about giving the principal chair of an important section to someone so young who had absolutely no experience—zero—playing on stage. He was even amused by Mel's embarrassment when her phone rang, the ringtone a blaring boom-boom rock.

She floated on air, an affirmation of how much she had turned her life around from an insecure daughter of an alcoholic preacher to a BSO principal, fiancée to a world-class composer.

She and Eduardo danced that afternoon in his living room to Piazzolla. They danced that night in the common area of her apartment building to Bartók's *Second Violin Concerto*. They danced the next day down the aisle of Market Basket to Muzak and then ran upstairs to his apartment and put on Elvis's "Can't Help Falling in Love." Standing opposite each other, they moved slow motion into dance embrace, eyes closed, cheek to forehead, letting the music absorb them, govern them, first slowly, then slowly again, and then a quick long step followed by an erect stop, chest to chest, thigh to thigh, losing herself in his embrace the way she lost herself in his music, descending into a slow coda that extended into prolonged stillness.

Her soft personality and musical talent won over most of the orchestra, but the assistant principal, who also auditioned, remained hostile.

Melody and China give the orchestra pretty, cheery, and youthful faces on which TV cameras routinely focus during live broadcasts. In an effort to lower the average age of its audience below forty-eight, Melody and China are featured on the orchestra's brochure, China blowing into a raised oboe, her face open and excited, a tight embouchure, Melody behind her, eyes closed, head tilted forward as she connects the music with her inner feelings and projects them through her bow.

Melody established her reputation after Clara Schumann's *Piano Concerto in A-minor*, which has a brief section where the principal cellist plays with the pianist. Critics talked about how Melody combined the emotional longing in the piece and forgot to mention the pianist. A *youtube* video surfaced of her playing the Haydn cello concerto that had been buried in the Prague National Museum until 1961. Edwardo amateurishly filmed her playing with a downloaded recording of the piece without soloist, making her its authoritative interpreter.

China established her reputation when the principal

oboist allowed her to play the opening of the adagio of Brahms's *Violin Concerto in F-major*. It's only a few lines of rich melody, which the soloist repeats later, but China played it with such beauty that the guest conductor had to wipe her tears to be able to continue reading the score.

That seems a distant past to Melody, whose fingers now stumble over every passage. Although the musicians in the hall number over eighty, Melody hears a church-like emptiness, hollow voices echoing off the walls. She hears cell phones ringing from both the carpeted and uncarpeted sections of the hall, distressed words uttered in short, halting beats two or three tones higher than usual.

Eduardo enters, and she races straight up to him as if she hadn't broken up with him six weeks earlier.

"No one knows what's happening."

"Lavender," Eduardo says as he inhales. Melody turns away embarrassed. She had gotten up early and gone through every self-confidence and tension-reducing ritual, including a bath and pleasuring herself in it. Orgasm freed any block to music in her head. Once, her father had caught her. She panicked. He looked at her indulgently as she covered herself with her hands. She wanted him to punish her to acknowledge her shame, but he never said anything but sweet words to her.

She and Eduardo would often make love in her old-fashioned, cast-iron, claw-footed bathtub, deep enough for two. Her brownstone Fenway apartment had high ceilings, heavy wood moldings, wide-planked hardwood floors, and a working fireplace. They made love to music, classical or rock or an odd piece from a remote part of the world that Eduardo had dug up. Some nights she couldn't sleep without a series of orgasms, urging him not to stop, embarrassed at her greed, craving one more until desire drained out of her trembling toes and music rang triumphant in her head. But after telling him to go away, she relied on her fingers, and she knows that Eduardo knows what she did that morning as soon as the faint scent of lavender assails his nostrils.

Quarks know the link between music and love, transposing rapid arpeggios and lush melodies into movement, rhythm, action.

"The news people are blaming FAS," Eduardo says.

"The whole trip is up in the air." Melody tries to infuse him with the anxiety spread around the room. "Your première! The New World Compositions!"

"Music is more than instruments and compositions," Eduardo says, detached. "Musicians lose instruments all the time."

He dresses the part of a young intellectual artist, wearing comfortable-fitting, light brown corduroy trousers and a dark brown tweed jacket over a charcoal turtleneck. Though hazel-eyed and relatively light-skinned, he projects Brazilian dark, wearing his curly hair longish and sporting flimsy Left Bank glasses. His manner is genial, his movements that of a chivalrous young South American gentleman, though he grew up in Massachusetts, a rising star of musical composition, with feature articles about him in *Gramophone* and *Stereo Review*.

"Brazil is my only chance to redeem myself," Melody says. "If I don't play—"

"What is music?" Eduardo asks rhetorically. "Is it a bunch of people with cellos and oboes?"

She stands speechless.

"Music is fundamental to our being. Astronomers talk about music determining the shape of the universe. During its first milliseconds, the Big Bang created shock waves that gave the universe its shape. On the crest of these giant waves, we have lines of galaxies, while in the troughs, empty space. These waves move through our bodies."

"So, we don't need our instruments, is that what you're saying?"

He answers in the reasonable meter of a *menuet*. "I started asking myself, why a perfect fifth? It must have filtered into us, just as waves of galaxies are an average five hundred million lightyears apart, which is their version of a fifth. Music runs through our genes, not just our ears."

"Too heavy." Melody flaps her arms like a gull. "We've just been robbed. Are you that dense?"

He turns serious. "The music is you."

Mel hears the essential notes of her solo again—B, E, E-flat, D-flat—in those four words. The solo begins high on the cello's A-string, wild and harsh like his voice, moves abruptly to the dark low C-string, and then jumps everywhere.

Walter approaches Eduardo. "We need sane, rational voices. The lieutenant wants to talk to everyone. Sit with Maestro Borges up front."

Walter, considerably larger than Eduardo, makes it seem as if he has his arm wrapped around the young man's shoulder, though he is only making the type of open-arm gesture performers use when accepting applause.

To Melody, Walter appears like a Beethoven symphony—proud, Germanic, grand but with vulnerability in the middle—while Eduardo resembles a Debussy piano trio: melodic, rational, ethereal.

When Walter and Eduardo leave Melody standing alone, Maestro Borges appears at her side, disdain and scorn dripping off his face.

"It's you and that militant bass player."

Melody shakes her head in vigorous rejection, but she is too stunned to get words out of her mouth.

"First you tried to sabotage the trip with your atrocious playing," Borges says *sotto voce*. "Then you gave the robbers inside information. But I will crush you and your radicals."

Borges begins walking away, then turns back. "You'll pay for humiliating me in front of the world."

"Take seats everyone," Walter yells twelve minutes before the first body is found.

Melody, shaken by Borges' accusation, ends up with China in row E while their friends, Tito the bassist and Felix the principal clarinetist, take the front row, all sitting on original chairs installed in 1900 when Symphony Hall was built. America's grandest concert hall was the first major structure to use acoustic science since Roman Empire amphitheaters and remains, acoustically, among the top half-dozen halls in the world. The shape of Symphony Hall's golden balconies, the indentations in the ceiling, even the red velvet on the railings, were designed for acoustics. The chairs are not comfortable. Some would be cramped for a chimpanzee. Many of the original leather covers and horsehair padding lasted over a century.

With more open gestures, Walter ushers Borges and Eduardo on stage. Maestro Borges wears an expensive dark sports jacket over a loose, immaculately-ironed pastel shirt covered with green stickmen designs of cats and dogs, a silk scarf tucked artfully under his shirt. His pants are crispy informal. While most musicians wear winter boots, Borges sports light Italian leather.

Melody sees Lowell looking around, as fascinated at being on the broad stage as a hick in the big city. He takes off his coat and throws it on a chair. He hitches up his beltless pants, brushes the residual frost off his nose with his index finger, and walks to the edge of the stage. Lowell has not dressed or groomed for the event, but even if he had, Mel thinks that his appearance would not have turned out much different. He wears beige and brown, his hair in disarray. He has dark, bushy eyebrows and large facial features. His earthy manner and muddy enunciation make it obvious that his mailbox is not crammed with invitations to gallery openings and ballet galas.

"First of all, I'm sorry about the robbery," he says to the musicians. "Boston loves the Pops."

"The Boston Symphony Orchestra," Walter says from his seat.

"That's what I meant." Lowell turns back to Walter. "Doesn't 'symphony' mean the same thing as 'orchestra'?"

Walter rolls his eyes. Lowell fumbles with a piece of paper in his hand, realizes he hasn't written anything, and then continues.

"It looks like a professional job, which means we have to limit the number of suspects." He gazes around with his finger on his chin, his other hand tucked under the supporting arm as if calculating a geometry problem. "I want to ask if you have any insights."

"I know who did it," a woman's voice shouts from the left.

Eyes turn to her.

"That creep who hangs out across the street."

A handful of musicians voice agreement.

"He's been staking out the place for months," says the sole female bassist. "He leans on a parking sign watching how everything works and then disappears."

More nods of affirmation.

"Who's this?" Lowell asks the group.

"We all know him," the original voice says. "He's a weirdo who hangs out across from the stage door."

"You have no proof," Melody says, strength in her voice. "Never accuse anyone like that no matter how weird they appear. He's a nice man."

"He might have worked with someone in this room," the assistant principal cellist replies, specifically not looking at Melody. "He was there this morning."

Lowell tells one of his men on the side of the stage to find the guy right away. Then he turns toward the first voice. "That's the kind of thing we need. We have to check out every hunch, every suspicious person."

"This isn't the job of an isolated creep," another says.

"We all know it was FAS."

Almost everyone agrees.

Tito the bassist, tall and lean with a trim black beard, comes to a half-standing position and speaks *con forza*. "Let's not jump to simplistic conclusions."

"We're concentrating on the anti-agreement radicals," Lowell says, "but we don't want to rule anything out."

"You know who helped them? Those electricians," another voice says.

Murmurs of agreement.

"I saw one of them in our lounge looking at the instruments," a violinist says. "He didn't have any work there. He must have been planning the robbery."

"They were here last week," Walter explains to Lowell. "They're from Everett. I'll get their names."

Melody sees Maestro Borges sitting silently on stage with crossed legs and an enraged face. She hears people in front of her breathing.

"How are you going to get our instruments?" a woman demands in a voice as high as the violin in Messian's *Quartet for the End of Time*.

"We have to work together, bring out every detail systematically." Mel notices that Lowell does not respond to the woman's halting syllables of hostility.

A woman stands, her voice a dark *coloratura*. "These are not instruments. They're not wood and reed and string. They're our intimate friends. We know them better than we know our own bodies. We understand their different moods, their reaction to heat and humidity, how they respond to other instruments. We know how they resonate in different rooms. We've sat with them hour after hour in practice rooms and living rooms and bedrooms. Our relationship is honest and clear. You can never lie to your instrument."

She begins to cry, silencing the room.

"Let's keep focused," Lowell says. "Strong emotions

have been associated with flatulence."

A stunned quiet descends on the hall.

Walter jumps up. "We're supposed to participate in a friendship concert on our arrival. It's more a social event, giving us a chance to unwind. It's not important musically. The Tuesday performance is the huge diplomatic event and the source of our problems." Walter looks at his watch. "Forty-seven hours from now. Rio is two hours ahead. We need eleven hours on the plane and one night's sleep. If we don't solve the case by midnight, I'll cancel."

Melody closes her eyes, muttering to herself. "There's no way robbers will stop what I will do."

"We didn't want to go," Tito says, directing his accusation toward Maestro Borges, who doesn't flinch.

Mel feels the atmosphere in the room become an unfocused *bourrée*.

"We start by making music a priority in schools," Tito continues. "We help creative people so they don't have to work as dishwashers."

"We all heard the rap," a musician interrupts.

Tito pushes on, his forceful tone filling the large auditorium. "We can't let our art be governed by capitalists. By agreeing to play in Rio, we were agreeing to screw every artist and musician."

The same musician stands and tries to shout him down. "We can't taint ourselves with politics."

"That's exactly what we've done." Tito's shouts are louder. "We should have spoken up for ourselves."

"Tito's right," a string player says, rising to her feet. "WBUR surveyed opinions after Friday's concert and found solid opposition to the deal. Almost all of us were against it as well and against the government forcing this on us."

Maestro Borges jumps to the front of the stage, his face red, his accusing finger pointing at Tito. "You socialist! We have to fend for ourselves. This is the real world. Without this agreement, they'll overrun us and leave us with nothing. You can't return to the good old days, because they're gone forever. The music business has been destroyed. This is our last chance."

Walter stops the argument with a raised arm. Everyone sits, including Borges. However disagreeable Borges is, Mel recognizes him as a quark.

"This handsome young man," Walter points at Eduardo, "is premièring a work in his home country, and this talented musician," he points at Borges, "is conducting the orchestra in his home country."

"Good to meet you again, conductor," Lowell says. "I went out with a girl once who said her father was a conductor, so I asked her, 'For which streetcar'?"

Lowell chortles, but no one joins in. "You know," Lowell explains, still chuckling, "they call them conductors, too."

The musicians look at each other. Walter's face is as excited as a bassoon solo.

"Hey," Lowell says, holding out his arm, his sincere voice disarming ill will, "I'm on your side. Work with me, and I promise to do everything I can to solve this before midnight."

"Maestro Borges is not our main conductor," Walter explains. "He's a guest conductor. This program initiates a new level of cultural exchange between our two continents."

"When were the instruments packed?" Lowell asks.

"The musicians left their instruments downstairs after last night's concert."

"Except for one person who came this morning," Lowell corrects.

Melody realizes he is talking about her.

"The instruments were crated and loaded in that warm truck," Walter says. "Because we're supposed to have a welcoming concert right after arriving, the transport officer separated the instruments from the luggage. The luggage was going to the hotel while the instruments were going with us straight to the concert hall."

"This was different than usual?"

"He usually delivers a trunk to each person's hotel room, but it seemed logical to send the instruments directly to where we're playing the friendship concert. We usually ship four tons of equipment and two hundred people, but this time there was far less equipment and only eighty-five people. Imagine if we had the Tanglewood Chorus. We didn't even have the orchestra's physician. The State Department was taking care of that."

"So this drama began with last night's concert," Lowell says. "Did anything unusual happen?"

"Guards had to stop a fight between a protester and a subscriber," a voice says.

"Actually, a woman was moaning after the last chords of Saint-Saëns's second movement," says Felix, the Taiwanese-American principal clarinetist.

"Second movement," Lowell repeats. "Eighty-six percent of people have only one movement."

Walter raises his shoulders and looks down his nose at the lieutenant.

"Her interruption was a vocal protest against us," Felix adds in his Asian accent.

Lowell puts his hand on his stomach. "Tell you what we'll do," he says, receiving sudden inspiration. "We'll interview everyone who works here, beginning with you," he gestures inclusively at the musicians, "just for a minute or two. We'll divide you into groups. Sergeant Franck will take that group. Sergeant Barber will take this group. Sergeant Carter will take that one. Tell us any hunch you might have. Speak candidly."

A musician jumps up. "They killed Milton!"

The hall erupts into screams of horror, panic, and disbelief.

"Listen," the musician says, reading off his Android. "A

New Hampshire newspaper delivery man found a body in the open trunk of a stolen car on the side of a small road. He was naked, a bullet hole through his forehead. A sign identified him as the BSO transport officer and declared that they have a list of everyone who works in Symphony Hall and cooperated with the arts agreement."

The musicians sob and hold hands.

"Everyone loved him," someone says.

Melody explodes with grief. She reaches out to China and looks at the stage. Even Eduardo's face is transformed into terror, his hands trembling.

"Why Milton?" Mel cries out.

It was the universe, not music, that had attracted Melody to Eduardo. Two years earlier, he heard her play at a wedding. Neither she nor Eduardo knew the happy couple. He was with his girlfriend, who knew the bride from work, and Melody was playing with an amateur string quartet, whose first violinist was a friend of the groom.

As soon as Eduardo walked into the reception hall, his ear picked out her cello. Then he looked around to find where the sound was coming from. He moved closer and stared at Melody, which didn't go down well with his girlfriend.

When the quartet took a break, Eduardo came up to Melody and started telling her about the shape of the universe, the curvature of space-time, the four fundamental forces. She didn't understand a word, but he spoke with such zeal and radiated such intensity and optimism that Melody was transfixed. She heard multi-phonics in his voice, harmonic tones an octave above the bass note. She knew right off that he was a quark.

As the event wound down and the musicians put away their instruments, Eduardo asked where the quartet would play again, and it just so happened that they had another engagement the following month. Two engagements in two months was two engagements more than they had played since they formed. They were a group of four young women who spent more time talking and nibbling than playing.

Melody smiled and continued packing, mad at herself for not saying something sassy—mad at Eduardo for not stopping her from leaving.

He came to her next event, which featured a Prokofiev piece. Melody's delicate left hand moved masterfully on the fingerboard while her right hand bowed both securely and loose. He hadn't seen anything like it. She phrased quick passages without gearing up.

At the reception afterward, Eduardo invited her to what he said was a most exciting event, a star party on the university roof next to the observatory. He put his hand over his mouth and spoke through his fingers. "Saturn is in opposition."

She thought it was something negative.

She peeked through the telescope and saw Saturn high in the sky with its rings spread open.

"What you see are photons generated by the sun two and a half hours ago, which traveled nine hundred million miles to Saturn, were reflected, then traveled another eight hundred million miles to reach your retina," Eduardo explained.

She was impressed, though she didn't want to risk asking what a photon was. Using the excuse of wanting to look into the telescope again, she moved close to him. He put his arm around her and sang, "When that ring hits your eye like a big pizza pie, that's amore."

They went to a café, where they talked for half the night.

"My mother died in a fire ten years ago," she told him.

"I heard the hurt in your playing. And your father?"

"It took years until I allowed myself to have fun. Even now, when I'm out having a good time, I think about her."

He listened without interrupting.

"We belonged to an evangelical church." Mel never called their group a sect.

"You believed in being fired with the Holy Ghost and all that?"

"It's not like that. Religion calms emotion. Bible study makes you logical. Fundamentalists are orderly, reasonable people. Religion is intellectual. Only in despair do people become devout."

She spoke with her eyes directly on him, absorbing his every gesture, every slight facial movement. She transformed his face into sounds, combining overtones and resonances to create a full canvas. Eduardo was her music.

"I might even be more logical than you," she said.

"I can tell that you consider every action. I saw you spending a few moments connecting to the music before playing."

"It's a paradox. I have to concentrate to become an empty channel. I don't allow my eye or my ear or my thoughts to wander."

Eduardo's vocal range convinced her that he was an exhilarating person, his timbre bringing words out of her that she had shared with no other, his tempo an *allemande*, showing personal depth. He had the habit of covering his mouth with his spread fingers, which she interpreted to mean that words were not important. She covered her eyes with her hair so that no one would notice her.

"I can tell by people's tone if they're speaking from the heart," she said. "My mother borrowed a three-quarters cello when I was six. It spoke to me. I've had a bow in my hand every single day since. Other kids wanted to smoke or drink beer after school, but I wanted to practice. I lied about how many hours I practiced so they wouldn't think I was strange. My mother cleaned houses at night so she could buy me a full cello two years later, the cheapest one. Cheap cellos are harder to play, so it was good training. We saved our pennies until we could afford a down payment on my Carletti."

"We can live dishonestly in a fantasy world," Eduardo said, "or we can experience and live what we feel."

He invited her to his apartment. She said yes without thinking, astonished at herself, relieved that she hadn't said no.

They began with a desperate embrace as soon as they walked in the door. Then, moving apart, they exchanged small kisses until they became full-mouthed and reckless. He lifted her shirt out of her pants. She closed her eyes and gave his hand room to move. Was she giving herself too easily? When his fingers reached under her panties, *Der Meistersinger* overture burst in her head and drowned out all doubt.

He lifted her off the floor and carried her to his burgundy sofa. They undressed each other, and he lowered himself on top of her. Ceasing their frenzied writhing for a moment, he moved back to look at her with delight and desire, illuminated by the light of the outside streetlamps. She didn't shave her legs or underarms, since she was almost hairless.

As he stroked the inside of her thighs, she stopped him by taking his hand.

"That's the way you hold your bow," he said.

She gave her head a teasing shake. He circled her clitoris until her body convulsed in orgasm, the first in a series. He entered her rashly, plunging deeper and deeper until the final throes when they gasped together. E-flat major, the key of Beethoven's *Eroica*, rang in her head.

Rolling onto their side and looking at each other at the same moment, they convulsed with laughter. She shoved him mischievously and gave him a kiss on the cheek as if they were old lovers.

"When I met you," he said, "I saw a beautiful composition, both wild and trained, surrounding a hub of pain, and I was so greedy, because I wanted it for myself. I'll write music as strong and as clear as you."

They were awakened by the sun shining through a

hanging crystal, diffracting rainbows on their faces. He put his fingers over his mouth. "I knew how you'd make love when I heard you play. Sex and music are the same: rhythm, melody, harmony." He gave her a kiss and embrace. "Saturn high in the sky. I'll make love to you every day we're together."

And he just about did.

For the next two days, they hardly left his apartment, making love a dozen times.

"Do whatever you want," she told him. It seemed as if she was reverting to her childhood when she did what others wanted. But by telling Eduardo to do whatever he wanted, she didn't relinquish control but took it, squashing shyness, a state in which she was out of control. With Eduardo, she gave kiss for kiss, push for push.

Cadenza: *a showy passage, written or improvised, that high-lights a musician's talent.*

Partita

Seventy-eight minutes before the bomb, Walter takes Lowell up the backstage steps to his second floor office.

Lowell cannot fathom why robbers would use toy guns and then kill someone.

Except for a clear, polished Shaker table that serves as a desk and ornately-framed landscape oil paintings with brass lights mounted over them, Walter keeps a working office. The carpetless, windowless room has a bookcase, chairs, and a row of filing cabinets with papers tossed on them, revealing that Walter is a hands-on manager of the pre-computer school.

"What kind of information do you expect from the musicians?" Walter asks. "We were all on the bus. Your men should be questioning potential murderers and robbers. This could waste valuable time."

Lowell tells Sergeant Rodrigo to bring in Melody, since she was at the loading area with Milton.

"Milton has a camp in the woods where he has no contact with the outside world," Walter tells Lowell. "I discovered that he did a novitiate as a Trappist."

"The truck driver made him out to have an itchy lizard."

"A true art lover would rejoice as much in a week of abject abstinence as in carnal excess."

"When it's money," Lowell says, "police investigations

are predictable. Throw in a guy who strokes a violin the way a horny teenager pets a centerfold, and everything gets out of whack."

"FAS agitated the musicians' union to stop us from going, but the union's constitution forbids them from taking a political stand. I met with a high-level FAS delegation, and so did Louis, the big boss." Walter raises his head reflectively. "Respectable people, ladies and gentlemen from local liberal organizations, like Mr. Cline who's been a trustee for twenty years. Three other people had their names on seats, and one gave a million to endow a musician's chair for life."

"Let me guess, the government spiced the pot."

"FAS also pressured the Teamsters and our own players' union. We have tight union rules, so the arts agreement won't impact us. The presidential liaison for the arts, a fellow named Cage, said that he would resign if the Advancement of the Arts Agreement went through, but last week he switched and enthusiastically supported it. He surprised everyone. He got daily updates on FAS, came every day to see if things were on track. He was even here this morning."

Walter eases his facial muscles, puts his hands behind his head, and speaks slowly. "A handful of CEOs arrived with a Republican senator from Georgia and met with Louis and me to make sure we didn't cave. We didn't give a hoot about the senator—such a daft idea sending a Republican to Boston—but a couple of the businessmen belong to our Higginson Society, so we were squeezed on both sides. No organization that depends on handouts can upset big donors."

"You added up the totals," Lowell concludes, "and the anti-agreement people didn't ante as much as the government."

Money is hardly on the commissioner's mind when he phones Lowell. "Homeland Security are dropping us in the sewer. They had a special agent investigating those anti-agreement groups. He left for Washington on the seven forty shuttle from Terminal B."

"He bolted at the most important time?"

"They're recalling him and blaming us for not protecting the Pops."

"It's like a lion fleeing when the gazelle ruffles his whiskers. Can't we pick up those FAS people ourselves?"

"We don't spy on law-abiding citizens. Got that? We never had a reason to keep track of FAS. The local feds have already nabbed many of them. They're scrambling, going way outside protocol. If they hadn't elbowed us out of this, we wouldn't have let such a thing happen."

Lowell tells the commissioner that the baggage truck is in Malden. "I imagine they didn't leave it in front of a police station with greasy prints all over it."

"Check out every possibility," the commissioner says. "The last thing we need is someone accusing us of not being thorough. I'm sending a crowd to New Hampshire to check the body. The Pentagon is trying to get satellite photos of the truck. With all the money they spend on satellites, you'd think they'd be able to spot a thirty-foot truck moving down an empty street, but the more information they collect, the less they know. I have to tell the mayor everything."

"I'm sorry for you. Did you know the instruments are worth fourteen and a half million?"

The commissioner gasps. "That could buy a new computer system for headquarters. Who would guess that people would lay out as much money for violins?"

"The robbers. What kind of guy is the FAS leader?"

"It's a she. The feds already have her in a vise in the basement of Government Center and are working her over, but she breathes fire, and they're getting burned."

Special Agent Dufay never, ever, expected to talk to the vice president of the United States. Salaried slightly above the middle of the federal hierarchy, Dufay has been stationed in Boston for the past month monitoring FAS, the populist movement mobilized against the arts agreement. He is opening the door of his Arlington, Virginia, home when the vice president phones. The VP has to repeat three times who he is before Dufay clicks his heels and calls him "sir."

"What the hell happened?"

"Sir?"

"The robbery. Don't you know?"

"I just landed in Washington, sir."

"Jesus. What are you doing here?"

He tells Dufay about the heist in two sentences. "This is a major embarrassment. The president wouldn't think of appearing on an empty stage."

"Cage told us to leave Boston."

"I never trusted that man," the VP says. "Everything about him grates me. Those Boston radicals shafted us just by swiping instruments. How long will it take to find the robbers?"

"Depends." Dufay regrets the word immediately. "Right away, sir. A few days."

"You got a few hours. I don't care what you have to do. Get those instruments today, or I'll make your most exciting job a guard inside a museum of sixteenth century religious art with a loop of a Gregorian chant playing in the background."

"Sir, a few hours is all I need."

Fifty-eight minutes before the bomb and three hours and eleven minutes after the heist, Melody opens Walter's office door.

She senses a serious, almost austere atmosphere, as if she's walking into the den of the Holy Inquisitor probing for heresy. Walter and Lowell—large, middle-aged men sitting on either side of the office—don't look too different. Walter is a bit larger and a bit older, more serious, both men avuncular but with a projection of male power that makes Melody uneasy about entering. If two foxes urinated in a doorway, would a hare be eager to cross?

"Come in and sit down," Lowell says. "We have to work quickly."

She registers his baseline voice as a sonorous B-flat.

"Our principal cellist," Walter announces with his arms outstretched. "A most talented musician."

Melody certainly doesn't feel talented, never felt she was anything but a mediocre musician. She enters flat-footed like a Tai Chi practitioner. The sect had taught her self-defense, which she had to use just after moving to Boston when a big guy approached her at night. Before he finished his demand for money, she attacked his eyes. In one swift, automatic move, she kicked the back of his knee, running off as the man hit the sidewalk.

Melody takes a simple armless chair that forms an equilateral triangle with Walter and Lowell. She sits forward like a cellist, not using the back of her chair.

"I'm recording these conversations so we don't miss anything," Lowell says gently.

"We're used to being recorded." She doesn't look up.

"Melody is performing her debut solo in Brazil." Walter speaks in crisp beats.

"So it's a double loss for you."

"Quartet loss." Melody hears her voice quivering. "We lost Milton, I lost my cello and my chance to solo, and we can't inaugurate the New World Compositions."

"Melody is the fiancée of the bright young man whose work is being premièred in Rio," Walter explains.

Walter's comment makes her feel awkward. She slides her palms face-down under the outside of her thighs.

"We've been together almost two years, but now we're just friends."

"His name is Eduardo," Walter says. "He was on stage with us."

"Why were you at the loading area this morning?" Lowell asks.

"It was only because of my cello."

"She put in yet another night of practice," Walter says.

Melody hears an upbeat bounce in Walter's voice.

"Melody, you were in a different position this morning than the others. You might have been one of the last to see Milton alive. Did you see anything suspicious?"

"I didn't see anything," Mel says. She should have taken a beat to think before answering. "I really didn't see anything." She feels her fingers tighten again. "I loved Milton." Saying his name brings her to the brink of tears.

"Someone in your position would be able to signal as the truck was leaving."

She hears a loud dissident chord and shivers. She doesn't hear blame in his voice, but she can't answer, just gives a hazy head shake.

"You also defended that guy who stands outside," Lowell says.

"People jump to conclusions without evidence. Social psychologists have shown that you can judge people's intelligence by their appearance but not their honesty."

"You know the guy?"

"Everyone knows him. People who attend classical concerts tend not to be criminal masterminds."

"It's you who's jumping to conclusions," Lowell says. Then he makes a realization. "It's you that Borges blames."

She hears Maestro Borges' accusation in her head. "He's a blameful man. Great musician but . . . I can't believe it about Milton."

Lowell waits. She remains silent. Then he speaks with

approving tones. "You have crisp white teeth, ideal for fine chewing, an often overlooked component of digestion."

It throws her off. "A lot of musicians did not want to go," she says. "They opposed this advancement of the arts thing. Life for creative people is hard enough."

"And your feelings?"

"I have to go. I haven't been playing well recently, and I made a decision to change that this trip. Critics are unforgiving. I've practiced the piece to death. China and I come up for tenure this month. I absolutely have to go." Her voice trails off like Vaughan Williams's *Lark Ascending*.

She raises her head and flashes an imploring look at Walter, who returns a reassuring gesture. She massages her fingers, trying to rub the tension out of them.

"So, this is your make-or-break moment. What did you do after last night's performance?"

"Walter was standing at the stage door, as he always does when the applause ends. He led us to the tuning room and reminded us that the bus to the airport would leave at seven."

She turns her gaze to Walter, who gives another approving nod.

"Walter came up to me and Felix."

Walter jumps in. "The principal clarinetist."

"Felix is an awesome musician," Melody says. "He's the first to show up for performances and the last to leave. He doesn't just study his part, he knows every section's music. He has to play as many little solos during concerts as I do. It always creates anxiety. Walter reassured us about the trip, because we were doing everything as a group, and the Brazilian government was taking absolutely no chances with our security."

"And then?"

"Then . . . well . . . then Eduardo walked me home."

"But you're just friends," Lowell says.

"The robbery and murder stunned us all," Melody says, articulating a secondary theme. "I have to go. I have something special I have to do."

Her left fingers are opening and closing on her right wrist, her practice-without-a-cello pose. Lowell sees that she's quite muscular.

"Why would anyone kill Milton?" she asks.

"This is Eduardo's second BSO commission," Walter says. "He premièred his first piano sonata in Sanders Theater when he was thirteen." Walter sounds like a clumsy trombonist playing a 2/4 march.

Melody looks down. Eduardo's musical skill was low on her pro and con list. "Eduardo, China, and I jam together," she says. "When an oboe and cello play, the oboe is an octave above the cello."

"What's the value of your instrument?" Lowell asks.

"It's a fairly new cello, a 1928 Carletti. The insurance appraised it at eighty thousand last year."

"How come you guys like old instruments?"

"Even with all our technology, we can't produce string instruments with the tonal qualities like those from Cremona three hundred years ago." Melody's eyes focus on nothing. "Cellos come in different sizes. Italian cellos are smaller than the French and German, and they're made of different woods. Mine has a light varnish and deep resonance for its size."

"Every cello sounds different?"

"That's what makes an orchestra. A tuning fork has perfect sound, but who would listen to an orchestra of tuning forks? We tune to the same vibrations per second but have a combination of sounds and overtones on that pitch. The BSO tunes slightly lower than other orchestras, 435. That's the vibrations per second on middle A. Deeper sounds like cello convey passion. When we're passionate, our pupils dilate and our voices drop a pitch."

"Strings do the most work," Walter says. "Conductors ask the winds and horns to stand and get applauded but rarely ask individual strings. Except Melody."

"So, what's the name of the guy who stands around?" Lowell asks.

"George."

"George what?"

"I don't know."

Lowell thanks Melody. She rises without looking at him, walking out faster than she walked in.

Maestro Borges flings open Walter's office door at 10:28 a.m., forty-nine minutes before the bomb. Borges walks deliberately, his back straight, head upright, face directed forward, a serious expression that Lowell guesses Borges wears even in happy times. His deep features are etched in his dark face as if molded by the wax museum. His nose begins straight, then makes a sharp angle until it is stopped by his face. His cheekbones are carved perpendicular to his nose, and his narrow mouth is a wavy line halfway between his chin and his nose. His straight hair is parted evenly down the middle, hanging past his ears. The timpanist says that he gets his cue from watching Borges' hair as it bounces to the tempo he wants the orchestra to keep, beating the kettle drum every time his hair drops.

"I came to give my assistance." Borges is both demanding and threatening.

"Maestro," Walter says, too politely, his open arms extending half as wide as the room, "you can inform this fine policeman. He doesn't know music, but he's a sincere man."

Lowell watches Borges take the chair on which Melody had just perched, his body vertical or horizontal, making ninety-degree bends at the knees and hips, his back not touching the chair, which Lowell figures must be how musicians sit, his pants creased precisely, no wedding ring, though he wouldn't be the type to wear one.

"Mr. Conductor, you seem to know who stole this great

moment from you." Lowell uses his formal voice.

"That girl who just left," Borges says, somber and dour.

Lowell pegs him as a person who's fastidious about how his eggs are cooked.

"She sought to sabotage the ceremony by her atrocious playing. She and her Trotsky-worshiping comrade Tito supplied inside information to the other FAS radicals to steal the instruments. I didn't imagine they were also capable of murder."

Lowell surmises that the hatred is personal. "You got proof?"

"I attempted to assist her, but she belongs in a high school marching band. You should have stopped those extremists from attending those meetings. Homeland Security has a dossier on them."

Lowell wonders how Borges knows that. "What happened after last night's concert?"

"We finished with the Tchaikovsky *Fifth.* The orchestra played sluggishly—I couldn't get them motivated—but the audience jumped up in applause."

"That's why orchestras play war horses," Walter says in a mini rant. He had told Lowell that he was seventy-two, but his hair has no hint of gray, no sign his strength is waning. "You just make a lot of noise, and most people walk away as if they've had an artistic experience, whereas they've bought a fifty-cent emotion from a junk store. Fewer and fewer people appreciate music as fine art, fine as in thin, subtle. Noise is not synony-mous with *forte.* Noise is not music. Music is love—sometimes you play piano, soft, and sometimes *forte,* strong."

"I can't imagine you make love anything but strong," Lowell says.

"Of course I can. Piano is harder to play because it's stripped to the basics. But you never make noise."

"My wife makes noise," Lowell says.

"In her case, it's art."

Walter gives Lowell a poignant look. It takes him a while to get it.

Their eyes turn to Borges, whose grim face has been rotating between each speaker as if they're playing tennis.

"I've lunched with the vice president as well as cabinet members," Borges says. "I know Brazil's foreign minister personally, and I've played before our president several times. I can make life easier or harder for many people. The BSO approached me last year. I met with the artistic director and agreed to go."

"The arts agreement wasn't passed last year."

"We were initially to première the New World Compositions. It was convenient and fitting to expand the concert to an international celebration." Borges shifts the weight of his hips and turns his wrist. "I've been trying to tell that to the media, who have lambasted our participation. Every day a recklessly distorted editorial appears in the *Globe* or the *Times*."

Lowell thinks that Borges is a guy who reads the conditions of a software upgrade before clicking "Agree."

"We open the program with 'The Star Spangled Banner,'" Walter says, "and then the Brazilian president bestows the Medal of Arts on the Maestro, the highest honor."

Lowell acknowledges with a head nod, and Walter continues, his voice excessively admiring. "The Maestro renounced our chauffeur in order to go on the bus with the musicians."

"Of course," Borges says. "I don't put myself above anyone."

Lowell has the opposite impression.

Borges' face transforms into an amiable smile. "At least now you can return our baggage."

Walter continues, again like a panegyric. "This concert will be televised and distributed. There's a lot of money on the line."

Borges holds his head too still. Lowell watches him swallow, realizing that Walter wants to make Borges look bad, perhaps to get back at him for disparaging Melody, whom Walter demonstrably likes.

"The business aspect of this concert will determine the new way artists are compensated," Borges says. "No more subsidies." He stands. "Last week, Cage, the liaison for the arts, became convinced of the Advancement of the Arts Agreement and became an enthusiastic supporter. Artists will stand or fall on their merits."

"Seems like they're not standing too good right now," Lowell says.

"You can't sit around here," Borges blurts, his attitude not an act. "Do something. Get those FAS terrorists before midnight. Interrogate them, find the instruments before they murder others. You should return our luggage in the meantime."

"Where does your brother Guru live?"

Borges takes a defensive breath. "We're staying at the symphony's guest apartment in Back Bay. Why?"

"He was at the loading area this morning," Lowell says.

Lowell sees Borges' arms move forward subtly, ready to attack or defend.

"Is that where he was?" A plastic smile. "The State Department wouldn't allow him to come. My mother is meeting me in Rio."

The officer in charge of knocking on doors along St. Stephen Street sticks his head into the office. "Nobody saw or heard nothing. The robbers seemed to have materialized out of the steam rising from the sewers and faded into the frozen air."

"Are we that inept?" Borges says, marching indignantly toward the officer.

"Our guys were thorough. They practically hauled every nineteen-year-old who lives on the street out of bed and shook them awake. No one gave us nothing."

"These people are like the mafia." Borges' face is fire red. "Everyone's afraid to talk."

"The robbers' key was surprise," the officer says, "working fast and not making any noise."

"Unlike my wife," Lowell says.

Borges whirls toward him. "What are you going to do now?"

Lowell regroups with the four sergeants after they finish questioning everyone who was on the buses to the airport. The interviews go swiftly, since the musicians have no substantive insights, only accusations against the nebulous group of anti-agreement activists, the electricians, and George, who stands across the street.

Lowell brings the musicians back into the auditorium. Walter, Maestro Borges, and Eduardo return and sit on stage while the musicians take seats in the auditorium.

When everyone is seated, Lowell asks Walter out loud, "If you received all these threats, why didn't you take precautions?"

"The State Department organized it. Homeland Security screened everyone. The Brazilian government was protecting us during the visit."

"And getting the instruments to the airport?"

"We left that in the hands of Brighton Hauling. They've been doing our moving for the past fifteen years, and we've never had a problem."

"Here you have your own guards. The airport is untouchable, the buses had an escort, and Brazil would be blanketing the city with security. That leaves one weak link: the truck with the instruments packed conveniently into separate crates."

Rodrigo walks calmly onto the stage. He asks everyone to seek a convenient egress. People don't get it. They're still in shock.

"We should relocate beyond the confines of the building," he repeats.

The musicians sit dumbfounded. Rodrigo whispers to Lowell, who turns quickly to face the audience.

"Get out!" Lowell yells, throwing out his arms in urgency. "Everyone, out of the hall!"

People jump over seats and race to the dozen exits, running muddled and jumbled.

Melody sees Eduardo on stage shaking his head, unable to believe what's happening. China yanks Melody's arm.

"Eduardo!" Melody yells, breaking his daze. He looks around, disoriented.

"Move!" China screams.

He remains bewildered.

"Eduardo!"

He walks unevenly to the edge of the stage.

"Jump!" Melody says.

He leaps down to the front seats. Melody grabs him, and the three run out the front entrance behind everyone else.

Raja is waiting nonchalantly for Melody. He rolls onto his back. Melody scoops him up and runs with everyone else across Mass. Ave.

A van with "BOMB SQUAD" painted prominently in Boston Police blue arrives just in time to hear the blast.

"It's in the Hatch Lounge," one of the musicians says.

The assistant principal cellist speaks loud enough for everyone to hear: "Melody, weren't you alone in there with Guru?"

After their first date following the Saturn star party and their two days of carnal obsession, Eduardo disappeared for two weeks. Melody, bewildered, running a gamut of emotions, read information about him on the web and walked his street. She dialed his number but never pressed talk. She studied two of his piano compositions from the music library, searching for him in the music, transposing one for cello.

Then he knocked on her door with papers in his hand. "I wrote this for you," he said. "I saw how you play and thought it would fit you."

Mel didn't know which leg to put her weight on, let alone what to say. She kept him standing in the hallway while she looked at the computer-generated score.

Melody rarely listens to recordings. When she wants to hear a piece, she opens the score, and the music flows off the page—the exact music, not someone's interpretation. But she was so flustered that her eyes couldn't comprehend what she was looking at.

"A quartet for cello, violin, oboe, and piano," he explained.

Mel took a long time to focus.

"Do you have time?" Eduardo covered his mouth with his open fingers. "If we get an oboist and violinist, we could try it in the room downstairs."

She went to get her phone and closed the door on him, realized what she had done, and ran back to open it again, still forgetting to invite him in. Melody phoned the Ukrainian oboist she played with in their amateur group, urging her to come right away and to bring a violinist, but she said she was out with friends and would come later.

"Right away," Melody said with emphasis.

"Got it," the oboist said, and arrived ten minutes later with a Korean-American violinist.

Their presence calmed Melody. After the quartet tuned, they played the first section precisely but without feeling. Each person remained internal, absorbed in his or her individual score. The music suited Melody perfectly, her fingers quick and clean. Eduardo had included rapid runs, trills, and three-string arpeggios. Mel tackled them on sight reading.

Halfway through the piece, Melody got it. She sensed what Eduardo wanted to say through her bow and slid into passion, articulating the piece on sight and expanding those feelings on the returns. As soon as she slid out of mechanics, she brought out the others' emotions, and they began making music.

The piece was in G, a key associated with childhood. It finished quietly, without resolution. Though he had never voiced it, Eduardo had written the theme of Melody's life into the music, and her playing intuited it. He was not adept at expressing emotions in words, since their sounds often clanged inharmoniously, but the piece he produced, wild and shy and wounded all at once, gave voice to such a range of emotions, including her inchoate longing, that between her understanding and expressing the inner sense of his composition, they consummated a sacred partnership.

The others remarked on how Mel and Eduardo fell into a pocket and played in unison. Eduardo became all business, making changes to the score. The three women suggested other modifications, and he incorporated them.

"It's a reasonable work," Eduardo said, "written for Mel's logical mind."

Most composers are pianists. Some try to get a wind or a string instrument to do what a piano does. Mel saw that Eduardo had an ear for each instrument and how it was played. She could take Eduardo's polished score and breathe life into it, because he wrote for her—or about her—and they understood each other.

"I've been thinking about a larger work," he told them, "a new way of composing. We four converged from different countries to unite in the New World and make music together."

That short piece, Melody's piece, which integrated elements of late Romantic artists like Mahler and Dvorak with contemporary minimalism, became the precursor to the New World Compositions, the series of new compositions that express in music the history of the Americas since the arrival of Europeans. Eduardo began organizing orchestras across the Americas to grant commissions to over three dozen composers. Melody was to première the first piece in Rio.

Afterwards, Melody and Eduardo returned to his apartment.

"You wrote about my mother dying in the fire," she said.

"You told me about it."

"Yes, I told you, but you understood that it wasn't an accident."

Portamento: Literally, carrying, now meaning the slide between notes, a type of glide or glissando. Singers are often encouraged not to slide up notes, since it comes across as sappy sentimentality.

Second Movement
Largo

Forty-two minutes before Melody swears to find the instruments, the bomb squad cop holds a piece of burned cloth in front of Lowell's nose.

"When I heard it, I thought it was a cheap pop—phosphorus nitrate sprinkled with sulfur and charcoal. Some kid could have taken the 'T' from Chinatown with a pocketful of cherry bombs, wrapped the snatch in newspaper, and shoved it into a plastic bottle."

He and Lowell move amid the debris that the bomb has spread around the first floor lounge, where Melody and Guru had talked. The bomb had been placed in a trash barrel. Except for a few pieces of wood and plastic scattered around four or five overturned tables and chairs, the room is remarkably intact.

"It didn't crack a window," the cop says. "Look at the burn—it's sophisticated." He points at the garbage can. "The guy who put this together knew his ammo. He made more noise with a half-pound of dust than the average Joe bomber makes with twenty. He configured it to do nothing but make noise. See? It didn't even burn the carpet. It's a high class stunt grenade."

Lowell studies the garbage can, unsure what to look for. He looks at the other garbage cans and observes that they have new liners.

"How was it set off?"

"Electronic spark, cell phone trigger. You could push the button from Swaziland. The pulp inside," he shakes his head, "that's expert."

"First the heist, then the body, now the bomb," Lowell says. "What's next?"

"These Boston Pops types take themselves seriously," the bomb squad cop says. "They write contentious articles about the meaning of a pause between two quarter notes."

"The heist and the bomb weren't meant to hurt anyone."

"The burn says that whoever did it is no loony."

"I'll bring the orchestra members back into the building as if nothing happened and make it our operations center," Lowell says. "It isn't the Pops."

The musicians balk when Lowell motions for them to reenter Symphony Hall.

"Maybe they'll kill another one of us," a musician says.

"The bomb squad certified the building as safe," Lowell insists.

"I'm not going back in there," another musician says.

"What about Milton?" someone cries. "Look what these people are capable of."

"What if all of us didn't make it out of the building before the explosion?"

Raja jumps out of Melody's arms and runs off at the sound of distressed voices.

"The bomb wasn't meant to hurt anyone," Lowell says. "Only frighten."

"Who can tell what they'll do next."

Walter steps forward, holding his shoulders upright. "Reentering is the noble action. We walk back in with our heads high to show that we will not yield to anyone's threats."

The musicians acquiesce to Walter. They follow their concertmaster to the downstairs lounge. Concertmaster Goldberg, also called "first violinist," is the orchestra's leader and foremost violinist, since composers write many bars of solo violin within larger works. She determines the up and down bowing for the violins and takes charge of tuning the orchestra. When an orchestra doesn't like a conductor, they look to the concertmaster.

Once they enter the building, Walter turns to Lowell. "Garbage is the last thing the crew does. They're the last to leave, and they take it out after they close up."

"That means the noisemaker was put here this morning."

China approaches Lowell and Walter as they poke around the loading area. She is wearing light-colored jeans that fit snugly around her legs and a pastel blouse that matches the rosy hue of her face.

"Melody and China are our junior members," Walter says with an open expanse, "absolute artists. In their capable hands we entrust the future of artistic music."

"Mel and I have been friends since we were hired," China says. "Many musicians don't know each other, even if they share a music stand for ten years. Mel's going through a tough time now. She can't have someone throwing another dart at her."

"You think I have darts up my sleeve?"

"I think you do your job without an agenda. That makes us friends."

China is vivacious, her attention turned outward. Lowell recognizes her as one of the rare people who can give reliable eyewitness evidence.

"Did you notice anyone besides police hanging around this morning?"

"There was a guy standing near the reflecting pond of the Christian Science Church."

"From that angle he could see the truck leaving the loading area," Walter says.

"Why did you notice him?"

"He was standing in the middle of nowhere, bundled up in a black parka, like most people in January. I got on the bus just before seven and sat next to Mel facing south, so I didn't see when he left."

"You play the—"

"Oboe. I've had a double reed between my lips since I was six."

"Is that what makes you talk fast?"

Her laugh is expansive. "Some people move so slowly they seem to be standing still."

"What's your oboe's value?" Lowell asks.

"I have an African Blackwood Loree, silver keys. The French make the best oboes, but wind instruments aren't as expensive as strings. Mine is worth seven thousand."

"Do you have any frustrations or difficulties with others in the orchestra?"

"The most frustrating aspect of an oboist's life is reeds. We make our own."

"How many in the orchestra are sympathetic to FAS?" Lowell asks.

"Those in the arts tend to be liberal," she says. "The arts agreement is like giving away our rights to shareholders, but some musicians are oblivious to the world."

The three move through the unadorned basement hallways. Lowell notices that the backstage and basement of Symphony Hall are utilitarian. Parts of it resemble the inside of a World War II battleship. It was even painted battleship gray at one point, but now thick coats of eggshell beige cover the brick and cement walls. Noticing that the basement extends under most of the block, Lowell asks Walter how they keep it secure.

"We have fifty-two surveillance cameras. Every door is alarmed, so whenever one is opened, it flashes on the guards' monitors. This hall is completely secure."

"Are the guards always here?"

"At least two security guards in the building every minute, day and night. They track everything. They also take care of medical emergencies. We have six defibrillators in the hall. Physicians volunteer to be on call during concerts. They discreetly assist several times a month."

"What's with all these trunks?" Lowell asks.

"That's how we normally travel," China says. "We pack our clothes and instruments in them, and they turn up in our hotel rooms on our arrival. Everything is organized."

Lowell pokes around. Wires and pipes crisscross the ceiling. He observes tables and chairs stuffed into the corners.

"The Pops," Walter says. "They unscrew the rows of seats in the main section of the auditorium and squeeze in as many of those tables and chairs as possible. They get in almost as many people as during BSO concerts. Then they serve them fizzy wine and wrapped sandwiches from the kitchen just off the auditorium."

"The Pops season is short," China says. "Principals of sections like Mel don't play Pops. We go to Tanglewood for the summer."

With the straightened spine of a parade soldier, Walter explains that the Pops began in 1885 to give musicians fulltime work. The Esplanade Pops is a separate orchestra of free-lancers. Arthur Fiedler began the Esplanade concerts on the Charles River in 1929 and stayed as head of the Pops for fifty years.

"Once, while Fiedler was vacationing in the Yucatan, he was asked to conduct an orchestra of Maya Indians. They couldn't afford shoes, let alone decent instruments, but they played Beethoven and Brahms. The BSO and the Pops perform two hundred and fifty concerts a year." Walter takes a breath. "Plus a lot of rehearsals, depending on the conductor."

He puts his hand on China's shoulder, a patriarchal gesture. "Stay around the building for now. The orchestra will have another meeting soon."

"I was planning to be on a plane for Rio de Janeiro, so my dance card is empty."

She has a wink in her eye that says, in the end, life is a joke. There is no joke on Walter's face. Lowell has a joke tucked away, but no one else laughs.

As China walks away, Mrs. Schutz approaches with sheets of paper. She is a short, dignified woman with gray hair who wears medium heels and a plaid wool skirt below the knee, even in summer.

"Here's the list we presented to the State Department," she says. "One piccolo, three flutes, three oboes, one English horn, four clarinets, three bassoons, one contrabassoon. Five French horns, four trumpets, three trombones, and one tuba. Only small percussion, since we were renting a set of timpani and chimes in Rio, plus two harps. Sixteen first violins, fourteen second—plus the soloist—ten violas, nine cellos, and seven double basses."

She hands the paper to Walter. It is clear to Lowell that Walter runs the orchestra but that Mrs. Schutz runs Walter.

Walter hands the list to Lowell. "She arranged the list in their traditional order down a conductor's score—winds, brass, percussion, and strings."

Lowell studies it, unsure of the difference between violin and viola.

"Horns, as in animal horns?"

"That's how they evolved," Walter says. "You will have the pleasure of interviewing the Czechoslovakian soloist. Shall we go meet him?"

Sergeant Rodrigo walks up to them. "You don't have to search for that man who hangs around. He's standing right across the street."

They begin converging on Symphony Hall mid-morning. They walk up the stairs from the Green Line subway or down Mass. Ave. toward the neo-classical brick building. They come by car and by bus, people in their fifties and sixties and seventies wearing long coats, lined boots, scarves, and colored wool hats. They gather outside the front entrance, standing alone, in couples, or in small groups.

As the crowd grows, they spread around the corner to Huntington Avenue. College students join them. By 10:00 a.m., soon after the bomb, people take over the right southbound lane in front of Symphony Hall, forcing the police to call for crowd control.

They come out for their orchestra, the BSO, one of the world's most richly supported orchestras. Last time the BSO had a capital campaign, the city rallied and gave up a crisp $150 million. Many orchestras struggle to raise $150,000. The BSO has the biggest budget of any US orchestra and the highest ticket prices. Its musicians are the second highest paid of any orchestra, second to the Met Opera orchestra.

They arrive at Symphony Hall dressed for a cold vigil, many coming from the area's churches, where news of the robbery was broadcast from the pulpit. They come with grave faces, and they keep moving to keep warm, although the sun has taken the sting out of the city's frigid morning. A low pressure system over New York exposed the city to a jet stream straight from the Arctic, but it's a bright day, clear and dry. If the temperature wasn't so bitter, it might well have been a Sunday for brunch and a stroll.

The music lovers who come bring others, a crowd that increases just because it's a crowd. Passersby, seeing the gathering on Mass. Ave., stop and stand around as well, and they, too, cheer for the orchestra. The police try to keep the crowd confined near the sidewalks so at least one line of cars can pass either way on the broad street, but that becomes a struggle, and soon they give up.

The BSO is one of the country's oldest musical organizations, though not as old as the Handel and Haydn Society, which began in 1815, before the height of romanticism, and commissioned Beethoven to compose an oratorio.

The BSO does not flaunt the list of composers who have watched their pieces performed or performed them within its walls or the soloists and conductors who have stood on its stage. Listing the great performers who have not played in Boston would be easier.

Composers used to take the first seat in the first balcony right over the stage, close enough to read the music off the viola stands. Now they sit on the ground floor or backstage and are called to the front after their piece is performed.

Although many lament that classical music is dying—a perpetual complaint—the overall number of people attending concerts is stable, including a new crop of young people. Employment for future classical musicians is as good or bad as it has ever been. The arts bring in four times as much money as all sports combined.

"The classical crowd don't take to being pushed around by the police," Rodrigo says when he, Lowell, and Walter step outside, thirty-two minutes before Melody begins investigating. He points to the gathering around the hall. "Protesters you can get rough with, but no cop shoves around a silver-haired Bostonian."

Walter raises his arms with inflated drama. "These are our people. You can't push them around."

Lowell gestures for Walter to cool down and let others deal with the crowd. He looks across from the stage entrance and sees Sergeant Franck's massive black hand grabbing the shoulder of a man leaning on a parking sign. Lowell observes that the mysterious man looks to be in his early sixties, wearing an expensive camel hair coat over a soft beige cashmere turtleneck. Lowell, standing without a coat, believes in trusting first impressions. He notices the movements of a man not used to being bossed around, whose stature doesn't cower when confronted by police.

Franck pushes the man across the street as if he were a lawn mower, bringing him face to face with Lowell.

"Do you mind telling me why your man grabbed me?"

Lowell asks his name.

"What's your name? Who are you?"

"Lieutenant Lowell, Boston Police. And you are . . . George."

George falls silent. Lowell watches him take in the situation and consider how to respond.

"I'm a Boston resident. You work for me."

Franck moves George to the wall. In one steady motion, pushes his back against it. Lowell stands in front of him.

"Boss." He makes a slight salute. "George what?"

"George Fredrick Handel. You tell me what you want with me."

"I'm sure you know what happened."

Again, George ponders the best response. "I heard on the news."

Franck releases him.

"At this initial stage, I'm looking for information."

"I don't have any."

"Why does George Fredrick Handel hang around over

there?"

"That has nothing to do with anything."

"Look, boss, we've had a murder, a bomb, and a robbery. I have to question everyone. I've even questioned the conductor."

"You're wasting your time with me. I'm a bystander, and I'd like to leave."

He starts to turn, but Franck's hand grips his elbow.

Lowell strokes his unshaven face and takes a couple of seconds to assess the man. "I think you should stay a while."

"You can't keep me."

"You a lawyer?"

"These are straightforward rights. Everyone knows them."

"I'm keeping you as a material witness."

"You can't do that."

"I'll show you what we can do." Lowell motions to Franck. "Take our boss inside to one of the rooms, and get someone to keep him company. If he wants anything, give it to him as you see fit."

Franck moves George by the elbow to the door. George looks back. For the first time, Lowell sees an expression of panic on the man's face.

"I thought George Fredrick Handel only hung around Symphony Hall at Christmas time," Franck says.

Lowell steps back inside the stage door, shuddering off the cold. He sees Borges pacing, ready to yell. Lowell ducks past him.

The commissioner phones to tell him of the nervous calls he's getting from Washington.

"Ask them why their special agent took off," Lowell says.

"The feds are stepping way over the line, snatching FAS people out of their homes and interrogating them roughly. Stay away from that."

Alan Ostinato, the sergeant who picks up the phone at the Malden police station, knows Lowell from Chelsea High School. Lowell asks after his son, but Sergeant Ostinato, sensing an unenthused voice, gives him his chief's phone number right away, finishing with synthetic pleasantries about getting together.

"Lieutenant, you were a leader even then," Ostinato says.

Malden is a blue-collar suburb fifteen minutes by train from downtown Boston.

Lowell gets right to the point with the Malden police chief. "You know about the symphony heist?"

"I'm hearing it on TV. Professional hit."

"The robbers left the truck in front of your police station."

"My police station?"

"It's a long silver truck with 'Brighton Hauling' written on the red cab. Can you inspect it? We might be looking for hairs."

The Malden chief mobilizes immediately, calling his investigators and telling Alan Ostinato to isolate the truck on Commercial Street.

"Can I ask you something?" Ostinato says before the chief hangs up. "Did I let you down when I messed up that flea market case?"

"Jesus, that was ten years ago."

"Eleven and a half. I still feel sensitive about it."

"Listen, Al, don't bring up past failures in front of your boss."

"See, you believe I was a failure. That's what kept me from being a leader."

"You're not going sissy on me, are you, Al?"

That shuts Ostinato up.

The chief is on the scene in minutes. He steps out of his tinted-window SUV and walks around the parked truck, his gloved hands behind his back. Al Ostinato, a tall, gawky guy with a pensive face, stands around with hunched shoulders, hands in his pockets, making the chief feel uncomfortable. He puts up with Ostinato's looming silence for five minutes until the crime investigators arrive. They slide on examination gloves and hop through the truck's rear gate with flashlights.

"Everything's neat here, four metal crates," one of them tells the chief.

They open the crates one by one, finding luggage in each.

"They must have worked fast," the chief says.

"If the baggage and instruments were separated," Ostinato reasons, "they could have rolled the instrument crates off in a couple of minutes and dropped the truck here before anyone reported the robbery."

The chief dials Lowell at 11:45 a.m. "At first look, I'd say they told it like it is. They must have known which crates contained instruments. Personal belongings untouched. Why would they want to mess with people's underwear? I'd say they either took a big risk leaving the truck in front of a police station, or they were making it easy for us."

"There's a third possibility," Lowell says. "They want to make us look like idiots."

"We need an hour or two to go through it. If we can't find anything by then, we'll be singing 'My Fair Lady'."

"Oh, don't tell me you're into classical music as well."

"Sure," the Malden chief says. "We got class here. Malden may not be Cambridge, but we ain't Revere or Saugus either. I've been to their concerts. You ever go?"

"I'm trying to tell the difference between violins and violas. How's Al doing for you?"

"He's all right when he doesn't get too sensitive."

"Funny how we change over the years but don't change. Call me if you get something, especially if that something is nothing."

"Check around to see if anyone saw the truck pull up," the chief says to Ostinato after he hangs up.

"I always knew what I wanted to do in life," Ostinato says, "but I could never pull it off."

"What's that got to do with anything?"

"I've been thinking, that's all. I always wanted to be good at something."

"Why don't you try being bad at something first and then work your way up?"

"It's just that—"

"You keep going on, and I'll take you off the bagpipe band."

It's a threat the chief uses often to ground his sergeant, and it works. Ostinato makes a resolute face and gives a crisp nod.

The chief looks at the two cameras strapped to the outside of the station pointing along Commercial Street. "We must have caught something on tape," he says.

"Those cameras haven't been working for dogs' years," Ostinato says. "I mentioned it a couple of times."

"What else do we have?"

"Those cameras could have really helped."

"Someone around here must have seen something. Get on it, Al. Go find their instruments while you're at it."

"Yes, sir!" Ostinato salutes, resolute, and marches directly to his computer.

"Any little thing," the chief says to the guys working the truck. "Lowell doesn't have much to go on."

"If they were bold enough to dump the truck in front of a police station, you think they'd leave an address book?"

"Confidence and carelessness, they run around the

playground holding hands."

The chief asks three of his men to go to the T station half a block away and ask around.

"What are we supposed to ask?" one of the guys says. "Did you see anyone today?"

After questioning George, Lowell and Walter walk past the musicians' lounge in the basement, which is near the loading area. Lowell picks out Tito the bassist from amongst the musicians.

"You had a lot to say against going to Rio."

Tito becomes confrontational. "I'm head of the Players' Committee. The government set up FAS." He stands straight, his face always looking like he has just showered. His large Adam's apple bobs with each word.

The other musicians huddle around the scene.

"You got information to back that up?"

"History," Tito says.

He begins an animated rant against capitalism. "They want to bust our unions, use independents instead of hiring people, take us back to the black days when musicians worked half the year and couldn't support their families. The level of musical performance has increased dramatically since unions. Many 1950s recordings sound amateur. My friend Art Verra, the timpanist, was the only one with the courage to refuse to go to Rio."

"How come you decided to go?"

"I have to support Melody. She's got a baboon on her back. Borges stopped her at every rehearsal and chewed her out during her solo. She sat up front, as soloists do, and she played progressively worse after each insult. A couple of people in her section agree with Borges out of jealousy. Almost everyone else is against him."

"Why were you late this morning?" Lowell asks.

"I had to pick up Felix." Tito points at the principal clarinetist. "I misjudged the time."

"You make that trip every day, right?"

"Never early Sunday morning. It was just a few minutes, not a big deal."

Lowell turns to Felix. "Aren't you always the first to show up?"

"Actually, we arrive early to warm up our instruments," Felix says. "But we're not playing today."

"Why question us?" Tito says. "The government is the predator."

Lowell turns to Walter. "What side are you on—predator or prey?"

Walter responds like a sage. "We appreciate the hawk, its power, its beauty, its ferocity, yet we mourn the sparrow in its claws. What good is a harmonic life? You need dissident chords and tense progressions to make life beautiful."

Rodrigo approaches, handing Lowell a phone. Lowell ducks into a corner to talk to Amy. Rodrigo hears him apologizing.

"I've wrecked my daughter's chances of a happy life," Lowell tells Rodrigo afterwards. "She goes out with these no-commitment types, which gives her the heebie-jeebies about staying a single mom and not being able to do anything else."

"It's tough to bring up your kid in a city like this where there's so much choice," Rodrigo says. "Where I come from, there was a handful of girls, and every guy knew he'd be hooked up to one of them, and he wouldn't have another chance. Very simple."

Eduardo never mentioned Melody's mother again, but several months into their relationship, after Melody played an unstaged *Simon Boccanegra*, a story of forgiveness and redemption, Melody returned to her flat with Eduardo.

"I was away at my first competition in Dallas and was so excited when I won. I stayed at the Y with the other kids. A policeman woke me up in the middle of the night and said he was driving me home. He said there was an accident, but he wouldn't say more. He didn't take me home but to the police station and put me in a small room. A woman I don't know told me that my mother died in her sleep. Asphyxiation. She didn't feel a thing, as if that made it all right."

Eduardo listened carefully.

"The county offered psychological services. I went several times, but I didn't see the point in sitting and talking about myself."

Eduardo asked about her father.

"I never blended with my uncle's family," Melody said. "I played cello in school as long as I could before going there to dinner. I got my teacher to recommend me to a boarding school, and I never attended another competition and rarely took the cello outside my apartment. I learned accounting, but the cello became my friend, a real friend. We talk to each other every time I pick up the bow."

Melody took out her wallet and showed Eduardo a photo of her mother, a miniature of the one she kept in her practice area. At the competition, she was offered management, reserved for the most talented, unheard of for someone her age.

"I never played my instrument in front of other people again, until the night I met you."

The first ruckus at 11:49 a.m. comes loud and fast, beginning in the front lobby and spreading throughout the first floor. They number about twenty, students who never attend school, jeans and rough beards, storming in like a SWAT team, screaming slogans against the government. Two have posters, three-word denunciations of the Advancement of the Arts Agreement. Most just yell, the f-word prominent, filling the entire building with chaos.

"Don't f*ckin' go!" they shout. "Don't f*ckin' sell out!"

The few police in the hall react quickly, running after the dispersed protesters but unable to nab anyone. It takes several minutes for the small army of police stationed outside to storm in and give chase, but they have a hard time arresting the agile protesters, entering a game of hide and seek. Two cops run down a hallway, and a protester jumps out behind them, jeering. Then the cops chase the howling protester the other way. The musicians stand by and watch. Even Tito, who knows the young people, is troubled by their actions.

"You shouldn't be in here," he chides them.

"You shouldn't either," one says. "Supporting f*ckin' capitalists."

"You want to be controlled by Yahoo and Microsoft?" another protester says. "You want Fox to decide who gets heard and who gets paid?"

"This will turn us into zombies," the first protester says, "sitting in a stuffy recording studio playing easy listening for ten bucks an hour."

"We agree, but Symphony Hall is a sacred space," Tito says.

It takes a better part of thirty minutes until the police either chase the protesters out of the building or arrest them.

"You can put your f*ckin' handcuffs on me," one yells. "But hundreds of others will follow and liberate the arts. We won't take your greed."

Twenty minutes before she becomes determined to find the instruments, Melody enters the basement lounge. The musicians are trickling into the large, plain lunch room, which has tables and chairs on a faded rug. Melody finds Eduardo talking nervously in a corner on his phone. He looks up, sees her, and hangs up. The two sit together, both somber.

"They think I signaled the truck. Borges is accusing me," Melody says.

"Your involvement in FAS makes you suspect. It also puts you in a position to solve the case."

Her forehead tightens. "What are you talking about? What could I know that the police don't? Tito was active. I only went to a few meetings."

"Tito is too fiery. You have the most to lose if the orchestra doesn't play on Tuesday. We have eleven hours to find the instruments."

"At least now you're taking this seriously. When the government turned the trip into the arts agreement ceremony last month, it put me in a double quandary, because playing the solo would support that fraudulent business deal."

"You seemed resolved last night."

Melody notices that his mouth and eyes droop and that he has shed his detached, intellectual attitude.

"I talked to Tasa, the FAS coordinator, before the concert. She said this was my opportunity. I would be more useful to the artistic community if I went and triumphed. I felt liberated. I have a reason to play. I want to do more than make a pleasing tune."

"What encore did you prepare?"

"The Boccherini Allegro," she says, referring to the *Cello Sonata in A-Major*. "If the audience applauds enough for a call."

"Walter was worried about you."

"He arranged the trip. I don't know how the baggage truck escaped his plans." She tightens her fingers. "We have to support him—you know what's under that fortress."

"This is the type of situation Walter is built to handle."

"He and Milton always argued, but they really liked each other. No one could talk to Walter like Milton did." She slumps in her chair. "It hasn't sunk in yet that he's gone."

China arrives, bringing joy and banter, which annihilates the gloom. Felix joins them, and lastly, Tito, completing the coterie of five spunky young musicians, all quarks. They sit around a table in the center of the basement lounge.

China turns to Felix and Tito. "You guys almost missed the bus. You're both usually so precise."

"Why is everyone making a thing out of it?" Tito says.

"Did you notice a guy dressed in black standing across the street?" China says, her tone a steady G.

"There wasn't anyone," Tito says. "I know, because I looked around to see if anyone else was late."

"China saw the guy before seven," Melody says. "He must have signaled the hijackers and left by ten after."

"Did Guru tell you about his April Fools' joke?" Felix asks her like a clarinetist laying down a slippery ground for Gershwin's *Rhapsody in Blue*.

"He says a bunch of crazy things."

"He might have been used unwittingly," Tito says. "He's been obsessed with FAS. This has nothing to do with our distrust of his brother, the maestro. I wondered if Guru was the FAS mole. I'm sure we had one."

"Let's not turn this into a witch hunt," Melody says. "You have to be extra careful before you go around accusing people. No one will give that simpleton a second thought."

"Exactly my point," Tito says, *fermata* on each word.

Melody hears the Coke machine turn on, people pacing, chairs squeaking, fluorescent lights humming.

"Mel, why don't you find out what Guru knows?" China says. "He's always around here."

"Let's leave it to the police," Melody says. "He's not as stupid as he makes out."

"Who? Guru or the lieutenant?" Tito asks.

"Both," China says. "The lieutenant observes. Guru remembers."

Tito turns to Eduardo. "When you heard last month that the première of the New World Compositions had been transformed into this capitalist farce, were you upset?"

"We couldn't stop the government by pulling out."

"That's not the point." Tito's cheeks turn blazing pink. "The musicians who refused to play for Hitler were not going to stop the Nazi war machine, but they had to take a stand. Grieg snubbed the Orchestra Colonne to protest the Dreyfus Affair. Pablo Casals declined to play in any country that supported the Spanish fascists. I wondered several times if it wouldn't be better to do what Art Verra did and refuse to go. If we had all done that, we could have had an impact."

"Tito, you talk like a Handel aria," China says. "You go on and on at a high pitch, repeating everything eight times."

"Our way of life is in peril," Tito says. "Musicians were pivotal in the revolutions that changed Europe in 1848. We can do it again."

Melody notices an unfamiliar guy sitting at a table across from them who lowers his head in E-flat minor guilt.

"I was called to sub for Art Verra," the guy says. "Orchestras have a person who books musicians. He calls around and finds someone free for the engagement. You discover later what you're playing and for whom."

"Refusing work is a luxury freelance musicians can't afford," China assures him.

Tito shrugs in acquiescence. "Borges used the BSO organization to strong-arm us. He has a secret agenda besides that fraudulent media deal." His voice changes into the derisive baritone in *Carmina Burana.*"I mean, Advancement of the Arts Agreement."

"He hasn't been straight with us," China says, "but the robbery is bringing the plight of artists into the spotlight."

"It's incredible that FAS outfoxed the police," Melody says, "given the significance of the trip."

"It's you who is accusing without proof," Tito says. "The heist brought attention to the cause, but we don't do murder and military-style raids. The government and Borges organized everything." Tito speaks as if plucking two strings on his bass in a finale. "They would be the first place to look for a robber, a bomber, and a murderer."

"But the government wanted to hurry through their treaty," Mel says.

"The government isn't monolithic," Eduardo says, his fingers over his mouth.

Melody hears "Mars" from Holst's *The Planets.*

Other musicians walk around the room talking. Melody remains seated, and Tito sits next to her, on and off his phone. In the middle of one of his calls, he turns to Melody. "There's something wrong with Milton's body in New Hampshire."

"What do you mean?"

Tito talks more into the phone. Melody knows that one of Tito's friends went up to New Hampshire to investigate the murder, because they don't trust the police.

Tito clenches his fist and hangs up. "The guy wasn't murdered."

Baroque: Initially a derogatory term given by the classical era for the overblown frilly music of Bach and Handel's time. Both eras believed they were close to ancient Greece.

Divertimento

"Milton was a music connoisseur," the assistant principal cellist tells Lowell through her tears, twenty-six minutes before Melody swears to solve the case. She is a small, dark woman who speaks with a Russian accent. She had waited for Lowell outside Walter's office until Lowell returned, saying that she has relevant information.

"Milton sat alert at rehearsals. I've seen him stand the string instruments upright against the wall and talk to them. He knows when I'm playing near the bridge, playing too much vibrato. He knows when I'm stressed at home, and he treats my instrument like a man treats a woman he loves."

Her curling index finger pulls Lowell out of Walter's doorway into the corridor.

"It's Melody," the woman whispers after she shuts the office door so Walter can't hear. "She's afraid the world will see how awful she plays. See how stupid she is? Caught in the loading area and the bomb room."

The contempt in the woman's voice is overly apparent. "Imagine, giving herself the name 'Melody Cavatina'!" she says, her voice growing louder. "I played professionally for ten years before even thinking of auditioning for the BSO, let alone principal. She has absolutely no training. She's pretty, that's all."

She lowers her voice again to a conspiratorial tone.

"When we were ready to go to the airport, I saw her in the street waving. She was signaling the robbers."

Lowell looks at her fingers and imagines the neural firings traveling through her arms that make her fingers fly up and down the strings.

"She doesn't belong in the orchestra," the Russian says. "Maestro Borges tried to help her, but she doesn't have it in her. She helped FAS rob us to avoid playing. She comes from a cult where they pass around rattlesnakes and drink each other's blood. Nobody knows who she really is."

Lowell understands that Melody's enemies are histrionic, but he cannot discount their accusations. "Tell me, what's the difference between a violin and viola?"

The Russian blinks. "Size. The smaller the instrument, the higher the tone. Each string instrument has a range. A violin plays the higher notes while a bass plays the low ones. We read from different clefs, like the top and bottom lines of a piano score. Composers run their score from one string section to another, from bass to cello to viola to violin. Higher sounds project more. That's why you hear a soprano towering above the chorus."

"And why do they call it a double bass?"

"The bass has many names. All refer to that six foot instrument that's three octaves below a violin, but our bassists can play every note on the piano. They play in unison with other string instruments, or with tuba and bassoon."

Lowell thanks the woman.

When an officer brings him a razor and a belt, Lowell tells Walter to have everyone else who works in Symphony Hall come down for interviews. Walter delegates the task to Mrs. Schutz while Lowell makes his way to the bathroom sink.

He opens the hot water faucet until a quiet cloud of steam accumulates at the bottom of the basin. He fills his cupped hands with water and dunks his face, dripping on his shirt. He threads his belt through his trouser loops and tightens it, jamming his stomach under it like a camper would squeeze a sleeping bag into its stuff sack. But Lowell is no camper. He holds his belly cheerfully, slapping it with two hands in satisfaction. He opens the door to the toilet and examines its height. He has been known to phone the management of an establishment that has improper toilet height. He envies Japanese toilets, though he has a hard time getting up from a squatting position.

Maestro Borges is waiting in the hallway, his eyes in a throat-slitting mode. Lowell wraps his hand around his chin reflexively in case his throat is the one in which Borges is interested.

"I just discovered that the liaison for the arts told Homeland Security to leave town," Borges says in a controlled yell. "I never trusted that man. You must round up all those fascists yourself. Right now."

"You know where they are?"

"That's your job. First, bring back our luggage."

Meanwhile, Walter descends to the basement lounge. The musicians stop their solemn conversations and gather. Others in the tuning room crowd into the lounge, everyone standing around him like downtrodden Hebrew slaves encircling their Samson.

"Why doesn't everyone go out for a while," Walter tells them, his worried face mirroring the atmosphere. "Let's meet back here at. . .." he looks at his watch, "half past noon, and we'll see where the investigation is at."

"You think they'll find the murderer and return our instruments soon?" someone asks.

"Probably not soon," Walter says, "but we might get a better idea whether we'll solve the case by midnight. The police found the car that was used in the robbery. The Homeland Security specialist will be here in an hour. Their people have already made many arrests and are narrowing the field of suspects."

"String instruments can't take this cold," one musician says. "It loosens the sound post, then the string tension damages it."

"Even if we get them back, they may be unplayable," another player says. "Only Milton knew how to handle our instruments."

"If I don't get my Peggy back in my hands," a violinist says, "I don't know the point of living."

"Go out," Walter insists. He turns to Melody. "Lowell would like to speak to you again."

An unnatural silence is directed toward her.

Mayor Bond is new at his job. He's the first minority mayor in Boston, having won a bruising campaign with the support of black and Hispanic voters as well as liberal Boston intellectuals. He ran on a firm anti-expansionist platform. With another news-generating spike in housing prices, plus several freak problems that caused endless traffic jams, his complaints about too much urban growth created a populist stir that energized his campaign. A climate scientist by training, his genial personality directed him toward politics, which he thought was the only avenue to save the world from catastrophe. Bond comes from Dorchester, whose hills George Washington fortified with cannons in 1776. It became a streetcar suburb in the 1800s and merged into Boston in 1870.

During his four years on city council, Bond had been planning his mayoral run, not his ultimate ambition. He first tried to decorate City Hall, an ugly 1960s building across from Fanueil Hall, by painting it fire-engine red and cobalt blue so it would look like a giant toy. The *Herald*, a tabloid that opposed him, called the idea "kindergarten leadership." Bond backed down, but that didn't stop him from putting into place drastic measures to, in his words, "Green the grid, the car, and the home," which made him as many enemies as friends.

When he gets a Sunday morning call from the vice president, he is silently ecstatic at the possibilities. He phones his secretary and his speechwriter, and the three converge quickly on City Hall, Bond's car led by two motorcycle patrolmen.

"We have to handle the situation skillfully," he tells them as they enter the elevator, "remain in the center of action. This is a chance to gain prominence and do something big."

As the three walk down the vacant corridor, the sound of their heels echoing off the tile walls, a city reporter for the *Banner*, an African-American newspaper, is sitting on the bench outside the mayor's office.

"Are you calling the city council?" he asks Bond.

"I don't want to worry a bunch of people," the mayor says with a politician's smile and a meaty handshake.

The reporter brushes the mayor's arm. "Especially those angling for your job," he whispers and slaps Bond's back.

Mayor Bond sits in his office ready for interviews, but besides two phone inquiries, no other reporters come, neither the radio stations nor local TV. It takes a couple of hours until the *Banner* reporter tells them, "All the press are at Symphony Hall. That's where the action is."

Bond jumps up and tells his assistants to get their coats.

"Why didn't we realize that?" his secretary says. "We have to be close to the police."

"It will be my first time inside that building," Bond says as they prepare to leave.

Walter's watch beeps for twelve noon as he drapes his arm lightly around Melody's shoulders, comforting her as they walk to his office, where Lowell waits. Walter has gone out of his way to be sweet to her recently, but she hasn't told him about Borges' accusation. Nonetheless, Walter must have sensed her unease.

"Borges is brash but innocuous," he says. "He handles stress like a trapped snake."

She enters the office, her feet planted firmly, expecting conflict.

"Let's go for a walk," Lowell says. "It's hard to sit with a woman whose face belongs on a fashion magazine."

He turns her by the arm and walks her downstairs, Walter one step behind, passing through the first floor hallway. Lowell glances into the glass displays of old pictures and sheet music. Lowell's casualness worries Melody. Walter opens a door, and the three walk into the main hall. Mel hears nothing but their shoes on the floor. Symphony Hall's heating fans make no sound.

"Are you part of FAS?" Lowell asks.

She missteps, then catches herself. "I've gone to a couple of meetings."

"Why didn't you tell me before?"

"I haven't been involved for a while."

Lowell strolls toward the stage, his hands behind his back. Melody and Walter follow.

"Do you know their leaders?"

"They try not to have leaders. Everyone is supposed to be equal. Tito took me."

He wanders into row D. "What did you do for them?"

"There were things going on in my life. I did honk and wave on street corners during rush hour. Most people didn't pay attention, but Maestro Borges saw us demonstrating in Copley Square the day he arrived in Boston while he was being driven to his apartment. I recognized the BSO's car. He got out and yelled irrationally at us, calling us all kinds of names. He didn't know me, and I've never figured out if he recognized me when we started rehearsal that afternoon."

Lowell turns and stands inside her space. She tries to step back, but Walter is behind her, sandwiching her between the two large men.

"How do you get along with him now?"

"Well, I mean, everyone says he's a first-rate musician. He records a lot, and every orchestra is trying to hire him."

"That's not what I meant."

"He adores Eduardo's music." She tries not to express emotion, her fingers opening and closing. "He stopped us several times in rehearsal to explain the piece so we would get the right mood. He said that a lot of recent music was a waste but that the New World Compositions represent a link with the past."

"Get back to the conductor."

"He's specializing in modern composers. He had been doing German opera. Do you know opera, Lieutenant?"

"Opera is people in grand outfits giving their lives for stuff that winds up being a mistake. In German opera, the mistake would be catastrophic."

She envies Lowell. He has an openness, a clarity, a lack of subterfuge. She's felt like a fraud the entire time she's been with the BSO. She has to get to Rio, stand up, and own her life.

"From an orchestra perspective, opera is different, because you work anonymously in a pit," she says.

"You and the conductor."

Melody looks down. "As I said, I haven't been playing well, and he's a perfectionist, so he hasn't been happy with me."

"Were you waving your arms before you got on the bus?"

"I was saying goodbye to Guru, that's all. Really." Her fingers become rock solid.

"And what were you doing in the bomb room when everyone else was in the auditorium?"

"I was . . . well, I mean. . . I was there with Guru."

"Why there?"

"It was just circumstances. I didn't mean to go there. It just happened."

"So, you were at the loading area this morning, then

next to the bomb. It would be a relief for you if this solo of yours were postponed, and you belong to the FAS movement trying to stop the BSO from going. That makes you very interesting."

"That's a pretty chintzy train of logic," Walter says, "going from Melody practicing an extra night to robbery and murder."

"I don't know anything about the robbery," she says, "absolutely nothing. I have no idea about it. I mean, it's something that I absolutely did not want to happen."

An urgent tremolo in the high strings stabs the side of her head. She wishes he would leave her alone. Without thinking, she cries out, "There's something wrong with Milton's body."

"How do you know?" Lowell says. "The medical examiner just phoned me. It wasn't even Milton."

China and Eduardo wait for Melody. As soon as she comes to the stage door near Mass. Ave., the three exit, their coats and hoods making them anonymous amongst the gathering crowd of bundled BSO supporters who stand around awaiting news. Raja is there, too, looking up at Melody. Bengals are more like dogs than other cats. She bends down and strokes his stomach.

"I know you want to be in the action, but don't stay out in the cold, honey. Go back home." He puts his paw on her hand. "Don't worry, I'll be all right."

The three musicians walk toward the Charles River, Melody's feet hitting the pavement ponderously to the tragic music from *Metamorphosen* by Strauss, written at the end of World War II.

Two cars drive down the street honking. The passengers hang their heads out the windows as they shout joyful slogans against the arts agreement as if they are sports fans whose team just won.

"They're blaming me!" Melody says outside the Little Saigon Café. "First Borges, and now Lowell. You should have seen Borges' red face."

"The police are shooting in the dark and seeing if birds fall out the sky," Eduardo says. "Borges is perpetually hostile. I can't imagine that Lowell could solve the case."

"I shouldn't have said anything about Milton's body. He made me nervous, and I blurted it out. Now he suspects me even more."

The musicians enter the empty restaurant. Eduardo points to a table near the window. Bright light projects through the glass, conflicting with the traditional carved-wood Asian décor. Alternative rock music from the sound system clashes with everything in the room.

"I absolutely won't let them blame me," Melody says. "I won't remain passive."

She sits, concentrating on Eduardo, wondering where he would sit.

"The solo is written for your fingers and force of attack—every note. It shows you off and catapults you to a new level. No one knows your style better than I do. It stretches your skill, but I knew you would break it. When you play it in front of everyone, you'll discard that destitute feeling you've been wearing of not being good enough."

She wonders if she should apologize. She thinks of how beautifully the cello blends two melodic lines in the final minutes of the piece.

China watches Eduardo as if she, too, wonders where he would sit. "You made cello our strongest section," she says to Melody. "Everyone knows what you're capable of."

Eduardo seats himself beside Melody. She places her left fingers around her right wrist as if fingering the high notes below the neck of her cello. The interval between notes shortens down the strings. Close to the bottom of the fingerboard, the notes are separated by a fraction of an inch. Melody uses fingers on her wrist to accompany the music she hears, either through her ears or from her brain's temporal lobe.

She turns to Eduardo. "Before Mozart, the Paris Opera commissioned a competition of *Iphegenieen Tauride* between Glück and Niccolò Piccinni. Glück went first and was such a success that Piccinni wanted to withdraw his score. That's how I felt—I wanted to withdraw. They wouldn't let Piccinni withdraw. His opera was a disaster, and he faded into obscurity."

"But you told me that you have to go," China says.

It occurs to Melody just then that her father had never heard her on stage. He may have different opinions, but he was always a kind and sincere man. She has to get to Rio. She will stand before the world and make her dedication to him. She will heal the hurt.

Melody sees China sitting opposite observing Eduardo. Though clumsy at self-expression, his voice is easy for Melody to read. He asserted once that talking about emotions is a futile exercise in self-absorption that never produces resolution. His language is music, a medium he shares with Melody, even if she is deliberately distancing him.

The Vietnamese waitress comes over, unenthused about having early customers on a winter Sunday. She taps her order pad, and Melody recognizes part of her solo in the tapping, a frenetic beat followed by a delicious legato, four notes expanded and inverted and played inside out.

They order vegetable *pho*. The waitress collects their menus without a word.

China points out the window. A steady trickle of people is joining the crowd at Symphony Hall.

"It's inspiring to see all this support for music," Eduardo says.

"I don't know how the classical crowd got the reputation of being stuck-up," China says, *con brio*. "Perhaps there's some universal justice in the robbery."

"You won't care about universal justice if you don't get your Loree back," Melody says.

Eduardo puts his hand on Melody's bowing hand. "Mel, you've got to clear your name. This could get ugly. Even if they find the instruments, the police might stop you from going because of your involvement in FAS. They have nothing to go on except FAS. Guru might know who placed the bomb, but he'll only talk to you."

"Nonsense. I don't know anything. Guru doesn't know anything. The FAS people don't know anything. The robbery and the bomb and the body came from some extremist group no one knows."

His hand is icy, but she keeps hers under his, glad for the contact.

"Someone in FAS must know someone who knows someone," China says. "FAS is a network."

"Guru would tell you about his brother who was coordinating with Liaison Cage and the government," Eduardo says,

"You called Guru a simpleton."

"You did. Then I thought about what Tito said, that FAS had a mole."

"Which proves that it was a distant group," Melody says. "Otherwise, the government would have known about the robbery through the mole."

"Maybe they did know," Eduardo says. "Your contacts will solve the case faster than Lowell. We'll support you. Then we can go to Rio on our terms, inaugurating the New World Compositions but shafting their so-called Advancement of the Arts Agreement."

"Mel, look me in the eye and swear that you want desperately to go to Rio and that you're committed to ferret out the truth," China says.

"I don't want to get involved."

"You are involved." Eduardo removes his hand as the

waitress sets their soup bowls in front of them. "You're in a pivotal position, the most suspect person," he says, using head voice. "You just said you won't stand by and let them accuse you."

"FAS people trust you," China says. "They'll lead you in the right direction. They wouldn't give that information to the police, because they want the police to fail."

"I'll get New World Composition musicians to help," Eduardo says, blowing on the soup steaming from his spoon. "Our people have day jobs in diverse areas."

"I'll hang around Lowell and see what the police are working on," China says. "Sergeant Rodrigo likes us. Tito knows everyone in FAS."

"You're throwing me an impossible task," Melody says. She looks at her soup and realizes she has no appetite. She wraps her hands around the bowl to warm them, her stiff fingers tapping the four notes, quick-quick, slow-slow.

"The piece I wrote for you was an impossible task, but I knew you'd master it."

"I'm not sure what to do. First, we have to find Milton. Lowell said the body wasn't his. How could he not know what happened?"

"I'll get my people to track him down," Eduardo says, his face shedding its somberness, which had begun when he heard that Milton was dead. Now he shovels in his soup as if he hasn't eaten for a week. "I'll phone everyone and tell them that you'll be the central person."

"Why pretend to kill someone?" Melody asks.

"Because the world doesn't listen unless there's death," Eduardo replies.

"And since the body isn't Milton," Melody says, her fingers loosening, "who is it?"

Vibrato: A quickly varying pitch either between notes or close to a note's central pitch. Vibrato goes in and out of fashion over the generations.

Variation on the Ground

Eighty-two minutes before the ransom call, a suited figure appears in Walter's office doorway.

"I'm Cage."

"Is that a fact?" Lowell says.

He is sitting alone at 12:21 p.m. behind Walter's desk staring at the general manager's diploma on the wall.

A forty-year-old, clean-cut WASP with a hard nose, Cage parts his hair like a standard politician. He strides in and faces Lowell. "I am the Presidential Liaison for the Arts. I'm in charge of the Advancement of the Arts Agreement in Rio."

"You must be a most unhappy man."

"How's the investigation?"

"We've only been at it four hours, Mr. Cage, not much so far."

"So what?" Cage doesn't understand Lowell's Boston accent.

"So *far*, f-a-h, far."

"You don't have many leads," Cage says, an answer rather than a question, causing Lowell to believe that Cage has more to tell than to listen. He doesn't project unhappiness.

Walter enters the room, eyeing Cage disapprovingly

from head to toe.

"I'm getting ready for a press conference," Walter says.

"Is the big boss here?" Cage asks Walter.

"I told the trustees that I'll take charge."

"Excellent," Cage says in an unenthusiastic tone, suggesting to Lowell that he is sorry to have to deal with Walter. "We just received word from the Brazil Philharmonic that they are willing to lend their instruments for the concert. It's a generous offer."

"Very generous," Walter says perfunctorily.

"Plus, the vice president will immediately make available a seven-million-dollar cultural fund for musicians."

"Sir, money is not the issue. Someone is dead. The robbers have threatened to destroy our instruments. Our musicians have a second instrument, often a third. Wood and brass players use different instruments for different pieces. But I'm sure that every single musician will refuse to go until they have their own instruments back in their own hands. We'd rather sit here scratching our heads and rubbing our bellies. We should never have gotten involved in this, and we will not move an inch without our instruments. Period."

Without waiting for a response Walter stalks out, muttering under his breath, "Doofus."

"You must have expected that Walter would react that way," Lowell says. "Why did you send off the special agent?"

"I didn't. He and his assistant were scheduled to leave at the same time as the orchestra. He's on his way back to assist you."

"You mean take over?"

"Work with you."

Lowell senses a non-credible voice. "The evidence is so fresh I can smell it squashing around our feet. This is our case. The commissioner is giving me all the people I need."

"The special agent kept tabs on FAS. It's his case for the taking."

"I think it would be really stupid if they called it their case. They'd have to admit they were in charge of security to begin with. They won't do that. But you know that."

"I can put them in any position you want."

Lowell puts his hand on his belly as if receiving inspiration from it. It tells him that Cage doesn't play straight. What does this guy want?

"Or else we can declare this a terrorist act," Cage says, his voice cocky, "then the FBI would take over."

"Terrorism isn't fake corpses, toy guns, and wise guys with firecrackers. Terrorists don't ditch a truck in front of a police station."

"The FBI gets involved in art theft, and we classify instruments as art."

"It's federal only when art crosses state lines. The instruments are probably within five miles. You're assuming it was FAS. We have no proof."

"Are you doubting that FAS did it? Who else has the organization? Do you have a team investigating the New Hampshire body? What about the bomb?"

"Weren't you initially against this deal?"

Cage strides to the bookshelf. "We need to get with the times. It might be hard on a few struggling artists initially, but the overall good is unquestionable. It makes sense to have music and art compete in the marketplace."

"Are you trying to convince me or you?"

He walks back toward Lowell. "Libertarians have been trying forever to get rid of all funding for the arts. We have to be practical or lose big. If you don't have a clue about the heist, you should concentrate on the body and the bomb. I'm sure there are tons of clues at both those sites."

"The investigation has to be systematic and coordinated."

"You're responsible," Cage says, like a politician. "I'll tell the special agent to respect that."

"If there's confusion," Lowell says, "the small intestine mucosa loses its alkalinity, a dangerous situation."

"I beg your pardon?"

"The main digestive action takes place in the duodenum. It's a small tube between the stomach and the intestine. Bile is fed into the duodenum by the gall bladder. That's the secret of good digestion."

Cage changes to good-old-boy mode, his voice both be-wildered and patronizing. "The special agent can provide valuable intelligence."

He walks out.

"Intelligence," Lowell says to himself. His eyes return to Walter's diploma. He puts his fingers halfway between his sternum and his navel and feels a strong, steady pulse. Lowell's eyes widen as he takes in the rest of Walter's office. It contains nothing musical: no instrument, no sheet music, no music stand or music book, not even a radio. It could be any corporate office.

Lowell calls out to Rodrigo. "I want to talk to that pretty blond again."

"China? You think she has information?"

"We're not looking for information. We're after intelligence."

Dozens of FAS supporters arrive with homemade placards and join the BSO supporters outside Symphony Hall. They have no permit to demonstrate, but they negotiate with the police, who erect a cordon of blue barricades next to the Horticulture Building and ask the protesters to stand behind them.

News of the robbery reinvigorates FAS. Before the heist, most supporters had given up hope of stopping the Rio ceremony. On that chilly Sunday, they stand well dressed and dignified, and they keep moving to stay warm. Except for the

handful who bring posters, they look identical to BSO supporters. Several are symphony subscribers. One carries a placard
that reads, "MAKE ART, NOT PROFIT." Another has a well-
used rainbow poster that says, "CLASSICAL MUSIC
ROCKS."

As the crowd swells, so does the anticipation. Even
people who rarely or never attend BSO concerts join in
solidarity. The police have to station officers outside both the
Mass. Ave. and Huntington entrances as people defy the cold
and filter into the street. Protesters and supporters merge.

A reporter interviews one violin-carrying student from
Boston Conservatory, located a few blocks away. "The arts
agreement sucks," he says, bits of shiny metal glittering around
his ear. "I'm ready to lend my violin to the orchestra." He lifts
the black case for the camera.

"This was an outrage against the city of Boston,"
another bystander says into a newswoman's microphone. "They
robbed us all—they bombed us all."

"God bless the BSO!" a bearded man in the middle of
the crowd yells out.

People cheer.

"God bless classical music!" another man shouts from
behind the protest barricade.

The crowd cheers with even more enthusiasm.

A group of young people near the subway entrance
begins to chant, "Bring them back, Bring them back," which is
taken up by the entire crowd for a minute before ending with
yells and applause.

Pretzel and balloon venders arrive and work the crowd.
Buskers performing in the subway for quarters come up into
the cold sunshine and take up strategic positions, strumming,
blowing, and beating their instruments for the gathering.
Jugglers and street actors who perform in Harvard Square in
summer come, too, so the assembly becomes a mixture of
tattooed twenty-year-olds and aged symphony gentry.

A woman in gypsy garb sets up a psychic reading table. Food trucks arrive like a wagon train. A group of college girls in red aprons go through the crowd distributing condoms. Jehovah's Witnesses offer *Watchtower*. A busload of Koreans snap photos. Four young guys wave signs that link atmospheric carbon to depleted testosterone. A man with a sandwich board and a megaphone warns about the four horsemen of the Apocalypse. Even an ice cream truck shows up, sounding its jingle, its product warmer than the air.

China, Eduardo, and Melody return to Symphony Hall amid the growing crowd.

"Look at the raw emotion here," Eduardo says.

China taps him on the arm. "Good for you for noticing. Having no instrument to play, that's pretty emotional, whatever you think of instruments."

Melody points at Eduardo. "He says all kinds of stuff, but he writes for instruments." She takes hold of Eduardo's arm, a familiar gesture, an unconscious reflex. "What kind of music could you write for no instruments?"

Tito's friend has driven up to New Hampshire and stays among the police surrounding the body.

"Tito told me to keep you updated," he says to Melody on the phone.

She listens to the scene as he describes it.

"We're congregated on the side of the country road where the body was discovered."

The other civilians, he says, are standing back, but he advances to the front line among the police and looks inside the stolen car's trunk. The large, naked man is stiff. His eyes are closed, his skin looks like dried chamois, and he smells of ammonia.

"I knew there was something wrong the minute I saw the body," a cop at the scene says. "But I couldn't put my finger on it."

"It took me a while to get it as well," another cop says. "A bullet hole right through the head but no blood."

Mel winces at the words.

Tito's friend says that another cop is studying the note lying on the man's belly, which threatens the same fate on the entire orchestra as happened to its transport manager. The cop is describing the scene to someone on the phone. He looks up and announces, "This guy was stolen from the morgue. He's a homeless PTSD vet who refused to go to a shelter and died in the cold two days ago."

"They must have driven him here," a sergeant says, "then opened the trunk so someone would find it."

"Who would do that?" Melody asks. "Who would want to impersonate Milton?"

"They're putting him back in a body bag now to examine him," Tito's friend says. "No one bothered to dress him. The police don't want to screw up, so they're doing everything extra careful."

"I don't understand what this means," Melody says.

"We all know that we have to get you to Rio," the fellow replies.

She steps out of the building and looks for her streetwise cat, but Raja is nowhere, probably scared off by the crowd.

Melody's first stop in her investigation is Arlington Street Church, adjacent to the Public Gardens, which has remained a fortress of liberalism since William Ellery Channing delivered fiery speeches in the 1830s against slavery and inspired the Transcendentalist movement of Emerson, Thoreau, and others. The handsome brownstone building has little interior embellishment except its superb Tiffany glass. Although New England is identified with Puritan intolerance, many Boston and Cambridge congregations call themselves open churches, several embracing undocumented immigrants and left-wing causes. When the arts agreement was announced the previous month, churches were quick to join liberals in making it their central issue, a cause on which they would never compromise.

Melody climbs the Arlington Street Church's stone stairs at 12:40 p.m., seventy-three minutes before the ransom call. She is directed to the second floor office. Reverend Hammond seems to be waiting for her, his bare arms radiating a golden shine as if he is carrying an armful of sunshine. His nineteenth century office, a large, square room with a high ceiling and dark stained wood, is crowded with books and papers.

"Melody, what do you make of this?" His belt tenor voice has a slight reverb from the marble floor.

"I'm bringing the same question."

"The police were just here accusing me, threatening to throw me in jail. You can't imagine how aggressive they were."

He wears staid clothes that give no hint he is— according to right-wing radio commentators—a Marxist revolutionary, nor does his attire describe his calling. The clergyman stands tall and has a crisp, suave, gentlemanly manner.

"That's probably Homeland Security. If they're coming here accusing you, it means they haven't a clue themselves."

"I was so ecstatic that the BSO isn't going that I didn't care who they were or what they said."

Melody hears the upbeat movement of a Mozart piano concerto covering Reverend Hammond's head like an aura.

He looks down for a second. "I'm sorry. I should have

been more sensitive about your solo."

"Did we have a mole in FAS?" she asks.

"I thought so after that spontaneous one-hour demonstration at Downtown Crossing when we faced those extra police. We knew how many police are usually there." His tempo changes to a slow, thoughtful *sarabande*. "Only a few of us were involved in planning the action. One of us must have been informing."

"Do you think the informant found out about the robbery?"

Hammond sits on the edge of the desk near where Melody is standing. "You're on the same track as those federal agents who came before you, pointing your finger at FAS just like they were. The robbers had to penetrate the police protection around Symphony Hall."

"There weren't any police around the baggage truck. Whoever planned the robbery had to know that."

"Or arranged it that way," the Reverend says. "Those faceless corporations who came up with this agreement and then sold it to the government want to make us look like thugs and scoundrels. They can say that FAS is ready to destroy a national treasure, which is what the press is calling two-hundred-year-old instruments. After that unfortunate's death in New Hampshire, they can label us fanatics."

Melody had seen Reverend Hammond on a Channel Two debate the previous week. Without much thought on the BSO's part, their principal librarian, a mild-spoken proper Bostonian responsible for providing sheet music to the players, found herself in the role of spokesperson and had to defend the BSO's decision. She was clearly flustered by Hammond's persuasive discourse. After the show, the orchestra received a barrage of letters, phone calls, and forwards of identical email blasts urging them to reconsider the decision to play at the Rio ceremony.

"I feel certain that no one in FAS was involved,"

Hammond says. "Perhaps the robbers are looking for a ransom?"

"If it's money, they'll knock on our door faster than the police can track them down. They know the instruments are worth more today than tomorrow."

"You and Tito would be the most likely to have been the conduit, because you two had a foot in each world."

"You were chiding me for making the same accusation. Tito and I were only part of FAS, which you say had no part in this."

"There are two or three secretive groups not part of FAS. They think we're too conciliatory, so they stayed outside our coalition." The reverend switches to the metered and symmetric tempo of a *gavotte*. "This could backfire on us. FAS has powerful enemies. Perhaps someone in the government engineered it."

"Wouldn't it be risky for the government to be involved in the heist?"

"Worse than Watergate. Oh, I forgot, Watergate happened long before you were born. The government prostrates before big business. I don't know anyone in our coalition smart enough to sabotage the arts agreement so easily. Someone inside Symphony Hall might have known how."

"At least one woman was involved," Mel reasons. "The two toy gunmen and the lookout China spotted near Symphony Hall were guys, plus a guy to steal the cars, two more to steal the cadaver—we're talking about a gang of eight—that's probably the extent of it. Big groups can't maintain secrecy or discipline and foul things up. The success of the evangelical movement depended on small groups. Mega-churches were divided into clusters of six or eight who met and developed bonds."

"The robbers must have been professionals."

"If they were professionals," Melody says, "they wouldn't have used toy guns, wouldn't have been gentle with the drivers, wouldn't have set off a harmless bomb, and they wouldn't have dumped the truck at a police station. Well organized, no doubt about it, but hardened criminals? I don't think so."

"Prove it wasn't us," Hammond pleads. He jumps up and takes Melody by the shoulders. "Even a wrong accusation would taint the entire cultural movement."

"I know how destructive false accusations are."

Sergeant Ostinato from the Malden police phones Lowell at a quarter past one. "We discovered an eyewitness who observed the truck." His tone is all business, identifying himself as 'Leader of the Abandoned Symphony Truck Investigation."

"What exactly did he see?"

"The witness observed the truck," Ostinato says formally. "He was operating his motor vehicle behind it as it veered onto Commercial Street."

"Did he see the truck driver's face?"

"The witness was driving directly behind him and has no awareness of that."

"The truck driver was a lady," Lowell says. "We already know that she drove onto Commercial Street and parked."

Ostinato's tone is unwavering. "We *did* know that, but now we have a witness who can testify that the truck drove there."

Lowell shows considerable patience. "Doesn't finding the truck there prove that someone drove it there?"

Ostinato becomes hesitant. "It could be coincidental."

"We know it got there. What we're looking for is a face."

"The chief will knock me off the bagpipe band if I mess

this up. He told me to find the instruments," Ostinato says, his voice pained.

"Forget it, Al," Lowell says genially. "Continue what you're doing until you find the instruments. They're probably in someone's garage. Hey, you know why bagpipers march when they play?"

Silence.

"To get away from the noise."

Pause. "I don't think of it as noise," Ostinato says, his voice serious.

"It's a joke, Al, a joke. It's not really noise. I was being funny."

"Oh." Ostinato doesn't laugh, and neither does Lowell. "Sometimes I march to get away from the drums. Does that count?"

At the same moment, Eduardo reenters Symphony Hall. Mrs. Schutz tells him that Walter wants to hold a press conference with him and Maestro Borges.

The reporters are ushered into the large, low-ceilinged restaurant in the Cohen Wing, where dinner is served before concerts. The tables have been moved aside and the chairs rearranged in rows in front of a podium.

Before entering, Borges grasps Eduardo's forearm and speaks to him in Portuguese. "We need unity at this juncture, not criticism."

It comes across as an order.

At 1:30 p.m. Walter leads composer and conductor onto the podium. Eduardo walks loosely while Borges takes the steps of an inflexible aristocrat. Borges pays as much attention to having sharply-cut clothes and being crisply groomed as he does to a precise beat for his music. He maintains a serious expression and stands rigid, giving him the final post on the evolutionary line of *Homo erectus*.

Walter approaches a lectern covered with microphones, his eyes gazing out above the rows of seats like a five-star general, calling it a taxing time for the Boston Symphony Orchestra. He summarizes the robbery and petitions for information.

"The bomb was professional but non-destructive. We're not sure how the dead body in New Hampshire ties in."

"Will you solve this mystery in time for the ceremony?" one reporter asks.

"We're considering our options. We have eleven hours to get our instruments back. There's every reason to be optimistic."

"Who was killed?" a WBZ television personality asks.

"The police have just begun the investigation," Walter says like a stern TV authority. "We'll know soon."

"What leads are you following?" another reporter asks.

"We're exploring several assumptions," he says, but he won't be nailed down. He also dodges the question of the value of the instruments, although other experts have tendered a range of estimates between ten and twenty million.

Walter asks Borges to say a few words. His voice is requiem-esque with an undertone of hatred. "If we don't resolve this quickly, we'll empower anarchists and socialists. A few violent people are making us dance to their tune."

"Maestro, who exactly are you blaming?" a reporter asks.

"FAS radicals bent on creating chaos. They can't win legally, so they'd rather hold the world hostage with guns and bombs. What will they do next?"

Walter gestures to Eduardo, who comes forward and reverts to philosophy. "I'm eager to première my piece, but perhaps now we can have a chance to discover a new way of looking at music. It's more than instruments. Music is an expression of the life force."

The *Globe* music critic, one of the few female music critics, puts up her hand. "Were you angry at the government for butting in?"

Eduardo speaks with his body and moves with agility. "The New World Compositions celebrate the triumph of art and science. We also acknowledge the suffering and injustice against Indians and Africans. The first pieces of the cycle deal with conquest, disease, and robbing the Native people. As the pieces develop, so do their harmonies and sophistication."

Reporters scribble.

Eduardo continues to speak confidently, his hands helping him express. "We hope to create better dialogue among composers. Here in the United States, the San Francisco, Houston, Chicago, and Detroit symphonies are premièring selections from the New World Compositions. Other pieces are for quartets and trios. Someone is writing a polyphonic piece in conjunction with the Boston Early Music Festival. Four musicians are performing a string quartet on New York street corners and in the subway. Three naked women are playing lute, hammer dulcimer, and viola da gamba at Burning Man in Nevada on the theme of utopian societies, of which there have been many in the New World. That's for starters. Other pieces will be presented in Mexico, Costa Rica, Canada, and all over South America. We're assembling a jigsaw puzzle of our history."

"How many other pieces are finished?" the critic asks. She was a slash and burn pianist who couldn't live off performance, so she turned to journalism.

"This is a multi-year process involving composers from North and South America. Usually, artists, writers, and composers work in isolation. It's rare to have this level of creative collaboration, like Vienna in the eighteen hundreds or Paris in the nineteen twenties. Two of the composers, for example, are Native American and are integrating traditional tunes in modern compositions. The première of this cello concerto was to launch this musical experiment."

"It's fitting that a musical cycle that begins with robbing and killing a people ends up robbing and killing," the critic says.

"Most of the works are positive," Eduardo says. "The piece opening this fall in Philadelphia is about the development of egalitarian democracy. The San Francisco piece is about the achievements of Silicon Valley and takes themes from computer noises. One piece scheduled for Havana is not about the nasty Cuban-American relationship but sounds like Havana during the roaring nineteen fifties. As many aspects as possible of this extensive four hundred-year history are being explored in major, minor, twelve-tone, upbeat, downbeat, and off-the-wall."

Other reporters ask questions of Walter and Borges, but hard information remains scarce. When every reporter has asked a question, the three step down and walk from the room, even though a couple of reporters try to nab Walter for an exclusive.

When they're out the door, Borges takes Eduardo's arm. "I don't know why you wrote such a beautiful piece for that girl."

Eduardo draws back his arms to shove Borges, but Walter jumps between them and pushes Eduardo back.

"Don't respond! He's fuming at the world and flinging hatred everywhere." Walter turns to Borges. "You stay out of people's way!"

He grabs hold of Eduardo and heaves him to the basement lounge, where the musicians are milling around.

Walter stands at one end of the room and tells the musicians that the police are leaving no stone untouched. "The trustees have empowered me to take any action that will get our instruments back, including not participating in the Advancement of the Arts Agreement, as long as we don't make a public announcement against our government. Our priority is to find the instruments by midnight so we can inaugurate a new era in music."

"Walter, we're with you," a female voice bursts out, and everyone claps.

Walter stands straight, tall, and impassive. He is in his element.

After meeting Reverend Hammond, Melody phones others she knows in FAS.

"Why do you want to solve the case?" people ask her. "Everyone is celebrating."

Melody explains that the arts agreement has been compromised by the publicity the robbery generated. "If we get our instruments back, we can inaugurate the New World Compositions, which would be a boon for the arts."

People want to help, but no one has the slightest idea of where to direct her.

Coming out of nowhere, Guru runs up to her as she is walking on the sidewalk near the Duck Boats on Huntington Avenue. She hasn't seen Guru since they talked before the explosion. They walk the two blocks toward Symphony Hall.

"Was FAS part of your April Fools' joke?"

His laugh is perky. "That's already happening. April in January."

"When you told me your brother's secret this morning, did he tell you how he's making money?"

"He needs money for a secret organization," Guru says in his gay voice. "Brahms and Debussy were born into poverty. Donizetti went crazy. I'll teach soldiers and spies."

"You will? Then you should help me find the instruments."

"I taught policemen how to conduct investigations."

Mel hears Elgar-like exaggerated drama in his voice, but she cannot get a bead on what he knows. Talking to him is like listening to twentieth century twelve tone—she doesn't know what is central and what is decoration. He has high-functioning Asperger's Syndrome combined with an imagination from spy movies. As they approach Mass. Ave., Mel hears the happy noise of the crowd. A helicopter hovers overhead. Police are diverting traffic.

"The key to solving the case is collecting information."

"That's my specialty," Guru says, *capriccioso*. "Guru knows everything. Wagner married Liszt's daughter. Guru knows FAS."

"FAS was probably not involved. It must have been a group outside the coalition. Were you telling your brother everything?"

"I was debriefed by a Secret Service agent."

"Who was that?"

"He came to FAS meetings undercover."

"What did he want?"

"He wanted me to be a double agent. He tested me by asking about Milton. My brother wants Brazil to have a bigger orchestra than Boston. He wants everyone to have freedom. He needs more money."

"How will he get this money?"

Guru's innocent voice turns into a secret whisper. "Cash is king. It's a dangerous world. Everybody has to protect himself."

"Find out as much as you can from them, then come back and tell me. Our secret."

Walter returns to his office fourteen minutes before the ransom call and sees Lowell sitting behind the desk.

"You know what it smells like to me?" Lowell says. "An

inside job."

"One of our people? Never." Walter gives a backhand snap of his wrist. He takes the visitor's chair facing Lowell, who has littered the desk with notebooks, papers, and coffee cups.

"Someone who knows how things work here," Lowell says, "who knows how much the instruments mean to the players. He or she wouldn't necessarily have done the robbery but could be the conduit. Someone had to deposit the bomb this morning."

Walter runs his fingers through his remaining strands of hair. "I know every musician. Whatever their personal feelings, I'll vouch for them all."

"Even that revolutionary bassist Tito?"

"Many people have access," Walter says. "I deal with four unions. Most of our staff has been with us twenty years, thirty years—only a few come and go. Mrs. Schutz has called them—they're coming down—but why focus on us? What about the anti-agreement groups? They're the obvious suspects."

Lowell stands. "Why hasn't Guru come in?"

"It's usually harder to get rid of him."

Lowell paces around the room and asks Rodrigo to send someone to the apartment to pick up Guru.

"Homeland Security are working over the FAS people," Rodrigo says. "I'll take you to meet the special agent as soon as he arrives."

Lowell turns to Walter and asks how he feels about the Advancement of the Arts Agreement.

"Me?" Walter puckers his lips and shakes his head. "I don't take a political stand. My life is the orchestra, not politics."

Walter makes the statement directly. Although Lowell hardly relates to current events, he raises his eyebrows in surprise.

"You mean to tell me that you were in the middle of it but didn't care?"

"My concern was how our participation in Rio would affect the orchestra."

"And your verdict?"

"The orchestra has been through a lot over the decades. We've had people rebuff us, criticize us, write articles against us, and sue us, and we've made it through every one of those obstacles. What will kill us is indifference. When people criticize, they're engaged, but when they accept a mediocre performance, then the pillars of creativity come crashing down, and a new generation will have to begin from scratch."

"You don't mind if people insult your orchestra?"

"Last summer, I had a ticket to Bayreuth, Wagner's hall, for a performance of *Parsifal*. People make ticket requests three years in advance, and almost all are denied, but if you've been in the business as long as I have, people invite you. The performance lasts from three in the afternoon until ten at night. People bring dinner and eat on the lawn. When it finally ended, you should have heard the booing and whistling. People rose out of their seats screaming against the conductor and the cast. The performers were veterans, the top of the top, who stood there collecting abuse. They should have been proud of arousing such passion. How wonderful when people take music seriously. You have to maintain standards in the leading halls. It's hard on performers, but you have to be strict. Let your standards drop, and they'll continue to drop until classical music becomes Trivial Pursuit."

"What exactly is classical music?"

"What does it mean to you?"

"Something long dead," Lowell says, "not related to us."

"Good point. People call Toni Morrison novels 'classics'. The musical classical age ended around 1820. The current tendency is to be nice and include banal music in the repertoire, but that's a gross error. Janáček can stand on his own. There's a reason that certain paintings hang in a museum and freshmen read certain stories that are called 'literature'. Dropping standards to be inclusive hurts art more than failed innovation."

"Banal music, like a simple tune?"

"Any tune can be played artistically or banally, from 'Mary Had a Little Lamb' to Rachmaninoff."

"I like Christmas music."

Walter stops a beat. "I draw the line at 'Mary Had a Little Lamb'."

"It seems that when people get rich and successful, they turn to fine brandy and classical music."

"You got that backward. People become successful because they turn to classical music."

"And to you, what's the orchestra all about?"

"Hands," Walter says, "hands and wrists and fingers. Two hundred hands working together. Two hundred hands organized to achieve harmony. If a pair of hands is too forceful or too fast, it throws off the other hundred and ninety-eight hands. Soloists are the best on their instruments, but they're poor orchestra members, because their hands show up. You have to be part of the whole, not playing your own music."

Lowell observes Walter's resoluteness. he hardly listens to an orchestra. It doesn't matter who composed it, much less who plays it. To Lowell, music is background sound. But to Walter, it is life itself.

"The audience does something different than we do," Walter says. "The audience hears the music integrated and whole. The musicians are counting and following their own score. That's why it couldn't be any of us. We'd feel it if one of our hands was out of whack."

"Did you see Liaison Cage here this morning?"

"He came every day this last week to see if FAS was bothering us. He coordinated with Homeland Security."

Walter looks at his watch, but Lowell notices that he doesn't take in the time.

"Someone in FAS gave him daily updates," Walter says.

"He knew that you were under threat yet withdrew the special agent and left you wide open on judgment day. A bunch of musicians can run the government better than the people we have."

"You've got that too backward—musicians are the most practical, detailed people."

China knocks on Walter's door at 1:51 p.m. and enters without waiting to be invited. Walter and Lowell are both sitting. Lowell's eyes following her to her seat.

"You wanted to see me?"

"How did you get the name 'China'?"

"You've got hours to get our instruments, and that's what you want to know?"

"You gonna deny a grown man's curiosity?"

"My parents were beats in San Francisco's North Beach," she says as brightly as a gypsy jig. "They played music in those smoky jazz clubs and listened to avant-garde poetry in creaky third-floor Victorian flats. When *hep* changed to *hip*, they moved to an organic farm in Mendocino County. A doctor told my mom that she didn't have a Chinaman's chance of having children, but I came along when she was over forty, and I was well worth waiting for!"

She gives the type of smile that makes Lowell agree with her. He realizes she got her distrust of the police from her offbeat parents.

"You learned music from them?"

"Musicians grow up surrounded by music," China says, her mouth skimming each word. "They usually have a musician parent. Except Mel. Children have a sensitive age for learning music. My dad was a violinist who tried to be a soloist, but he couldn't get management, and he was too proud to play section, so he kind of threw in the towel."

"You think that pushing you to become a musician was his way of making up?"

"I pushed myself. I had to get it perfect. I practice three hours every morning without stopping. You know what it's like to work a piece to death, keep breaking it, then play it perfectly, passionately, and have people rise out of their seats cheering? You don't know, because it hasn't happened to you."

"I have a hard time just being taken seriously."

"I could have aimed for a secure career, but I knew I would be sorry until the end of my life if I didn't try making it as an artist."

"Why classical music?"

"Depth. Pop music can make you cry or feel elated, but artistic music touches a point beyond emotion. I like music beyond a reason, just as you like having sex without a reason. I assume you don't believe it's only for procreation."

Lowell waits for his bafflement to subside. "It's one thing to like music and come to concerts, but it's completely different to dedicate your life to it."

"Do you ask businessmen why they dedicate their life to making more money than they can spend? Do you ask yourself why you dedicate your life to hunting criminals?"

"How come you and Melody are keeping up with the investigation?"

"Hello? Didn't we just get robbed? Did you forget about that? Would you like us to be thoroughly uninterested?"

"Don't be cross with me," Lowell pleads. "Stress increases a man's risk of prostate cancer by twenty-four percent. Stress from you would triple the risk."

"Ever wonder if you're looking in the wrong place?"

"Where should I look?"

"The smart thief sits right under your nose."

"Or right under yours."

"Your nose is bigger," China says with a comic gleam.

Lowell watches her stand on her trim legs. "I can see that you have a strong vagus nerve," he says as if giving an anatomy lecture. "It stops excess gas and keeps the belly flat."

She twinkles her eyes and walks out, Lowell observing her well-angled sacrum, which gives her a gently rounded butt.

"Did you see how both these girls talk about practicing and playing?" Walter says. "They're artists, not note players. They establish a relationship between composer and listener. It must be like the relationship police develop with criminals."

Lowell picks up the ringing phone.

"This is the switchboard downstairs," an excited voice says. "We've got someone on the line saying they have the instruments and want two million cash."

The fire marshal declared that the blaze that killed Melody's mother was an accident. She knew it was her father. He was an alcoholic and a religious fanatic. He had been on an evangelical tour in neighboring cities, preaching that Jesus did not come to bring peace but a sword. He quoted the Bible: "A man will find his enemies under his own roof."

The sheriff, the father of her best friend, who had known her since birth, spent all afternoon with her telling her it was an accident. When she insisted, he took her to the burnt house and showed her that the fire was caused by candles left burning in wooden holders.

"My father must have gotten into a drunken stupor."

"He hadn't been drinking for seven years. He was an AA sponsor. He wasn't even in town."

The sheriff put his arm around her while she cried. She

nodded, but in her mind, she knew her father was guilty.

"My mom was going to leave the church to give me a normal upbringing. That upset him."

"He started making plans to move with you," the sheriff said.

She refused to believe it.

Her father could hardly talk. He didn't quite know where he was, said that if she would feel better blaming him, then go ahead.

"Get out of here," the sheriff told her. "Go far away and don't come back. You're a sensible girl. A talented musician can go far, but when the musician is a pretty and demure girl, she will be in demand around the world. I'll take care of your dad and come for you when you're a woman."

She practiced with fury to erase the brutal memory. An elderly teacher gave her a Bengal kitten. Melody named him Raja. He perched on the highest bookshelf and listened attentively to her practice. Raja's expression told her when she played from her heart. She played by herself, unaware that she was developing a revolutionary technique.

When Eduardo changed her name, it was the final break from her past, or so she thought.

After she was hired by the BSO, she was amazed that her playing enthralled the critics. She pressed her fingers on the strings as the notes dictated and bowed, no big deal. The daughter of a murderer deserved no praise. The psychologist told her that children often blame themselves for the death of a parent. The irony she was running away from was that she really *was* responsible.

Resonance: Strings vibrate by themselves when they sense a related pitch. Strings on instruments are generally a fifth or a fourth higher or lower than adjacent strings, accenting the phenomena.

Intermezzo

Fifty-six minutes before the electricians become the prime suspects, the switchboard puts the ransom call through to Lowell.

"You want the instruments unhurt?"

Lowell hears a grating gangster voice with a low-tech concealment, like a handkerchief over the mouthpiece. Lowell turns on the speakerphone so Walter can listen.

"It costs two million."

"Take it," Walter whispers.

"One million," Lowell says.

Walter shakes his head vigorously.

"You got nothing to bargain with," the gruff voice says.

"Take it!" Walter says again.

"One million," Lowell says. "I'll give you one million cash today. No questions, no investigation. You leave the instruments and pick up the million."

A short silence.

"You make a tempting offer. All right, one million." The voice loses its dominance. "We'll tell you where to drop off the cash."

"I'll hold my breath," Lowell says. "When you call, just ask for the Blue Boy."

The phone goes dead.

"Shall I prepare the money?" Walter asks. "The government will give it to us right away."

"I was testing to see if this guy was genuine. He called the switchboard. The guy who told us about toy guns phoned you direct. That's why I'm saying it's a job with an inside connection, someone who knows you're the boss, the real boss. There's a lot of difference between a legitimate crook and a stupid crook."

Lowell steps out the door and finds Rodrigo. "We just had a crank ransom call to the switchboard. Find out where it came from."

"We're getting people saying they've seen the truck or the car, but no one's seen it in the right place at the right time," Rodrigo says. He bends his head toward his collar to radio the information.

Lowell returns to Walter. "Who insures those instruments?"

"Northeast Casualty. The players have their own insurance as well."

"Track down the president of Northeast and tell him to advertise a million-dollar reward online to anyone who has information. The reward is only good today. We'll get a bunch more crank calls, but we might get something real."

Walter delegates the task to Mrs. Schutz. "If anyone can reach the president on a Sunday," Walter says to Lowell, "she will."

Sergeant Rodrigo pokes his head back in the door. "Interesting information," he says, looking at a piece of paper in his hand. "Those electrical contractors applied for passports six weeks ago. They have a credit card charge for Avianca Airlines. That's Colombia's national air carrier."

Through the open door, Lowell sees Maestro Borges standing outside the office, still red-faced and projecting rage.

"Those militants are standing across the street laughing

at you," he calls out to Lowell. "Some of them are in the musicians' lounge downstairs."

Meanwhile, Melody returns to Symphony Hall. She talks to her musician friends about her mission of ferreting out the truth. People are as generous to her as when she first started playing in the orchestra—most have gone through dark times of their own—but no one can suggest a new direction she should explore. FAS, they say, is the obvious culprit.

Walter doesn't deal with the crowd outside until 2:10 p.m., when Mrs. Schutz corners him in the corridor.

"There are thousands out there," she says with a dog-gedness that stops him. "What are you going to do?"

"It's not our problem. They're in the street."

Walter tries to pass by her, but Mrs. Schutz blocks him again.

"It looks so mean that we're not doing anything while they're standing in the bitter cold."

Walter eases back on his heels and scratches his chin. "They seem to be having a good time out there. They'll get in the way here."

"The mood out there being what it is, I bet you could take up a collection and raise fourteen point five million on the spot," Mrs. Schutz says.

Walter deliberates, his eyes turned toward the ceiling.

"Why don't you ask that nice young composer to help?" she asks. "He's a teacher, and he gives pre-concert talks here."

"Eduardo? Good idea." Walter says, straightening his shoulders in resolve. "He was going to speak in Rio anyway."

Walter follows Mrs. Schutz to the basement lounge, where Eduardo is sitting among a group of musicians conversing around a table in the center of the room. Melody is near the vending machines, soliciting information from musicians.

Felix is speaking to the others in his accented dialect. "When I see a new piece of music, I used to ask myself, actually, is this the next *Eroica*? Is this the pivotal piece that will begin a new musical era? But I stopped doing that. I don't know if I am correct to judge new compositions, especially those with pretentious titles like 'Meaning of Life,' or if I've simply become jaded."

"Perhaps Beethoven and *Eroica* are rare," China says.

Tito takes up the argument in his manly baritone. "We wouldn't recognize the next *Eroica*. A new *Eroica* needs to invent, reach for the moon, not because it wants to be different or rebellious but because Terpsichore, muse of music, has breathed her inspiration."

"Cut and paste composing software is cheapening music," Eduardo says. "With two clicks, you can take a theme, transpose it a third, and put it somewhere else. Clever."

"Maybe we're making a mistake looking for one composer to jump us to a new musical era," China says.

People look up at Walter as he comes toward them.

"Astonishing," Walter says. "I've never heard musicians talk about music. We usually talk about money and food."

"Emphasis on money endangers artistic expression," Tito says.

"Then you should give thanks for being in a financially stable organization instead of one that's forever wondering if they'll be able to play next year."

"Eduardo's been playing exciting bits of his friends' pieces on next year's schedule in the big orchestras," a string player says to Walter. The historic big five orchestras in the US are Boston, Chicago, Cleveland, Detroit, and New York.

Melody's phone rings. "Where are you?" she asks. "Walter wants us all here."

She walks out the room with her phone on her ear, Eduardo's eyes on her.

"Actually, our trip should not have been tarnished by this fraudulent deal," Felix says. "We have to go to Brazil and launch the New World Compositions. Mel must play."

"We'll go if the lieutenant and I solve the case today," Walter says. He turns to Eduardo. "Can you entertain a hall full of people? We want to get them off the street."

Eduardo stands and takes charge. "Let them in. I'll talk to them about music. It will be one thing off your mind so you can concentrate on the investigation."

"You'll be doing the BSO an enormous service. Mrs. Schutz will get the police to seat them."

"Leave the rest to me," Eduardo says. "I'll give talk after talk, and I'll also invite musicians who are part of the New World Compositions to come and play."

"We've only got twenty-six hundred seats," Mrs. Schutz says. "There must be ten times that out there."

"Put out a sound system and monitors," Walter says. "Those who can't enter will be able to hear. Let the TV crews have access. Let the people in!" he declares grandly to the room.

The musicians in the lounge say they, too, will go to the talk, since circumstances have given them a free afternoon.

Walter squeezes Eduardo's shoulder with his large hand, and Eduardo leaves to prepare the sound system cart.

Mrs. Schutz steps outside and asks the first policeman she sees to bring in his boss. An overweight, baby-faced sergeant walks into the front foyer. Mrs. Schutz explains that since they don't have ushers on duty, would he mind if his men direct people into the hall?

"We'll get a succession of audiences out of the cold and give them the opportunity to listen to a lecture or a performance."

The sergeant nods his flabby face, his cheeks wobbling, promising her in a heavy north Boston accent that he will arrange it and "not to worry about nothing."

Half an hour later, the police open Symphony Hall's doors and set up outside monitors and speakers above the marquee.

Lowell keeps George, the gentleman who stands across the street, waiting until seven hours and twelve minutes after the heist. He opens the door of an administrative room and sees George sitting coldly, a defiant expression.

"Are you prepared to cooperate?" Lowell asks.

George stares at him.

"He's managed to keep his mouth shut for three hours," the officer sitting with him says. "Didn't even open it for water."

Lowell takes a seat across from George. Normally, he would start with gentle encouragement, but unlike the anti-agreement activists from whom he wants cooperation, George has to be broken.

"I only want to know if you saw anything while you were standing across the street."

George looks around him.

"Don't leave me in the dark, George. Please tell me if you've seen anything."

George keeps silent.

"You like classical music. Don't you want to help me?"

George sits solid, his lips shut, breathing through his nose, his eyes turned away from the man speaking to him.

Lowell takes a better look, noticing a boring but expensive shirt, a couple of pimples on his large, slightly reddish face, an antique wedding band, but no other garnish. He lets a long minute pass.

"If you don't say anything, I'll assume you're withholding information, and I'll keep you here until I know otherwise."

"You can't keep me here just because you want to," George says without emotion. "You need a charge. You can't make me answer questions. It's written into our Bill of Rights to protect people like me from people like you. If you keep me here illegally, I will take action against you."

Lowell makes a show of losing his patience. "I'm glad you informed me about the Bill of Rights. I do have a charge against you. You've been drug dealing on the corner."

Blood fills George's face as he looks directly at Lowell's large eyes. "You're setting yourself up, forcing me to stay here, and then bringing false charges."

"Drug dealing. That's what people who stand on corners do, drug dealing or whoring."

"I'll sue you to kingdom come!"

"Kingdom come could be a while."

"You'll pay for this!"

Without looking back at George, Lowell steps into the hall, running into China's bright smile and Maestro Borges' livid face.

Melody leaves the basement lounge when she hears Wisteria's distraught voice at the other end of the phone. She remains in the basement at the bicycle rack near the organ bellows room and faces the wall.

"Where are you?" Mel asks, plugging her other ear. "Walter wants us all here."

"I can't come. I'm too upset."

"We're all upset."

"It's not Rio. It's not about my violin," Wisteria says, though hers is an exceptional eighteenth century French piece. She explodes in a mixture of cries. After a couple of minutes of indecipherable blubbering, Wisteria takes a long, sniffling breath. "I saw them doing it. Bishop. He didn't know we hadn't left for Rio, hadn't heard about the robbery. He didn't expect me to walk in the front door and find him humping another woman."

"Oh my God." Mel wanders toward the carpentry shop.

"The bastard couldn't wait." Full glottal stop on the "b" in "bastard."

"I'm so sorry."

"He jumped off her, startled, his thing gleaming wet, but neither of them said a word. I looked at the other woman, who lay frozen with her legs in the air."

Wisteria cries more. Melody doesn't interrupt.

"'Get out of here,' I told the bitch. 'You, too,' I said to him. 'I want you both out in two minutes.' Then I slammed the door and walked into the kitchen."

Melody waits silently, knowing there will be more. She's never heard Wisteria use profanity.

"You know what that bastard said? 'This is my house. You can't throw me out.' The nerve. I've paid everything on that house since we've been married. In fact, I've paid everything, period. I told him to get out before I grabbed a knife."

"I'm so sorry. On top of all this."

"You all knew, didn't you?"

"I didn't know."

"I'm sure everyone knew but me. She had a shaved, you know. Is that what he wanted?"

"Be level-headed, sweetie. Don't do anything rash."

"She wasn't even pretty," Wisteria wails. "I've got to change the lock. I've got to get a lawyer. I've got to think. But I'm not coming there."

"Leave it to me. If anyone asks where you are, I'll tell them that you're shocked and upset. Come and stay with me tonight."

"Thank you, Mel." Wisteria sounds relieved. "I wish I

had self-defense training like you. And I want so much for you
to succeed."

Mel hears her name on the public address system summoning
her to the security cubicle.

"Tell me more about George," Lowell asks as soon as
she appears.

Lowell wants to talk to her alone, but Walter follows
him as if he is Melody's attorney, shielding his client. Rodrigo is
about to take Lowell to meet Special Agent Dufay.

"You know why he stands across the street?" Lowell
asks.

"He's a patron of music." She hears herself hold each
syllable as if written with a dot above it.

Lowell leads them through the metal gate and down the
stairs into the basement corridor, entering an open concrete
area that fans out to the rest of the cavernous basement.

"Have you had conversations with him?"

"Once."

"Where?" He sounds like a dentist with a pair of rusty
pliers asking her to open wide.

"L'Espalier."

"He took you to the most expensive restaurant in
Boston?"

Lowell's tone sounds controlled, but his flat fifth tells
Mel that his mind just slid off its perch. Walter remains silent.

"He wanted to talk about music," she says. "Classical
music needs patrons."

Lowell is amazed that a beautiful young woman would
even say hello to an uptight older gentleman like George.
Lowell figures he's got a lot more going for him than George,
but women like Melody never stop to talk to him. He imagines

her deeper than her skin. He pictures her spleen and liver, stomach and intestines, guesses she has small, efficient kidneys and a non-fibrous bladder.

She, in turn, hears around Lowell the digestive noises contained in Beethoven's *Eighth Symphony*.

"And how is he a patron?" Lowell asks.

"He's a dedicated concertgoer." She holds a quarter rest and looks at Walter. "He bought me a Lamy bow."

"I don't know much about bows."

"The bow is as important as the instrument. I had just gotten hired. George asked about my instrument. I told him that I had tried a nice bow in Rutman's and was going to buy it after I paid off my car. The next day, there was a package for me at the stage door."

"How much is that bow worth?"

"An 1894 Lamy? It's light and balanced, and the frog fits my hand perfectly. It was about six thousand."

"He gave you a six thousand-dollar gift? Why didn't you tell me that before?"

"He didn't want people to know. Some bows cost twice as much."

"Someone who takes you out and buys a six-thousand-dollar present is more than, as you said, 'everyone knows him'."

"That was a year ago. I tried to thank him, but he wouldn't accept any thanks, pretended that it wasn't his gift, kind of avoided me. I asked Walter if it was all right to accept the gift, and Walter said yes."

Lowell looks at Walter. "So you know him."

Walter gives a noncommittal pucker of his lips.

"What else do you know about this man?"

"Nothing more than what Melody said."

"We still see him at the corner," Melody says. "He doesn't talk to any of us. He's an anonymous donor, and I felt obligated to respect his anonymity. They are the real givers, because they don't want anything back, not even recognition."

Lowell wonders how many businessmen would give six thousand dollars to lunch with Melody or China. For many, it would be the highlight of an otherwise tedious life.

"Why question lovers of classical music?" Mel says. "They're on our side."

"They're on your side, but whose side are the robbers and bombers on?"

Lowell thinks that these two girls can ask any man to do whatever they want, and the strongest would bend to them.

"She's a good girl," Walter says to Lowell as the two men walk back to the side door, "protecting the confidence of one of our benefactors. I'm sure what she says is true."

Lowell turns on a stair and stops. "We're both in positions of trust—you trust and I don't."

Sergeant Rodrigo is on the other side of the door with his notebook. "We discovered that the president of Brighton Hauling, a guy named Quadrille, made a large donation to the symphony last month."

"Most of our support is corporate," Walter says, waving his arms in a dismissive gesture. "That doesn't have anything to do with the robbery. Donors get their names in the program, and people study those names."

"Bring Quadrille here," Lowell says.

Special Agent Dufay disobeys FAA regulations and uses his phone while flying over Connecticut. He tells Lowell that he and his assistant are landing at Logan at 1:58 p.m. and asks Lowell to meet him at the Homeland Security office in Scollay Square.

Lowell and Rodrigo are waiting for them as they get out of their dark blue Ford LTD twenty-five minutes later.

Dufay and his assistant look like copies of 1950s TV

detectives—crewcut, deadpan, broad-shouldered. Dufay, African-American, and his assistant, flat-top blond, both wear trench coats with the collars touching their jawbones, brown leather gloves, the squiggles on the back of their gloves crispy straight.

Lowell shakes their stiff hands and follows them through the revolving doors.

"We know FAS inside out," Dufay says. "We'll nail them in a couple of hours."

Lowell thinks Dufay works out on weights.

"You've been spying on citizens for political reasons," Lowell says. "And you left town before all the crying."

Dufay gives Lowell a reproachful look as the guard waves the men through the turnstiles.

"We entrusted their security to Boston Police. Obviously, that was a mistake."

Lowell lets it drop. "I'm surprised at the organization of the robbery. They had little time to prepare, not to mention their in-your-face tactics—toy guns, truck at a police station, body from a morgue. The bomb was a sensational noisemaker. The whole thing doesn't make sense."

They enter the open elevator. Dufay's assistant pulls out a sheet of paper and speaks precise English to distinguish himself from Lowell's colloquial tongue. "Here's what FAS posted on their web page. 'Elation! Ecstasy! Euphoria! We stopped Rio. Joy! Joy! We must continue using any method until the whole arts agreement is obliterated'."

"Words," Lowell says.

"We didn't think these groups had the ability to deliver," Dufay says. "Thanks to inept police, they pulled off a spectacular raid."

Again, Lowell doesn't react.

The elevator door closes.

"This case is like being in a stuck in an elevator with a pregnant woman," Lowell says. "You press all the buttons and hope nothing exciting happens."

"Washington expects immediate results," Dufay says.

"Maybe Washington knocked her up. Do you know how many hearings you'll have to attend when it gets out that you've been spying on good citizens?"

"In an age of terrorism," Dufay says, stern-faced, "we have to be prepared. You can see that we were right to collect information."

"Isn't it called 'intelligence'?"

The two agents give each other a look of having to stretch their patience. The doors open onto the second basement.

"What point are you at?" Dufay asks in a way that suggests Lowell's work doesn't matter, but Lowell senses an undertone of desperation.

"The robbers knew how to pick them," Lowell says, "cold Sunday morning on a small street in front of the Braille Press. We didn't ask any of the blind people to identify suspects. The only better place for a heist is the Forest Hills Cemetery."

"They planned the robbery as soon as the news broke that the BSO would be playing," Dufay's assistant says.

"We're being systematic," Lowell says outside their office door. "If you go helter-skelter, the stomach muscles start contracting four or five times a minute, creating goop out of the chyme, and the whole system gets out of kilter."

The two men don't know what to make of Lowell.

"First, we interviewed each orchestra member."

"Of course, you wouldn't get much from them, since they were on the busses to the airport."

Lowell isn't abashed by the comment. "We've got to think of the possibility that someone inside had intentional or unintentional contact with the hijackers and bombers."

Dufay nods, slightly humbled.

"We're tracking down electrical contractors who worked there and acted suspiciously as well as the transport officer who was replaced by a cadaver. He doesn't know the difference between a violin and a vagina. There's also a suspicious guy who's been hanging around. We have him in custody."

"Fast work," a comment that sounds as if it's intended to make up for the previous putdown.

"He's hiding something," Lowell says.

When Dufay opens the office door, they are swamped by a wave of commotion, twelve or fifteen agents on and off the phones, men walking around with fistfuls of papers, young radical types being questioned.

"We've rounded up many in FAS," Dufay says. "The leader is in the next room being interrogated. Several coordinators are still at large. Bang a few more heads, and they'll lead us right to the instruments."

"I heard your agents accosted a reverend in his church."

"We've already lost a lot of time. We have nine hours."

"You go around threatening clergymen, and you won't be too popular."

Special Agent Dufay looks intently at Lowell. "I'm not here to win a popularity contest but to solve the case. Today."

Lowell takes his arm. "If you live on an island, don't make an enemy of the sea."

"Mel, is it true?" Milton asks in agitated vibrato.

"Didn't you hear?" She paces the basement near the loading area with the phone to her ear.

"Oh God," the transport manager says dramatically, "who's got his hands on my instruments? I can't believe it. And I'm supposed to be dead?"

"They're threatening to destroy the instruments." She stops pacing and concentrates on the blaring timbre of his voice.

"They're more than instruments!" He seems so distressed that he can hardly form words. "I can't believe that some thug would take them out of the crate and defile them. This guy drove up, told me the story, and handed me a phone."

"He's a musical friend of Eduardo's. We're trying to find the instruments. How could robbers have pulled this off?"

"First they'll steal instruments, and then they'll go directly after women." He shifts to a serious low *tessitura.* "I have no idea how they could have done it since it was outside Symphony Hall."

Melody hears in his voice the strong orchestral chords that open the *Emperor Concerto.*

"You packed the crates yourself?"

"Like I always do, but it was slightly different this time, because the instruments and luggage were separated. I saw to it that *everything* went onto the truck."

"Did you see anything abnormal?" Melody asks.

"You were there. Everything went exactly on time."

"In the past month, did you see anyone looking at things, checking how things work?"

"If I knew there was someone ready to pounce on my instruments, I would jam his balls down his throat," he says *sforzato.* "I can't believe this. There are always people backstage—visiting musicians, students coming for lessons, tourists. If I was suspicious of everyone who walked through there, I'd be a nervous wreck."

"When you finished loading the truck and went to the street to meet your lady friend, did you see anyone standing at the top of the street waiting for the truck?"

"I can't believe it, hostility toward musical instruments! There were chanting protesters with a sign."

Melody hears a woman's voice in the background, a low, breathy voice whose baseline is between F and F-sharp.

"She saw a guy in front of the Christian Science Church." Milton says. "He couldn't have been waiting for the service, since it starts at ten. He stood in the empty area in front of the reflecting pond. He was all covered up, and then he disappeared. Why are you playing detective?"

"Because if I can't play that concert, I'll be canned. You know that. Besides, the police think I'm involved."

"You're kidding."

"No joke. I refuse to be passive and let them accuse me. I've been talking to all the FAS members I can find, but they know nothing. Who did you tell that you were driving to New Hampshire?"

"Walter knew. And you."

"Didn't you hear about the heist on the news?"

"People have been telling me for years to get a phone here, but that spoils the reason for this place. My car radio was blurting out static, so we listened to Argentinean composers from my phone, Golijov and Ginastera."

"I had a similar radio problem. The antenna was broken."

"Hang on. I'll go outside and check."

He is quiet for a few seconds. "The antenna is missing altogether. Let me get a closer look. Someone unscrewed it."

"Simple, advance planning, every step. Chaos out of simplicity."

Milton phones Walter next. "Were you even a little sorry when you heard I was dead?"

Walter shouts into the phone the way long distance calls were carried out fifty years ago. "I don't know how anyone could have mistaken you for that homeless guy. I'm told that he was good looking, and he didn't have a big smirk on his face."

"I told you that the arts agreement was a curse. If you ever get the instruments back, no one touches them but me."

"Get back here as soon as you can."

"I shouldn't be surprised. Men are drawn to instruments because of their womanly shape. Five hundred years ago, string instruments were triangles and boxes and gourds. Those sly Italians put boobs and hips on them. Women weren't allowed to play them, because men believed that vibrating strings upset a woman's cycle, and the only thing more mysterious than music is a woman's cycle."

Special Agent Dufay leads Lowell into an adjacent room where Tasa Costa, the coordinator of FAS, is standing behind an interrogation table, two men with hard faces staring at her. She doesn't look up when Lowell enters. Tasa's main feature is an intense mass of black hair that comes out of her head in a semi-circle of curls. She stands her ground on two ample legs like a Sumo wrestler. Lowell thinks she looks like a statue of a voluptuous woman with a sword that you see under the bowsprit of a nineteenth century warship.

Lowell senses the tension in the room and understands that Tasa is in control. He asks the others to leave. When they comply, Lowell apologizes to her, recognizing that any unwise word could ignite the rampage lying under her tongue.

"You're working for big entertainment conglomerates," she says.

"Civilized people resolve differences legally. I want to find the instruments before someone harms them, instruments they've been playing six hours a day for the last twenty years, instruments they love as part of their lives."

"Instead of berating me, round up the head of the Presbyterian Church or the Speaker of the House and drag them into this room. They were as vocal as we were."

"I will drag them here if I think they can give us information," Lowell says. "I'll summon the bishop and the governor if there is even a minimal possibility they can help."

"How can you suspect us? None of us has guns or

training in guns to launch this kind of military operation." She keeps a serious, all-business façade.

"I believe you." He pulls a paper from his pocket. "What about Nuovo Mondo and New American Wave?"

"I haven't had any dealings with these people. Nuovo Mondo is a ragtag bunch of losers who occasionally bring out a half-dozen people to march and yell."

"Young guys?"

"They're women, white middle-class women who make crafts. They meet in one of their apartments. Talk to them yourself."

"And the New American Wave?"

"I doubt that it's more than someone who started a website last month. I've never seen any of their people, and I wouldn't know how to get hold of them. It's a phantom group, not part of any coalition. Governments create phantom groups to make the whole movement look like extremists."

Lowell remains silent.

"There's another group that refuses to be part of our coalition," she says. "Art Unincorporated. They march to their own tune."

Lowell lets out a finishing breath. "I'll ask them to let you go."

Lowell's phone rings as he steps out to meet Dufay. He sees his daughter's number on the screen, sighs, and presses cancel.

"All we got from her was hostility," Dufay says.

"The favorite word of political activists is 'struggle'," Lowell explains calmly. "They don't take concrete action, because that would help them win. Then they couldn't struggle against the system. It surprises everyone when they're effective."

Lowell's phone rings again. He looks at the screen and again presses cancel.

"We're rounding up more and interrogating," Dufay

says.

Lowell wonders if they will turn off all potential sources with their curtness, wonders if they have another agenda.

"We need FAS's cooperation," Lowell says. "It's counterproductive to harass this woman."

He steps back into the interrogating room and addresses Tasa. "An officer can drive you home."

"I can find the way myself."

She turns around and walks out, accenting the weightiness of her every step.

Rodrigo sticks his head in the door. "Amy is on my phone."

Lowell slumps on the interrogation desk and puts his head between his hands. "Tell her I'm interrogating suspects, and that I'll be interrogating for a long time."

"You'll have to talk to her sooner or later."

"It's always the same," Lowell complains. "She tells me that I can't do this and that I have to stop doing that. Then she says she won't let me do what I want. because she cares about me."

"Why don't you express that to her?"

"That's one thing I'm not allowed to do. She says I embarrass her."

"I can't see how that could be true."

When Lowell returns to Symphony Hall, a police lieutenant from the town of Everett phones. "I'm in front of the electrical contractor's shop off Main Street up near Malden."

"That puts them close to the Malden police station. The two stolen cars used in the heist were also close to each other."

"I'm half a mile from the Malden station. But their shop

is abandoned. My partner is knocking on a neighbor's door."

Lowell hears the neighbor say, "They left all of a sudden, three or four days ago, packed up and took off."

"You know where they went?" the cop asks.

"Greenwich, Connecticut. They were nice guys, kept to themselves like neighbors should."

Lowell thinks that an upscale town like Greenwich is not a place for workmen.

"They can't work there," a voice says.

The cop tells Lowell that it's the electrical inspector who's just getting out of his car. "Their electrical licenses aren't any good outside the state. Contractors don't just take off like that."

The inspector takes the phone. "I knew them, two brothers named Giordani, both licensed electricians, and another guy named Pat Piston, who was on their payroll. If they had a big job, they'd hire extra guys."

"What were they like?" Lowell asks.

"I should have suspected them. They listened to classical music. I'd go to inspect their work, and some big orchestra would be banging away on their stereo. They always brought a stereo, and they wouldn't play fluff like Mozart, which even working guys can tolerate, because it pacifies your brain, but the kind of furious music you'd expect to hear in the Kremlin. You ever hear of contractors listening to Shostakovich?"

"Who?"

"That composer who wrote for Stalin. When Stalin died, he said he was really writing against Stalin."

"You seem to know music."

"My wife played violin in an orchestra," the electrical inspector says. "Gave it up for the children."

"Our children run our lives," Lowell says with conviction.

Another neighbor says that Piston, the guy who worked

with them, took his wife and kids to Florida two days ago, driving a brand new car.

"I'd say we have strong suspects," Lowell says.

"If there's information in Everett," the inspector says, "I'll see to it personally that you get it right away."

"You know why violin players put their violin under their chins?" Lowell asks.

"No, why?"

"I don't know either. I wasn't giving you the first line of a joke."

"I don't get it."

"My jokes aren't going over today," Lowell says. "Maybe this is no joking place. It looks uncomfortable to stick a wooden box in your neck instead of on your lap."

Lowell calls the commissioner, telling him that apart from FAS, the electricians are the best suspects so far.

"I'll phone the Greenwich police," Lowell says. "You ever hear of Shostakovich?"

"Was he that Hasidic Jew who was mistakenly arrested in Kenmore Square?"

"You ever listen to music?"

"Music?"

"The classical stuff these guys play."

The commissioner's tone becomes less assured. "Well, the wife and I own a few classical CDs. She likes that stuff, you know, romantic strings while sitting in front of the fire with a glass of wine, the dog at our feet, but I can't say I know much."

"One of the musicians told me that knowing music isn't important. What matters is taking time to listen. I thought about that and told her this is how we'll crack the case, by listening."

"What are we supposed to listen to?"

"This is a symphony heist, and what does the symphony do? Make music."

"You might want to entertain the idea that the symphony also makes money."

"I thought they always lose money."

"That's the same thing," the commissioner says. "You have to make it to be able to lose it. Don't get off on tangents. Go into abstractions like music, and you'll miss things right in front of your face. What's new with that enraged vagrant?"

"Three-time losers break easier than urbane gentlemen. He's holding onto a secret."

"The electricians are our best suspects."

"Don't brag to the musicians about the CDs you own," Lowell cautions before hanging up.

Perfect pitch: The ability to hear a sound and sense the number of vibrations per second, thus assigning it a note on the scale. An estimated one in ten thousand people have this ability.

Pianissimo

At 2:52 p.m., eighteen minutes before the naked body appears on Harrison Street, Felix is lost in thought in one of the sound-proof practice cubicles in the basement. Melody knocks on the open glass door. The principal clarinetist turns his head slowly from abstract space toward the sound of the knock.

"I either practice or teach here, and I was thinking how strange to sit here without instrument. I never did it before," he says without losing his reverie.

Melody enters and closes the door. The honeycomb acoustic panels absorb the overtones in Felix's Asian-accented voice, the slippery "l" and "r" undistinguished.

"We've been relating to the world through music," she says, "playing someone else's tune, usually some eccentric German who died before they invented toilet paper."

"Actually, we learn to listen closely to music, each detail. I wonder if we can transpose that sensitivity to ourselves."

"Even though it takes years to learn cello, it's harder to express through words than through my cello."

"Many times words are useless," Felix says. "The word 'concert' used to mean to oppose, to contend. It gives whole new meaning to music."

"What would you like your clarinet to say?" Melody asks.

"Music is supposed to come from musician not instrument. Actually, right now I feel liberated. Since childhood, my life was my instrument. I didn't know what else was inside me."

Melody and Felix think silently.

"I never raised a voice against the arts agreement," Felix says finally. "My silence helped them."

"I don't know what else to do to find our instruments. You think Guru has real information?"

"Guru speaks in counterpoint," Felix says. "He wouldn't say boo to a goose, but his April Fools' idea sounds dubious."

"He was at the loading area when I turned in my cello, and he appeared again when we got back from the airport. I don't know who led whom into the bomb room."

"Guru has a knack for knowing where you'll be."

"I've always taken what he says as nonsense, but maybe I'm wrong. Tito thinks he might have been used by the government for their dirty tricks plot."

"Actually, the government is more complex than Tito believes," Felix says. "Many officials threatened to resign if the ceremony went through. Half Congress is against it. The other half wanted to push it through before people wake up."

"The bomb was placed this morning. We were the only people here."

"So were Liaison Cage and Special Agent Dufay. Why did he leave town?"

"He knew we'd be safe in the airport. Word of the robbery didn't reach him. He never thought about our instruments."

"Sounds like a *badinerie*, actually."

Five minutes later and one floor up, Eduardo walks on stage and introduces himself. There is no applause, just silent anticipation.

"The BSO general manager told me that the police—and there is a small army of them on the case—have solid leads and are working systematically. The robbers can't sell the instruments any more than you can sell this hall. Two are Stradivarius, and you can count the people gifted enough to play them on your fingers and toes. In the absence of news, I've been asked to talk about music. The favorite subject of composers is modern compositions that most concertgoers hate."

There is a ruffle in the audience. He's an engaging teacher, moving while he talks, making wide gestures and putting different stress on his words, but because of the expectation of the day, he hardly needs to work to get their attention. His fingers never cover his mouth when he's in front of the audience.

"To talk about modern music, we have to dip back into antiquity, starting with Pythagoras and his music of the spheres. He was the first to articulate musical theory, and he was such a dazzling lyre player that his recitals propelled his followers to euphoric heights. Modern scholarship says that the Greeks also ate psychedelic mushrooms, which might have aided Pythagoras's audience on the road to ecstasy."

A cackle rises from the audience.

By early afternoon, the crowd outside spills over into the side streets around Symphony Hall. The two motorcycle cops who drive in front of Mayor Bond's car manage to get him to the edge of Symphony Hall by going the wrong way up St. Stephen Street from Gainsborough Street, stopping as close to the building as the crowd permits. Flashing waves and smiles from the stone steps, Bond enters with his two assistants.

"How you doin', Mayor?" the security guard asks. "You going to get their instruments back before midnight?"

"I sure am. Let's start by seeing that one-of-a-kind lieutenant."

Walter and Lowell come down to the entrance to welcome him, Lowell finishing a slice of pizza on the stairs. Walter, inherently well-mannered, says how happy he is to see the mayor, and the mayor responds to his genuine appreciation. Bond makes open, expansive gestures, always ready to launch into a responsible energy speech.

"I thought we could coordinate efforts," the mayor says, adopting an earnest tone, "to get to the bottom of this efficiently."

"Homeland Security is working over the leftists." Lowell is careful to finish chewing before speaking. "Would you like to deal with the press?"

Bond's smile makes it obvious that it is, indeed, his aim. Here's his chance to the national spotlight. He has to be as cunning as the oil industry. "We're here to give all the assistance we can, to put the full force of city government behind the investigation."

Bond is used to being on stage and giving speeches, a natural politician, whose parents emigrated from Jamaica and sacrificed to give him a Catholic school education. A light-skinned man and an academic whiz, Bond speaks with neither a black nor a Jamaican accent, and if you didn't see his children, you wouldn't think he has African roots. He's easily the most intellectual mayor Boston has seen, but he makes a deliberate effort to appear like a regular guy.

"We appreciate every effort you make on our behalf." Walter's voice elicits a call for help. "We'll look to you as

Washington's point man."

"It's my personal pleasure to assist Boston's most beloved institution." Bond raises his hand like a crossing guard. "We all love the Pops."

In the auditorium, Eduardo continues to talk about new music. "The classical community's biggest problem is a narrow interpretation of worthy music. We like what we know, what we've grown up with, like aging hippies stuck in the music of the sixties. But it's such a satisfying experience when we open ourselves and listen to different music. Just the opening up to want to listen gives us a whole new feeling about life. It's the difference between being young at heart and being a stodgy old fogy.

"Try listening, for example, to the atonal music of the Kurds or to an Indian raga, and you will find that they are full of emotion and power. Many say that hip hop isn't music. The singers don't sing, they talk, backed by a bunch of phony electronic noise. But listen, and you'll find rhythm, harmony, and melody, the three pillars of music.

"Getting back to Pythagoras, the father of Western musical theory and science, he claimed that each planet plays a musical tone as it orbits, and he was able to hear it. The moon, closest to us, is the soprano of the system, while Saturn, the furthest known planet at that time, hums a bass. Can anyone else hear it?

"His theory was so ingrained that when Kepler—two thousand years later—developed the laws of planetary motion, he used Pythagoras's music theory to calculate a series of notes made by the planets as they moved through the heavens. Kepler discovered that planets orbit faster and slower depending on how far they are from the sun. He suggested that they make increasingly lower and higher sounds during their orbit, like a pianist warming up on scales. His thesis includes a musical score for each planet. Don't laugh—astronomers may arrive at a modern version of this notion, because music, movement, vibration is essential to the universe and innate to us. Listen, we're surrounded by music. Stop and listen. The universe is music."

Lowell and Walter continue working inside Walter's second floor office. The coffee has long since run out, but neither refills it.

"Did you tape last night's concert?" Lowell asks.

"We've taped every concert since recording became available. Musicians and conductors study them. Last night we played Schumann's *Manfred* followed by the Saint-Saëns *Cello Concerto,* which the Czech played, and the Tchaikovsky *Fifth.* A pretty standard program—an overture and a concerto followed by a symphony after intermission."

"Why don't you bring in the tape?"

"It's just the concert." Walter relaxes his shoulders. "I'll run down to the archive room in the basement and get it. We can listen while we work."

Maestro Borges joins Lowell at the urinal, making the lieutenant feel uncomfortable during one of his important occasions.

"Have you seen your brother?" Lowell asks before Borges can get an angry word out.

"Why are you interested in my simple brother? Why aren't you rounding up our enemy?"

Lowell looks straight ahead to avoid Borges' aggressive stare. "Your brother said he was playing a practical joke."

"His mind is not normal—you cannot take what he says seriously."

"Do you know the company he keeps?"

"He doesn't keep company. His world is imaginary friends, imaginary work." Borges' voice is loud and accusatory. "I doubt if he knows what I'm doing in Brazil."

"Your mother was visiting you there."

"Well, ah," Borges mumbles. "We're running out of time. Go after the militants."

Lowell zips and turns. "I understand that Guru knows about them."

"You yourself said how well the robbery was put together. My brother can barely put together a macaroni and cheese dinner with the package in front of him." Borges' body gives nothing away, but his tone is emotive.

"Will this arts agreement help your Brazilian orchestra?"

"What does that have to do with the investigation?"

"I'm trying to get a sense of the big picture."

Borges also zips. "We're in a new era. Artists who don't adapt will be left behind. Recent history proves that free markets work best. This will be true for the arts as well. Look how creativity was sucked out of communist countries. Our agreement creates two million jobs in entertainment in the first three years."

"So, where did Guru run off to?"

Borges' body quivers as he sucks in air like a sprint swimmer. Lowell isn't sure if he is defensive or embarrassed.

Borges composes himself. "Isn't he at the apartment?"

"He seems to have vanished."

Lowell walks out, leaving Borges open-mouthed.

China's bright face lights up the hall. "What's new?" she asks.

Meanwhile, transport officer Milton arrives at Symphony Hall and encounters Malden Police Sergeant Alan Ostinato as he parks the half-empty baggage truck in the loading area. The two men unload the four crates of baggage.

"I'm assigned to find the instruments," Ostinato declares. "I have to go underground."

Eduardo speaks to the audience with clear diction, but it feels as if he has a joke tucked away, which makes people pay attention so as not to miss it.

"Music used to be an essential science, on the same level as biology and chemistry. The seven-tone scale, the *do*, *re*, *me*, *fa*, *so*, *la*, *ti* that we all know, was established in mathematical terms by Pythagoras. Put your finger midway on a violin or guitar or piano string, and it vibrates twice as fast. It's an octave higher, the eighth note of the seven-note diatonic scale. Put your finger two-thirds up the string, and you have a perfect fifth, the *so* on the scale. Three-quarters and you have a fourth, *fa*. Four-fifths and you have a sixth, *la*. This is how Pythagoras came up with the scale, close to what we use today. He also thought that the intervals between notes correspond to the distances between planets, hence the music of the spheres.

"*Do*, *re*, *me* were the first words of each line of a poem that a medieval monk used to conform music notation.

"Until Darwin's theory of natural selection, which brought chance or probability into our worldview, humans thought the universe had perfect harmony. Life's harmony was reproduced by composers, but our growing knowledge is making us uncertain and perplexed.

"Mozart's world was not uncertain. People lost their teeth, smelled because they never bathed, and died young, like Mozart and Schubert, but their universe was utterly clear: right versus wrong, heaven above the clouds, and hell under the earth. We are far less sure of ourselves, so modern composers who write inharmonious music are in harmony with today's world.

"Baroque and Romantic music of the eighteenth and nineteenth centuries is founded on a grand design, a God-centered world. Composers tried to propel their listeners into the spiritual realm, even if, to them, that spirituality meant nature. Similarly, today's music should challenge us to become more aware of our world. It should invite us to dig inside ourselves and pull up feelings and thoughts we did not expect to find. We need to be still, receptive."

Eduardo speaks for half an hour. At the end, he receives loud applause.

"Before leaving," Eduardo says, "I want to tell you how lucky we are to have such a high level of performed music in Boston. A piece I wrote was played in the Midwest last year. The musicians there were exceptionally nice to work with, but as I listened to the performance, I couldn't help thinking, their orchestra would never fly with Boston audiences. Let's never forget how lucky we are to have the BSO."

Melody, China, Felix, and Tito come through the metal door next to the stage to find Eduardo after his talk and compliment him on his intellect.

"You're better than most heady guys," China says. "You keep people's attention."

Eduardo asks Melody if she has news.

"I'm talking to everyone I can," she says.

"I'm glad you're doing this," Eduardo says.

"I'm glad as well. It wipes out the feeling of passively accepting fate."

They all agree to go to Melody's flat, since it is only two blocks away, and discuss what to do next.

"I never thought about music as science," Felix says,

putting on his heavy brown coat and Russian-style hat. "I make music every day, but I still don't know what I make."

China pulls on her red gloves, and the group exits the stage door. Melody looks at the demonstrators, a couple of whom wave at Tito.

"The arts agreement used to be a political debate," Eduardo says. "It's turned into passionate support for music."

China takes him and Melody by each arm like long-lost friends, and the group walks a block down Westland Street toward Melody's Fenway apartment, a short distance from the robbery.

Tito says to Eduardo, "If you wrote about the scientific aspect of music, it might take away from the corporate rule of the industry."

"I wanted the New World Compositions to speak for themselves."

"They can't." Tito tightens the hood straps on his REI parka. "We all had to learn music just as we had to learn to read and add numbers. We even have to learn how to listen."

Although Tito's tone is usually accusatory, his face remains an even *largo*.

Raja is curled up inside the front door of Mel's apartment. He jumps up and watches everyone enter and throw their coats in a pile on the sofa. They pull the kitchen table to the center of the room, bringing chairs from the living room. No one touches Mel's practice chair which she keeps in the center of her chapel-like bay window, dominated by the last picture of her mother, taken at an amusement park the night her mother told her that they were leaving the church and Mel's father could come if he liked.

"I don't have much to offer," Melody apologizes as they take seats around the table. "I expected to be eating in Rio."

The others make noises about not bothering, since they'll be there for only a few minutes, but Eduardo opens cupboards while Melody hunts in the fridge, pulling out hummus and carrots. Being a hostess takes the edge off Melody's angst. Eduardo finds chips, salsa, and several bottles of wine, the same bottles she had when she stopped seeing him. He also sees Jell-O, which had been one of Melody's staples. Eduardo demeaned it, so she ate it only in secret.

Melody didn't cook when she was alone, didn't appreciate the social aspect of dining until Eduardo came into her kitchen. He introduced her to ethnic cuisine, brought ginger marinade, olive tapenade, couscous. He took her about town and did things with her that she never imagined: off-beat social activities, poetry slams, wine tastings, salsa dancing, lectures on genetics. He enjoyed a wide range of interests and shared them with her. She rubbed shoulders with creative types, folks from different cultures, went to art openings and Tibetan meditation, and, of course, they played and listened to music together.

Raja walks between everyone's legs, then jumps up to his high perch above the kitchen cabinets.

Eduardo opens a bottle of wine and lets it breathe. "Scriabin the mystic said that wine helps creativity."

Melody gives the group a summary of her investigation. "Whenever Guru talks to me about his brother, the maestro, he always mentions money. I assume Borges is mad that the lucrative rights of the televised ceremony might be canceled. None of the musicians knows anything. No one in the coalition opposing the arts agreement knows anything—I can tell by their voices—but FAS had an informant. He obviously wasn't successful at finding out about the heist."

"Depends on who he was informing," Eduardo says as he pours wine for everyone.

"You go, girl," China says. "We're impressed."

Tito raises his glass. "Here's to our symphony detective."

"Where's Wisteria?" China asks.

"She's paying someone $175 to come out today and change her lock," Melody says.

"Good riddance to bad trash," Tito says. "Her slime bag husband tried to pick up my girlfriend once. I said to myself, 'This guy is getting reckless'."

"She'll forget him next week," Felix says.

"No she won't," Mel predicts. "She'll take revenge."

Her own experience against her father tells her about a period of anger.

"Hatred loses its steam," Eduardo says. "When Berlioz won the Prix de Rome and lived in the oppressive Villa Medici, his beautiful fiancé wrote him announcing she was marrying someone else. He rode back to Paris swearing to kill them both, but he calmed down on the trip and, later, married a lame, grating, debt-ridden actress."

"Eduardo, it's reasonable to stop hating," Mel says. "But humans are not reasonable."

A warm winter light filters through the window blinds. Melody has few decorations and fewer chotchkies. Her apartment offers a comfortable wood setting, especially welcome in the winter cold. She keeps a tidy house and a working kitchen, orderly and sensible.

The musicians get on their phones while drinking wine and nibbling on olives, rice cakes, low-fat crackers, and whatever else Melody pulls from her cupboards. Eduardo phones musicians who are part of the New World Compositions, asking them to come to Symphony Hall and perform. Tito texts his leftist friends. Felix phones a kingpin in Chinatown who has tentacles in every illicit racket. China keeps in touch with Sergeant Rodrigo. No one has any new information.

Although Melody welcomes the break, she wants to get back to the action. Her investigation empowers her, chiseling away at her sorrow. Eduardo, too, has another lecture to give.

They walk briskly back to Symphony Hall.

"Walter's right about us being lucky to have jobs with the BSO," Felix says. "Most musicians make a couple of hundred here, a thousand there, spending twice as much time driving to gigs as playing. When they get sick, they end up in a clinic for poor people. Look what happened to Alban Berg. He was too poor to see a dentist and died of a gum infection."

"It's supply and demand," China explains as they walk on Westland Street. "Too many trained musicians and not enough posts. People don't need music like they need grocery stores and prostitutes."

"In progressive countries, musicians get benefits, like not being taxed," Tito says. "Here, you're guaranteed a hard life."

"It's worse for soloists, who live like nomads," Felix says. "Bela Bartók suffered the same fate, too poor to be treated. Only a BSO commission helped him die with dignity."

Melody hears in their voices the tune of the Helsinki Complaints Choir. She knows that Felix promised his wife that they would return to California eventually. He could send his résumé anywhere, and he would be grabbed up. Like all BSO principals, Felix is among the top handful of musicians of his instrument, playing with sensitivity and precision.

When the group gets two blocks from Symphony Hall, they hear the crowd.

"People have no idea of the stress of competition," Tito says. "During my audition, they had to call an ambulance when one aspirant passed out."

"Felix still sweats before a solo," China says, voicing what everyone knows. "It doesn't matter how many times he's played it, I'm sure to find him pacing backstage biting his nails."

"Before my first solo," he says, "I went out of my mind. Actually, I refused to go on. The concertmaster came backstage and slapped my face. Hard. She told me later that someone had done the same to her." He turns to Mel. "I can relate to what you're going through. I used to be terrorized that I'd botch it. But you'll come out the other side."

"You have to admire people with tattoos," Melody says

out of the blue. "They define themselves for the rest of their lives."

The musicians make their way through the throng of supporters. Tito asks Eduardo why he didn't include a bass solo in his composition. "Every other principal gets a lick, but you guys never let a bass speak." Tito's voice is *bravado*. "Break free from the cliché of keeping the tune with the squeaky violins."

"You're right. It was an oversight. I was told that one trio in the cycle is scored for tuba, bassoon, and bass."

"Low notes drive the orchestra with depth and drama," Tito says. "The bass got devalued, because it sounds like a thud on a stereo. The live bass sound is carnal, adult. That's why bass *pizzicato* became the foundation for jazz."

"Actually, recordings made orchestras stiff," Felix says. "Musicians used to be flamboyant. We don't allow any deviation today. You can recognize Heifetz or Horowitz, but it's hard to tell one contemporary orchestra from another. We still dress like waiters. Critics and audiences expect us to sound like their CD. That becomes our aim."

"If we don't find our instruments by midnight, we won't sound like anything," Melody chimes in as they come to the stage door.

She closes her eyes thinking that no orchestra will want her if she's fired. What's she going to do? Go back to accounting?

Mayor Bond's main aggravation is getting information. He wanders the corridors of Symphony Hall, but Lowell avoids him. The mayor relies on the commissioner, who stays at police HQ on Columbus Street.

Bond tells his secretary to call another press conference. "Those reporters out there are national."

His speech writer arranges a 3:00 p.m. conference in the

front lobby, chosen because it looks old, impressive, and properly Bostonian. When Bond steps into the foyer, the television crews' lights focus on him. The mayor wears his gravest face as he faces an array of mikes at the top of four marble steps that lead to the main hall.

"This is a difficult moment for our city," he begins, his eyes expressing a dedicated earnestness. "Some of these instruments are old and fragile. All have great value, foremost to the wonderful men and women who sacrifice their natural desires and pleasures in order to play this serious music, but also to the city of Boston, since this refinement counterbalances the sin and debauchery rife in our midst."

He stops and looks directly at the cameras. "I'm a scientist, not an arts person, but I was affected personally by this calamity, deeply affected. Be assured that I have mobilized city government to find the instruments today and bring the scoundrels to justice. I have ordered the police to be on high alert, and I declare to all citizens of this great city that we will leave no stone unturned."

Before he is finished, many reporters raise hands.

"Do you have any suspects?" a journalist for WBZ asks.

"Irv, I don't want to get into details, because it might jeopardize our work. We have been following several solid leads since the robbery."

"Can they resolve the case today?" Irv asks.

"We have the best investigator working on it. I'm optimistic."

"Is there truth to the rumor that the FBI will take over?" a Channel Five reporter inquires.

Bond assumes the kind of solemn face that makes it obvious he hasn't heard the rumor and is hostile to it. "I have been coordinating with Washington since early this morning, working diligently and harmoniously with my friends in the highest level of the federal government."

"Mayor Bond," says a voice in the back next to a set of

bright lights, whose glare prevents the mayor from seeing the man's face, "Can you tell us your favorite classical composer?"

You have to know Bond quite well, as the reporters do, to realize from his extra gracious attitude that he wants to walk back and strangle the reporter.

"Let's concentrate on the Symphony," he says. "This isn't about my taste or yours—it's about a city treasure."

"Are you a fan of Henri Mancini?" the same voice asks.

"Perhaps you're close to my favorite classical composer," Bond says with an open smile.

Bond turns to take questions from another part of the room, but the same reporter speaks up again.

"Can you tell us how often you attend the Symphony?"

Bond shoots a momentary glance at his secretary, then turns to the voice near the lights. He knows he's dealing with an enemy who will go to any length to embarrass him. He certainly wants to avoid the race issue—if Bond does attend the Symphony, he would be one of the few African-Americans who does.

"It wouldn't be right to divert attention at this crucial juncture away from the massive loss that our city has suffered," he says. "I want to repeat that the city government is mobilized. We will track down these robbers and bring them to justice."

"Has the emergency network been activated?" another reporter asks.

"If it can help, I'll activate it. If the sanitation department can help, I'll call on them as well," Bond replies. "Right now, it's a police matter, and I have directed the police to find the instruments today, whatever it takes."

The malevolent voice in front of the lights persists. "Why do the musicians play on old, fragile instruments? Wouldn't it be a generous gesture if City Hall offered to buy new ones?"

"Let's think about that at another time. Right now, I'm concentrating on getting their original instruments back."

"Sir, will this affect the Pops as well?" The voice won't let up.

The mayor offers another broad Bond smile. "Every musician is affected. When you know that they'll steal someone's fiddle, the guy who plays horn has to keep peeking over his shoulder. What kind of music can you make when you're always looking behind you? Musicians are in this together, never mind if it's the xylophone or the saxophone or the Pops. It's their collective behinds that are at stake."

"Another naked body has been found in a car parked on Harrison Street," the voice says again. "What do you think about that?"

Six weeks earlier, when the applause ended for the Stravinsky *Pulcinella Suite* and the orchestra was packing up, the sheriff, wearing a suit, came onto the stage and stood near Melody. She looked up and took an alarmed step backward.

China stood, ready for battle.

"It's okay," Melody said. "He's a family friend."

China wasn't pacified, but she stood back. She knew that Mel had no family.

"Would you mind going with me for tea?" the sheriff asked.

"Like yeah she minds," China said. "We're going clubbing."

"I'm going out to talk," Mel said to China. She saw Walter looking on from the side door. "I'll text you."

"I didn't come here because your father asked me," the sheriff said as soon as they were seated in a café. His voice had gotten darker over the past ten years. "I came on my own, because I know you're a sensible girl. It's time for you to acknowledge the truth."

"I did it," she said. She broke down crying. "I killed her."

"Sweetie, it was an accident."

"She lit candles for me. She had never done that before. She wasn't superstitious, but she knew exactly what it meant if I won that competition in Dallas. She may have even prayed to the Virgin Mary, even though we looked down on Catholics."

Melody had never voiced it so plainly. She had denied her own guilt for ten years.

"On top of that, I lashed out at my dad." She wanted to say more but couldn't get air past her larynx. She needed to apologize and atone, to take back a decade of blame.

He sat compassionately with her, his hand on hers.

What had she done to someone who was already in the throes of grief? She wanted to thank the sheriff, but she was having problems with her voice. Wasn't she supposed to feel relieved?

She stood to leave the café, her heels echoing off the empty room. When she exited onto the street, she heard the drone of the Saturday night city encasing the tall buildings.

China found her before dawn wandering across the MIT Bridge with her hands on her ears, trying to stop the hurting sounds, unsure of where she was going, what time it was, or whether she had eaten. She had a box of his letters, all unopened, in her apartment. He wrote once a month, and once a month, she tossed the envelope into the box.

Tempo: A most contentious aspect of performance. A piece has an entirely different meaning if it's played slower or faster. Some composers write the exact tempo they want at the beginning of the score.

Third Movement
Andantino

Two hours and fifteen minutes before George's confession, Lowell finds Cage.

The presidential liaison for the arts is sitting in the restaurant of the Isabella Stuart Gardner Museum, a few blocks from Symphony Hall. Cage is on his phone, sipping coffee with his legs crossed. He certainly isn't unhappy. Lowell goes to his table.

Cage stands. "This museum is one of my special places. Whenever I'm in Boston, I hang out here to cure my mind from the Washington hassle. I'll show you around."

"This is not my sightseeing day. Why did you insist on seeing me here? You should know better than anyone that I have to work on the case."

"The vice president wants to know directly from you how the investigation is going."

"He's been talking with the commissioner. Dufay also keeps him posted."

"Dufay is one of the best agents."

It takes Lowell a long silence to absorb the last comment. "Special Agent Dufay has been investigating the people and groups in and out of the FAS coalition, hasn't he?"

"His specialty," Cage says. "He's been collecting intelligence about potential threats since the arts agreement was announced. Nothing in his memos told us of trouble. Perhaps that made everyone complacent."

Lowell pauses again to absorb the comment. "I'm keeping Symphony Hall as our base, since that is where the robbers might call again."

"You think they'll call again?"

"Yes. And soon, while they have the world's attention. They need their say, a ransom or a soapbox speech about capitalism."

"The vice president is on edge," Cage says. "Imagine the chance he'd have for reelection if he crossed the media industry."

"Mr. Cage, it all depends on what happens between the inner and outer sphincters. We only have the conscious ability to control the outer, so a small amount of gas passes the inner sphincter, then sits in no man's land. We look around and decide whether it's socially acceptable to fart. Isn't that amazing?"

"What are you talking about?"

"If you deny the internal sphincter too many times, you end up holding your butt muscles tight, which leads to constipation."

Cage is silent.

"It's always best to let it out as soon as possible. Why didn't anyone protect the baggage truck?"

Cage coughs to bring himself back to the question. "You're right. It was a major flaw. No one thought about the instruments."

"To collect all the mistakes and excuses in this case, I'd

have to go home and bring a wheelbarrow and shovel. FAS must have been mad at you for changing position on the arts agreement."

"I honor free speech. I welcome different points of view."

"Takes a mighty man to wrestle down human nature," Lowell says. "Most men get upset when another man verbally assaults them. It's more than money—it's honor. If those in power wanted the deal so much, they might design a scheme to discredit FAS."

"Whoever wants to help artists would see this agreement as it is." Cage sounds like an insincere politician. "the vice president has directed me to be the press liaison."

"You'll have to compete with the mayor. Did you hear about the second body?"

Cage stops, dropping his conceited attitude. "Second body?"

"Found nearby."

Cage turns white. "How do you know it's related to the robbery?"

"The famous Mr. Anonymous phoned me. A sign on it says, 'We know you, too'."

"We know you, too?" Cage repeats.

"Now, if I don't get right back to work, worry will drive my intestinal alkalinity sky high."

Lowell leaves Cage gazing at a blushing marble Venus.

Before entering Symphony Hall, Eduardo stops at one of the large press trucks parked adjacent to the building and sticks his head in.

"I have some information," he says to the four men

inside. "A group of musicians is coming to perform the second concert in the New World Compositions, the series of musical pieces that the Rio concert was scheduled to inaugurate. The piece we'll perform was scheduled to be premièred next month on a Navajo reservation in Arizona, but the composer has given permission to air it now."

"We've already got feeds from the auditorium," one newsman says.

"The police are arranging the audience," Eduardo says, his fingers on his mouth. "The musicians will be here soon, and we'll start at 3:20."

"The lead item on the BBC was the robbery. It's become international news, and everyone's blaming FAS," another newsman says.

Eduardo re-enters the building and gives the signal to Mrs. Schutz, who directs the police to fill the hall with a new set of supporters. As soon as the crowd discovers that the hall is opening again, people begin positioning themselves. By this time, the crowd-turned-festival has spread down Mass. Ave. toward Back Bay. The police help install a large wireless TV monitor and speakers on top of an ambulance that had parked in the middle of the street and then became trapped by the people standing around it.

Melody has already reached the body on Harrison Street.

"This arts agreement is causing a lot of commotion," a policeman standing by a car parked at the scene says as Mel approaches.

She tells the policeman that she represents the orchestra and is working with Lowell. He lets her come forward for a closer look.

"It's just like New Hampshire," she says to the cop. "Big, bearded naked guy stuffed in a trunk."

She reads the note out loud. "We know you, too."

"What does that mean?" the cop asks her.

"It sounds like people giving each other private signals. Or a Haydn joke."

She watches a man in a white coat walking out of the building. He comes to look at the body.

"How did he get out here?" the man asks. "He was in my morgue."

"Maybe he needed some fresh air," someone says, and the others laugh.

"Someone must have pulled him out on that gurney over there," a cop says.

"Who was he?" Melody asks the man in the white coat.

"Unidentified. He was brought in early this morning, picked up off the street. We're examining him tomorrow."

"Just like New Hampshire," she says. "He's got to be connected with the heist. It wouldn't have been Christians, because Christians would have taken the time to dress them."

"It might become a war of bodies."

"Leaving bodies must be more than morbid humor," Melody says. "It must have a logical purpose. Everything has to fit together. Doesn't it?"

Guru phones her as she is leaving, his voice as excited as a tarantella. "It's international, the orchestra and the FBI and Art Unincorporated. I have to do my duty like a soldier and solve the case."

"Where have you been?"

"I'm in their safe house. They have me tied up, because I know too much. They're allowing me one phone call, and then they're taping my mouth. A nice policeman from Malden named Alan Ostinato was there, too. His chief ordered him to find the instruments. I know who did it. I told everything to the Secret Service agent."

"I'll come and get you. Lowell is looking for you."

Guru is too revved to listen. "They're trying to get me to join the movement, to be a double agent. They need me badly, but I have to get more top secret information. No one collects information like Guru does. I taught soldiers how to overcome fear. I taught Officer Alan Ostinato about the New World Compositions. Brahms was a loud, brash guy who stuck his beard in people's faces, but he loved Clara Schumann and caught a deadly cold at her funeral. He died for her."

Melody hears chatter, then someone takes the phone.

"Come to the Democracy Center near Harvard Square at five," the voice says. "I'll take you to the secret safe house where the great spy is being kept. He will save humanity from the dark forces. Do you understand?"

"I think so. You have Guru, and you'll give him to me."

"He's not going anywhere, since he's tied up. We're having a long talk—more like a long listen—about the international conspiracy. Understand?"

"I'll be there at five."

Gustav feels the whack on his nose before he sees the fist. He had approached his front door cautiously, asking, "Who's there?" and staying several feet away. Even when he hears his girlfriend's voice, he hesitates.

"Are you going to keep me out here?" she asks.

"I . . . just . . . didn't expect you."

"Let's talk. Face to face."

He approaches the door, still hesitant. "Talk about what?"

"About you and me."

He opens it a crack. A foot kicks the door wide open, and the blow to his nose comes from a blur of light. Gustav reels backward, feels three pairs of hands seize him, a knee on his kidneys, his face on the wooden floor. He doesn't even have a chance to put up his arms to mute the blows.

He cries in pain, not realizing that someone has shoved

a handkerchief in his mouth.

His girlfriend kneels and looks him in the face. "You're scum."

He musters his energy and moans through the handkerchief. She takes it out of his mouth.

"You used me, too," he says.

"Take good care of him," she tells the others.

He hears her leave, his television in the background giving news of the heist.

"How shall we punish a snitch?" one of the intruders asks.

"Jam his balls up his mouth," says another. "That's what the mafia does to a grass."

"I didn't snitch," Gustav pleads.

He gets a blow to the stomach.

"Tell us another lie, and you'll pick your eyeballs off the floor. Who were you informing?"

"I wasn't—"

The blow comes to his crotch as he tries to cower on his side.

"Who?"

"I don't know."

A punch reaches his ear.

"I talked to a guy on the phone," he says quickly. "I don't know who he is or what he does."

"What did you tell him?"

"Nothing," Gustav insists.

This time, it's his thigh.

"I said that Milton was going away and that everything was on track."

"Liar. You told him about the heist. It's better to tell us now."

"I didn't take any money for my work for you. The guy sent me money. He said he was on our side and was going to help after the heist, which he did. I was already risking myself by getting the cars. If they caught me, it would be my second, and I'd do time for sure."

They beat him more, demanding the identity of the one to whom he sold information. Finally, they conclude he doesn't know, beat him some more, and strip him.

"This is only a warning," one of them says. "You say one more word to anyone, and we won't be nice like this."

News of the second body reaches the crowd around Symphony Hall as, once again, one hour and fifty minutes before George's confession, Mrs. Schutz directs the police to open the doors and allows in another hall full of people.

The first musical group that Eduardo has arranged arrives backstage as the police seat the new audience. The media trucks parked outside the building on St. Stephen Street have live feeds from video cameras placed around the auditorium. They also have two men with cameras on their shoulders near the front of the stage. The footage is beamed to stations across the country, many interrupting their regular programs for a special broadcast of the unusual robbery.

The West Coast had awakened sluggishly to a January California storm. Combined with the standard Midwest winter, the day becomes a heavy TV Sunday. Even NFL playoff announcers keep their viewers updated about the heist. Since the TV crews have exhausted their reporting of distraught symphony goers, crying musicians, and FAS activists—either young guys with rings in their lips or distinguished gentlemen in Giorgio Armani coats—stations across the country broadcast the Symphony Hall feed featuring an *avant garde* group of musicians playing the second of the musical cycle dedicated to the history of the New World. One of the musicians, a techie by day, arranges for the concerts to be streamed over the web.

Part Native American, the composer of the piece, Sky

Horizon, holds a chair in the Brandeis University Composition Department, where Leonard Bernstein studied and played with Aaron Copland. Her composition is scored unusually for soprano and sextet.

Eduardo comes to center stage and introduces Ms. Horizon enthusiastically, saying what a thrill it is to have worked with such a talented and sensitive musician. "Sky is one of the brains behind the New World Compositions, an experiment in composing music of all genres, from delicate chamber pieces to rowdy hip hop played in ghettos and subways. One composer has written the film score of a major movie set during the Inca golden age. He researched and tried to recreate Inca music. Dozens of musicians are involved in similar projects. The compositions will be played across North and South America. Sky has become a sensation in Europe, barely able to keep up with the commissions she receives. She's also a beekeeper—she drives hundreds of hives across New England so they can pollinate our farms."

Sky comes on stage in Native dress, a simple leather skirt and bead necklace. Her rich, coarse black hair is pinned behind her neck, runs down her back, and brushes her bare arms. She points at the decorated tribal drums in the center of the stage. "You ever seen these in Symphony Hall?"

The audience responds genially. She is a slender, dark woman with a simple, pretty face whose pronounced cheek-bones make her look solemn, but when she speaks, people feel her warmth and enthusiasm. Although an extrovert on stage, in private, Sky is humble and timid.

"A college radio station recently replayed an old *Lone Ranger* show," she says. "You know you're a music connoisseur when you hear the 'William Tell Overture' and don't think about the Lone Ranger."

People laugh.

"On the show, a decent, upright settler family was being attacked by malicious Indians. The Lone Ranger, a symbol of the ideal American male—unsociable but effective at his work—arrived just in time to fight off the vicious savages and save the settlers. It's remarkable that white people, who killed Indians and robbed their land, were able to portray themselves as innocent victims and Indians as violent killers."

She looks around the room. "In the piece we're about to play, I try to express one aspect of our history in music. Many have heard about the conquering armies giving Indians blankets deliberately infected with smallpox. Then the white men dispersed the diseased people to other tribes to spread the infection. The first incident happened in 1763, not far from here, an epidemic that killed, by one account, a hundred thousand. While historians dispute the numbers and intentions, it's beyond doubt that our country perpetrated the worst act of biological warfare on a defenseless population. We stubbornly have not acknowledged this. It would be like if Germans denied the Holocaust."

Sky speaks with conviction but without emotion. "I'm not trying to blame anyone or make you feel guilty, but we need to get the history right. I wanted to capture the 1763 incident musically. The drums give the piece an Indian sense of time, which is different from our constant linear notion. Native time comes in cycles, as you'll hear, speeding up and slowing down.

"A flute solo, which begins and ends the piece, transmits the serenity of death. The flute is the high voice of the orchestra, while the cello, with its deep resonance, reminds us of Earth. The viola, played in the middle of the vocal range, speaks for those suffering and dying. The violin, played mostly on the high upper string, conveys the sadness of loss, and the piano, as usual, puts it all together. The piece is divided into eight sections, the soprano singing a declarative phrase announcing each section.

"Finally, people have asked me about my name. It wasn't the name I was born with but an identity to which I aspire. Do you like it?"

Applause.

"Native names are descriptive," she says. "Like so many rivers and towns that Indians named."

A group of five musicians comes on stage, accepts applause with Sky and Eduardo, and take up their positions. Instead of being dressed in musician black, they wear a mixture of colors. Eduardo sits behind the Steinway while Sky is the violist. The soprano, a tall, dark Native woman, wears a loose, flowery dress.

The musicians tune, then begin with a haunting flute solo played in the high register as Sky described. The drums enter quietly, and the soprano sings in a slippery legato, "They came with the sword of disease, which stabbed young and old, men and women." Then the strings take up the themes set out by the flute.

The piece, which holds a fairly classical structure, part European and part Native, a combination of rondo and rhapsody, lasts about twenty minutes and is not, as some had feared, a discordant modern composition. At the end, the audience stands up and cheers, and Sky is called back three times.

She stops the audience's applause with outstretched palms. "Another naked person was found in a car on Newbury Street. This one was alive and kicking but beat up. A sign claimed he was a snitch. We don't feel sorry for infiltrators and collaborators."

Ninety minutes before George's confession, Melody rushes to the scene on Newbury Street. The police have a shivering guy wrapped up in a sheet inside a patrol car. She wonders if the same people are responsible for all three naked men, two dead and one living. She invokes Lowell's name again.

"Young kid," a policewoman tells her. "Won't give us his name, and his name was the only thing he didn't have tattooed on him."

"Someone phoned the press," Melody says, "claiming he was a stooge. How did he get here?"

"Beats me. He was thrashed and thrown into a car like a fraternity prank."

"I recognize his face from last night's FAS meeting," Melody says. "But I don't know who he is. He must have been the mole."

"That makes sense. FAS discovered that he was an informant, and this was his punishment."

"But if he snitched on them, why didn't anyone know about the heist?"

Melody hurries to the Lucy Parsons Center, a left-wing revolutionary bookstore on Centre Street in Jamaica Plain. Tito has arranged for her to meet another young FAS coordinator who evaded being picked up by Homeland Security. He sports the requisite scruffy beard and Che beret.

Melody and Tito enter the storefront bookstore and walk between shelves of socialist books and anarchist magazines printed on cheap paper, stopping at a table in the back where meetings are held.

Mel asks the young man if the beat-up naked guy is Homeland Security's informant. They turn to the TV and see the fellow on the news.

"It's Gustav. He became active recently, coming to meetings and nosing around, but he's kind of quiet, not the one I suspected of being a mole." Che Junior speaks in a Johann Strauss Viennese waltz tempo without the usual militant rancor.

"What does he do?" Mel asks.

"Professional loafer, always in need of money. He didn't participate in demonstrations. I don't know much about him except that I heard that he was leeching off his girlfriend, a musician."

"Whoever beat him up must have thought he was an informant," Mel says.

"He wasn't at the meeting when we decided on the spontaneous demonstration and then found extra police stopping us. Someone low level isn't useful to the cops, since they're not in a position to influence policy, which the cops want from their stooges."

"The government could have had more than one informant," Melody says.

"Moles are usually gung-ho and active in order to get to know what's going on. I always thought Raymond was our mole."

Raymond is a vigorous organizer. Melody knows him by sight.

"If Raymond was the snitch," Che Junior says, "why would they need another? They didn't have time to devise a penetration strategy. FAS started organizing against the BSO when it became part of the Rio deal. I can't understand why Cage turned against us."

"He's a politician," Tito says. "Homeland Security is roughing up our people, innocent people. Makes me sick. Throw out the Constitution whenever it doesn't suit you, then preach law and order."

A young radical couple comes through the front door chanting positive four-word slogans for liberty and anarchy. "The BSO won't go!"

Three other people in the store chant with them, fists raised. Mel tries to ignore their simplistic slogans.

When the people calm down and high five each other, the activist turns to Tito. "It shouldn't be complicated to track down the group that did it. There are only a few choices."

"That's just it," Tito says, "the robbery didn't come from the movement. It's got to be Borges and the government, the whole charcoal-suited gang."

"But Borges was the most vociferous about our going,"

Melody says.

"It's the vociferous ones you have to watch. He's the kind of guy who makes money off natural disasters."

"Robbing the truck was a bold action," Melody says. "Borges is a chicken. Look how afraid he is, lashing out against everyone."

"You know what happened in Europe during the 1970s?" Tito says. "The CIA helped the right wing infiltrate the progressive movement. The infiltrators discovered who the legitimate leaders were, and the government killed or arrested them. The moles secretly took over and made the organizations militant, radical, obnoxious. They threw bombs and made it look like the work of leftists in order to discredit them. And it worked—the truth didn't come out until years later. Same thing happened during the Vietnam War when Nixon, Kissinger, and Hoover penetrated the anti-war movement with thugs who became leaders."

"It may be happening today with radical Muslim groups," Che Junior says. "Nothing can make you need a strong man and powerful military more than when you think you're in danger."

On the cab ride back to Symphony Hall, Tito says to Melody, "Everyone knows the composer's name. Most people know the conductor's name. A few people know the concertmaster's name, but until this morning, no one knew Walter's."

"Did the wine free your tongue?" Melody asks.

"Who talked to the robbers? Walter. Why did they call him?"

"Because he's the general manager."

"He made a comment to me that I haven't forgotten. Just as this whole trade thing was dropping on us, he said to me that his biggest accomplishment during the past thirty years was keeping the BSO the center of attention. That's what he said,

'keeping us the center of attention.' He also said, 'It's a dangerous world in Brazil—we've got to be on the offensive against
robbers'."

"He was saying that to reassure us," Melody says,
coming to Walter's defense.

"It's strange that this is happening during Walter's last
season. The BSO couldn't be more at the center of attention.
Reminds me of Bach going blind until ten days before he died,
then he miraculously regained his sight."

Back at Symphony Hall, Lowell and Walter are finishing
questioning a recently hired stagehand. Special Agent Dufay
and his assistant come into Walter's office and wait, their hands
clasped in front of their groins in the undertaker pose. Lowell
watches them, wondering if their emotional involvement is
blurring their judgment.

"That naked guy they found on Newbury Street with a
black eye and bruises was not our informer," Dufay says when
the stagehand leaves.

"If he's not your snitch, whose snitch is he?" Lowell
asks.

Dufay's partner shrugs. "They beat up and humiliated
the wrong man."

"We're homing in on a group called Art Unincorporated," Dufay says. "Their leader is a Dartmouth-educated
agitator in his mid-thirties named Arnold Honegger. He ditched
a career in economics for rabble-rousing. He's been to North
Korea to examine textiles. It took us a while to track him down.
His secretive group doesn't cooperate with FAS."

"How do you know that those who opposed the arts
agreement were responsible for the robbery, bombing, and

bodies?" Lowell says.

The feds let out a deep breath in unison.

"If you can't figure out by now that they were targeting the Rio ceremony, you should find another job."

"We have to be open to all possibilities," Lowell says.

"It's all about the Advancement of the Arts Agreement," Dufay says.

"There's also fourteen point five million worth of instruments on the line. The only clue they gave us was calling Walter directly."

"Anyone can find the name and phone number of the symphony's manager."

"No one in the orchestra could possibly be involved in this crime," Walter repeats. "Perhaps the person who called about the toy guns didn't sound like a brute, but that's a far cry from saying he had inside knowledge."

"Listen to your musicians," Lowell says. "The majority was either dithering about the trip or downright opposed it. Tito and Melody were involved in FAS."

"We're loyal to one another, when push comes to. . .." Walter's voice fizzles out.

"You know each player, no doubt about that, but can you see the forest?"

"We rounded up Honegger and those Art Unincorporated people," Dufay says. "When we interrogate them, they'll lead us right to the instruments. I'm sure of it."

Lowell is skeptical.

"Our guys couldn't find them until we realized they were standing right outside the building with posters," Dufay says.

"I won't allow you to bring them into Symphony Hall," Walter says, pointing his index finger. "I absolutely won't have it."

Dufay motions for Walter to calm down. "We'll throw them in a van and send them to Scollay Square."

"How long have you been in Boston?" Lowell asks.

"What does that matter?"

"Those are liberal people out there. They don't take well to police intimidation."

"It's those who oppose authority who better be careful," Dufay says.

Rodrigo enters. "Another piece of news—your daughter is downstairs at security. They want to know whether to let her in."

Lowell drops into his chair and grimaces.

"Life gives us no choices," he says to the group of men, his arms cradling his head. "We try our best and then get bulldozed by our own children."

Castrato: a voice with the power of a male combined with the pitch of a female. Ever shameful, some composers, like Mozart, refused to write for them, but castratos were superstars. Recordings of castratos were made around 1900.

Lamentoso

As Special Agent Dufay lectures Lowell about the terrorist menace, seventy-five minutes before George's confession, FAS coordinator Tasa Costa addresses the crowd in front of the Horticulture Building next to the Christian Science headquarters. The forceful Spanish woman mounts a wooden crate at the edge of the police barricade and speaks into a megaphone.

"Citizens of Boston, we want the symphony to have its instruments returned immediately."

Her tone is upbeat, eager. She makes an inviting gesture with her free hand, and people cheer.

"This trip was a disastrous mistake. The BSO should have withdrawn as soon as it discovered it was giving legitimacy to this media deal. We should never put profits above people. We oppose this wonderful musical organization being used as a political tool. Don't you?"

Many applaud.

"It's shameful that Boston, a bastion for liberalism and justice, is leading a right-wing alliance whose sole purpose is to put more money in the hands of the already rich. Concertgoers are the cultured and sophisticated voices of the community. We should be setting a positive example, not giving creative and artistic people an even harder life."

More applause.

"You have heard the corporate-owned media say that this deal creates equality. That's absolute nonsense. It removes restrictions so that entertainment conglomerates will create one giant box store that will ruin every small artistic organization."

Almost all cheer, clapping their thick gloves and hollering. Unlike most political activists, Tasa has the wisdom to quit speaking when she is on top.

One person beats a rhythm on an empty plastic five-gallon joint compound container, and the crowd follows his drumming with claps and stomps, sending rhythmic shouts down Mass. Ave. The gathering has evolved into a party, upbeat and hopeful, genial and amusing. A group of young people sing, "I love that dirty water/Boston you're my home," which was about the then filthy Charles River. Then they sang "Sweet Caroline," as they do at Red Sox games at Fenway, a few blocks away.

Melody and Tito arrive at the end of Tasa's speech and squeeze through the crowd to talk to her. She has a round, unadorned face and auburn hair that falls like a helmet around her large forehead and neck, accenting her vivacious personality. Tasa's large eyes look around joyfully.

The carnival music contrasts with Melody's serious thoughts.

"Mel, we're jubilant that this happened," Tasa says, "but the first thing I thought about was your solo."

"Everyone expected me to mess up and be fired," Melody says. Then she asks Tasa about the snitch who was beat up, but Tasa says she hardly knows him.

"Gustav was a loser, not committed to the movement."

"I can't understand how he ties in," Mel says. "He didn't seem to do anything."

"He was kind enough to talk to Guru. Come to think of it, he sided with Raymond at last night's meeting to scrap the protest here. It was the first time Raymond opposed a demonstration."

"That means Raymond didn't know about the heist. What difference would a demonstration make if he knew the instruments would be stolen?"

"All our people are ecstatic," Tasa repeats with the euphoric lyricism of Gounod. "Perhaps we fantasized a heroic act to stop the deal, but no one in our group would have even thought about the baggage truck."

"Walter thinks that if we get our instruments back, he'll be in a position to dictate terms to the trustees—going to Rio but not be involved in the political ceremony," Mel says. "They gave him complete authority. He's announcing it to the press."

"A major victory," Tasa says, giving Melody a hug. "That means the only thing up in the air is your solo."

"It also means that there's no reason for the robbers to keep our instruments."

"*If* the robbers were against the Rio trip," Tito says.

Melody and Tito reenter Symphony Hall. A few minutes later, Dufay leads a team of agents into the group of protesters. Two Boston policemen step in to see what is going on.

Dufay identifies himself. "We're taking a couple away for questioning."

"They haven't done anything wrong," a police sergeant says.

Even though goodwill has grown in the crowd, with the deal becoming a black ogre and the robbery bringing a sense of unity, the police step back.

"You have no right to do this," Raymond, the scruffy young protest leader yells as agents begin arresting people. "Brutality! Fascism!"

A couple of TV cameras rush to capture the scene, pushing their way through the crowd.

The agents ignore Raymond's insults.

"Citizens, don't stand for this. They are illegally abducting people," he yells to the crowd.

After they arrest a half dozen, all taken peacefully, Dufay turns to Raymond. "What's your name?"

"I don't have to give you my name. Ever read the Constitution?"

"Ever seen the inside of solitary confinement?"

"That's the goddamn way you fascists do things, threaten and shoot."

An agent goes to grab Raymond. He flings his arms to resist. Two other agents jump in, wrestling him to the ground and handcuffing him. Raymond hurls insults at them throughout. They bring him through the side door of Symphony Hall, half-carried, half-dragged between two ample men.

Walter stands, shoulders raised in determination, and absolutely denies that one of his musicians smacked a guy in the teeth outside the building. The hitter was, supposedly, not one of his big brass players but a slender sixty-year-old female violinist who never has a hair out of place. Walter knows that they definitely have the wrong person when the police tell him that she was tipsy. Not Wisteria. But, come to think of it, Walter hasn't seen her since the morning.

"You should have seen what she did with one jab," Sergeant Franck tells Walter. "She overheard some guy she never met make a male superiority comment, or at least that's what she called it. The guy didn't press charges, said it was kind of funny, laughed his dignity back inside him, so we're letting her go."

As soon as the police release the jilted Wisteria, she phones Melody. Wisteria's voice is so loud that Melody holds the phone a foot from her ear, which makes her remember how

China took care of her when her life fell apart.

"I threw the sheets out the window. It made me even madder."

"China and I are meeting musicians at Berklee. Join us—it might help."

Melody walks with China the two blocks to the Berklee College of Music, which specializes in rock and jazz.

"Today is my first *intermezzo*," Melody says to China as they make their way through the crowd. "The first day I haven't played cello. Even on vacation I practiced."

As they pass the Mapparium, they meet Wisteria, her handsome face distorted with rage.

"Being a woman is too uncertain," she says. "Men lie and cheat and take advantage of us, and we think it's our fault."

Melody hears an entirely different music around Wisteria. The pleasing tunes of Vivaldi are replaced by the erratic tones of modernist Christian Wolff. She's carrying a bottle in a paper bag.

"I'm ashamed that I was so needy," Wisteria says. "I'll never allow anyone to use me again."

"Play music," China says. "We play brilliantly when we're mad."

"You know what I did? I took all the silver that his mother gave us for a wedding present and put it in a box on the sidewalk."

"Wisteria!" Melody cries. "What a waste. Go and bring it back."

"I don't want to touch it again. Let some bum find it and binge for a week."

"You have to be rational," Melody says.

"I have to be myself first. There's only one person I have to live with for the rest of my life, and that person is me."

Melody listens carefully. Wisteria's dissident music becomes a focused tone, a straight sound that does not waver. The three women continue walking.

"A psychic volunteered her services to locate the instruments," China says. "She wasn't interested in a reward. Walter didn't want to mess with her, but Mayor Bond graciously let her walk around backstage and touch things."

"This is turning into an Offenbach *opera buffa*," Wisteria says.

"She has a better chance of finding the instruments than I do," Mel says.

The three talk with several musicians who are active against the arts agreement. None has any information.

"We can't let ourselves get frustrated," Mel says. "We need a clue to lead us in the right direction."

They return to Symphony Hall, Wisteria clutching her bottle and remaining outside with the crowd.

Melody and China find Tito and Felix in the tuning room, half a flight of stairs off stage right.

"I don't know what else to do," Mel says to her friends.

Eduardo arrives in between lectures. Uncharacteristically, Mrs. Schutz opens Symphony Hall's doors repeatedly to new audiences who listen to lectures from Eduardo or segments of his New World Compositions.

"Did Lowell give you any idea where the investigation is going?" Eduardo asks. She hears the carpet swallow his words.

"He questioned China and me again. He thought I was the conduit for George, since he bought my Lamy bow, as if a timid, middle-aged man could have pulled off this daring robbery. Basically, the police don't know, and I'm not sure what to do next."

"It's a perfect opportunity to talk to the mayor about music education," China says.

The others agree enthusiastically.

"Don't you find it odd," Tito says quietly, "that something like this happens just before Walter is about to retire? Haven't you heard him talking recently about the reason for existence?"

"That's because his life is changing in the fall," Melody says.

"He needs a feeling of accomplishment," Tito says. "It's convenient that this crisis comes along. He could say to himself, 'I'm a great man—look what I did. I saved classical music.' Walter's been keen on dynamic action to involve young people. This would be a good stunt."

Melody shakes her head. "Someone robbed us because they didn't like the trip or because they wanted to get rich."

"We need to read outside the ledger lines, another motive besides political and financial," Felix says.

"What are we blind to?" China says. "The robbery happened in front of a place for the blind. The bodies of naked homeless men demonstrate our social neglect."

"China, you give the impression that you know more than you're telling," Melody says, "which is unusual, because you don't have a problem announcing everything on your mind like I do."

"All I know is that Lowell hasn't much to go on, and yet it feels like it's right in front of us."

"That means you agree with Lowell that it's one of us," Melody says. "You can't just be thinking motive. You also need the ability to pull this off, and who has that?"

"Loving God," Lowell sighs when Rodrigo tells him that his daughter Amy is in the building. "I'm already getting grief from all sides. If I let her in, she'll launch into a diatribe about keeping my word. If I don't let her in, I'll never hear the end of it."

"Their generation doesn't think like we do," Rodrigo says. "My son doesn't want to speak Spanish or have anything to do with Mexico. He says we shouldn't be proud to be Mexican when the best thing Mexicans do is work as laborers."

"Be proud to be a laborer."

Lowell calls the guard downstairs and tells him to let Amy in. When she opens the office door, Lowell braces his shoulders and prepares his list of apologies. She stands in the doorway. He grabs papers from Walter's desk to show how busy he is and doesn't look at the expression on her face.

Rodrigo, who had talked to her on the phone several times but has never seen her, realizes that parents don't know their children. Instead of Lowell's account of her desperately seeking a guy, Rodrigo sees a woman who guys hit on constantly. She has a clear, light complexion, deep brown eyes, and long black hair that moves the air as she walks—the type of hair that men look at from behind, then hurry ahead to see the face that goes with it.

She remains in the doorway looking across at Lowell, wearing the flamboyant multi-colored blouse of a circus performer. He puts his hand on his stomach. She walks to the desk in front of her father. Lowell looks up, noticing that she is wearing mascara and a large dab of rouge.

Walter enters his office and sees her standing in the middle of the room while Lowell gazes up at her from behind the desk, as if both are on the verge of a Verdi father/daughter duet.

Walter comes to a dead stop and clears his throat. "I have to oversee the people coming into the hall to hear another of Eduardo's lectures."

He makes an awkward but prompt exit, even though it is his office.

Amy puts her arms on the desk and leans forward to address her father. "I think I can help you."

As Mrs. Schutz gets ready to bring in another audience, Melody finds Walter sitting at a table at the other end of the Hatch Lounge. Policemen are picking up the final fragments from the bomb and taking the last pictures. It has been over four hours since the explosion and over eight hours since the heist.

Walter has given over his office to Lowell and is twirling his fingers on a small circular table in the lounge. He seems in a reverie, gazing at the marble bust of Major Henry Higginson, the BSO's founder and financier. After the Civil War, the major spent his money and energy assembling an orchestra that would rival Europe, bringing European conductors and principals to Boston for the first seasons.

Melody senses Walter's melancholy and guesses he is sad to leave his beloved orchestra. Could Tito be right in suspecting him?

"Higginson was a common man who believed music belongs to every person," Walter says to her as she approaches. "He didn't want money or class to hinder art."

"Just as FAS believes," Melody says. "Art shouldn't be subservient to economics."

He gestures for Melody to sit. "Are we only curators of old music? Do we no longer create?"

"I've never asked you, Walter, what did you do before you became manager?"

"I did piano gigs. You have to be exceptional these days to be able to make a living, but I managed. I played rehearsals for opera and ballet, sight reading stuff." He sits forward, still reflective. "But to get married, I needed a job, so I got an MBA, and a couple of years later, I came here."

"You'll be hard to replace."

"Bless you, Melody. You and China are the brightest spots in my career, but everyone's disposable. You have an expiration date stamped on you, then you're thrown away."

"Not you! I hope you enjoyed being around music

during the past thirty years."

"I had to keep thinking about next season's schedule, players who were sick, missing sheet music, deadlines, guest conductors, and soloists with special peculiarities. Instead of listening for meaning, I had to make sure the orchestra didn't rehearse into overtime. Sometimes during open rehearsals, when the hall was full, I had to go up to the conductor in the middle of a piece and tell him to stop. My wife is going to ban me from wearing a watch."

"It must be hard to love music and keep it at arm's length."

"Many artists have a hard time in the real world. Like Shubert." Walter leans his chin on his hand. "There's urgency to Schubert—he's calling out to be understood, loved. There's no triviality in his music, yet he died a syphilis-ridden failure. His greatest works lay in a closet for thirty years until Mendelssohn blew the dust off them. Mendelssohn also revived Bach, who had been forgotten until Mendelssohn conducted the *St. Matthew Passion* in 1829."

"What good is finding his work if you're too busy to listen?"

"Just now, I've been thinking about writing articles and talking to schools. I want to take classical music to construction sites. We've disenfranchised two generations by giving them trash and calling it music." His voice becomes *allegro presto*. "Let young people have as much synthesizer noise as they want, but if we deprive them of real music, we're cheating them. We've convinced them that plastic jewelry is more valuable than gems."

"People in the orchestra have been talking about making music relevant," Melody says. "It's unacceptable in a city as diverse as this that the audience is all white."

"Eduardo and his New World Compositions group are fomenting a musical reawakening," Walter replies. "The BSO does outreach into Roxbury and East Boston, but we don't have the budget, and the players don't have the time. Seventy percent of classical companies are in the red. Everyone is vulnerable. The government should allocate five billion a year for art education. I think about how baseball teams give tickets to kids, T-shirts, baseball cards. An investment. When the kids grow up, they go to games themselves, and baseball games are more expensive than classical concerts."

"People think classical concerts are boring," Mel says.

"They are boring if all you know is boom, boom, boom." Walter sits on the edge of his chair, eager to express himself. "You have to get involved before life becomes interesting. Music wasn't written for people to listen to while shopping. Two whole generations have heard had only canned music. They think iTunes is music, that slick, sterile recording studio sound where overtones are enhanced electronically to x-bass, Maria Callas in surround sound."

Melody recalls Tito's accusation against Walter. "So you're ready to retire at the end of the season, and this robbery comes along."

Walter ignores her comment, changing his tone to a *lento* minor. "Only a few cities have a classical radio station—most of those play snippets of popular works and call it music for relaxation, like taking Valium."

"Walter, you need another challenge."

Walter continues as if he didn't hear. "The young fellow who's taking over has a musicology degree from Yale and an MBA from the Sloan School, full of new ideas."

"You think new ideas will draw people to classical music?"

"An attractive, skillful girl like you who makes music meaningful to people today will." he adds as quietly as a pastoral, "I want to make sure you're not let go."

Walter looks around the empty room at the bare tables and bars. The police finish collecting evidence. "I'll miss taking care of the folks. They've been family. Some I've known from the beginning, but I'll be free to experience music and be away from the business end of it."

"Is it possible to separate business from music?"

"I'm looking forward to having Glück and Glinka and all the rest speak again. Glück contributed more to opera than Mozart, and Glinka fathered Russian music—both have been overshadowed." He turns to Melody. "Eduardo may become one that later generations talk about. There was a time when people listened to living composers. Now very few we play are alive."

Mrs. Schutz enters and stands behind them.

"Every night, Eduardo's father and mother would dance together," Melody says. "I've seen it, his father's left fingers holding an unlit cigarette and his right hand around a glass of wine."

"Probably not wine," Walter says. "Probably amber whiskey in a tumbler, ice cubes rattling."

"Walter knows that time," Mrs. Schutz says. "There was a lot more dancing and a lot more drinking."

"And a lot more real music," Walter says.

"I'm bringing in a new audience," Mrs. Schutz says.

"Mrs. Schutz has chided me for thinking we should have left them in the street. Right now I have a crime to solve."

And then, as if on cue, a commotion emerges from the hallway, shouting and pounding. Walter rises, cheeks flushed as he charges ahead to the scene.

Sitting in Walter's upstairs office, unaware of the commotion below, Lowell takes a moment of silence to catch the words coming from his daughter's mouth. She had arrived at Symphony Hall at 3:55 p.m., ten minutes before the unruly protester Raymond was dragged in.

"I've been hearing the news," Amy says. "I thought you need someone to introduce you to FAS and take care of things while you work."

Lowell still doesn't register.

"We can start with a decent lunch. Soup."

"That would be nice. Rodrigo has been doing a poor job taking care of us."

Rodrigo looks away politely.

"Look at all this stuff." She points to the fast food containers. "I bet you've been eating cream donuts as well."

"Haven't touched them."

Rodrigo vouches for him with a sly smirk.

"Look how disheveled the office is. I'll go out and get soups and salads."

"That'll be great," Lowell says, though what he wants is a fat sandwich that oozes as you chomp it. And chunky French fries, Lowell's best food in winter, but not salty, since salt dehydrates the intestine. She lectures him whenever she catches him in his favorite eating mode—leaning over the kitchen sink devouring a thick, crumbling sandwich, then licking the overflow off his fingers.

"Dressing," he starts to say but knows not to finish the sentence. He will get olive oil and balsamic vinegar.

"You know these FAS people?" Lowell asks.

"Everyone knows them. They've been having meetings and demonstrations to support the arts. The guy I'm seeing is on one of their committees."

Lowell's wife had told him that their daughter had met a man at a contra dance, but Lowell wasn't aware that the venture has been successful.

"Would you like to talk to him?" she asks. "We can meet, and you can ask him questions."

"Perhaps with you present he'll be more open than those we've interviewed so far," Rodrigo says.

When Walter locates the source of the commotion, he is beside himself. Two men are dragging Raymond into one of the three green rooms. Walter storms in behind them.

"I told you specifically. I made it unquestionable. You're violating every right!"

"This is an emergency," Dufay says. "There's nothing to be upset about."

"I will not tolerate this," Walter says. "I have to think of our reputation. You're degrading this noble institution."

"We'll deal with him quickly."

"Get screwed!" the young man screams as the agents force him into a chair. "The people will unite and end this fascism."

"Shut up!" Dufay shouts.

"I allowed you to use this space for the investigation," Walter says, "not for persecutions."

Ignoring Walter, Dufay hits the table in front of him and yells at Raymond to shut the hell up. Silence. Another agent closes the door.

Dufay's tone is suddenly gentle. "What have you found out?"

"Honestly, boss, there's nothing out there. These guys don't know what happened."

Walter relaxes when he realizes that the belligerent protester is an informant.

"Who have you been in touch with?"

"I called everyone this morning to come down and demonstrate. Then I hit them up for information. They were all blown away by the robbery, every single one. No one knows nothing about bodies."

"No idea where the instruments might be?"

"Nothing, not from anyone. When they discovered that

the BSO was leaving the next morning at seven, they lost interest in having a demonstration."

"Why was that guy stripped, beat up, and left on Newbury Street?"

"They knew that someone was providing information. I guess they blamed that poor sucker. He wasn't anybody in the organization. That retarded guy, the conductor's brother, talked to him. A girl I hadn't seen for a while, Tiffany Rodgers, had a private conversation with Tasa."

"We'll check her out."

"Two things are guaranteed to happen at a leftist gathering—it will start late, and the microphone won't work."

"Good job," Dufay says.

"I got the steering committee to argue with each other at last night's meeting," Raymond says. "It's easy to get lefties bickering."

"Anyone suspect you?"

"Not at all. I'm the most devoted person there."

"You do it better than anyone else."

"If you ask me," Walter says, "his speech is thirty years out of date."

Dufay remains oblivious to Walter's observation. "We'll get you back out there. If you find anything, break cover."

Walter looks at his watch. "We have six and a half hours."

Someone opens the door.

"Get this jackass out of here!" Dufay yells.

"Get screwed, fascist!" the *agent provocateur* shouts back.

Two men grab Raymond as he continues hurling insults out both sides of his mouth. They bring him to the outside stage door, take off the handcuffs, and throw him into the street. He howls back at them, and then rejoins the demonstrators, who hail him as a hero for standing up to the authorities.

The final embers of a pale ocher sun are extinguished at 4:40 p.m. Its distant warmth, which had distracted the city from its chill, fades with it. The earth is closest to the sun in winter. If anyone could see through the tall buildings, they would find the planet Mercury, god of music, hovering above the horizon in the sun's fading glow.

The first impression Lowell has of Quadrille, the president of Brighton Hauling, is that he can't lift anything heavier than a Kleenex box. He is a short, emaciated bloke with a pasty Irish face, someone who can shop for his clothes in the boys' wear section.

Quadrille bounds into the loading door holding a manila file of documents. Walter steps forward and greets him, and the two look like an exaggerated version of Laurel and Hardy. Walter shows him into a small basement workroom near the chorus practice room and pulls up a chair with prolonged courtesy.

"Didn't you know this was a bigtime security trip?" Lowell asks without any warmup.

"We weren't given any indication to do things differently."

"But you knew this was unusual," Lowell says, hammering the point.

Quadrille puts up his guard. "You should have warned us instead of subjecting our people to danger."

"Did you or didn't you know it was a controversial trip?"

"The cops knew better than anyone. It's you guys who should have protected us."

Walter puts up his hands to ease the tension. "It's a failure on all our parts."

Lowell wonders whether Homeland Security's tactics

are getting to him. He shakes his head briskly and changes his tone. "I'm sorry I was severe, but no one seems to be taking responsibility. I'm frustrated by the lack of information." He sits in an empty chair, cradling his hands behind his head. "Do you listen to classical music, Mr. Quadrille?"

"As well as being one of our patrons, Mr. Quadrille has a season subscription," Walter says.

"You come regularly to the symphony?"

Quadrille throws off his confrontational stance. "Seats K14, 15."

"Did the symphony ask you for a donation?"

"I don't know why you're asking that," Quadrille says. "You should thank people who support the arts."

"Without doubt we do," Walter says, trying to smooth rough edges.

"I could have put the money in my pocket or hired another guy," Quadrille says, "but if we don't support Walter and his people, no one else will, and we'll have nothing to hand down to our children except money."

Lowell turns to Walter. "Why do you always have to ask for donations? The musicians say you get a pretty full house most of the time."

"Ticket prices don't cover half of what it costs to run the orchestra," Walter says. "The city of Berlin gives a hundred million dollars a year for their opera companies, but here we're not much different than the homeless guys outside 7-Eleven begging for change."

"Rock bands don't beg," Lowell says.

"That's the difference between art and pop. Popular music comes and goes. Art endures. We make forty million a year and spend eighty."

"How much do tickets cost?"

"You can line up for rush seats for nine bucks cash, sold before the performance, a Boston tradition of frugality. Or you can pay several hundred for galas, another Boston tradition."

Lowell turns back to Quadrille. "You're insured, I take it?"

"Fully insured." He opens the folder on his lap and starts turning pages. "We've had to report damage a couple of times, but we've never been part of a robbery."

"In these past months, has anyone asked about your role in this trip?"

"No one needs to ask. People know that we move the symphony, and if they don't, it's on the home page of our website."

At 5:20 p.m., Lowell enters the BSO administrative office where George, still in his camel hair coat, sits next to a cop who looks as if he's just out of high school. Lowell assesses George's expression, which has turned more somber, his arrogance extinguished.

George acknowledges Lowell's entrance with a distant nod. The young cop stands, puts his hand on his cheek as if it is an automatic gesture to cover his acne, and Lowell sits in his place.

"Doesn't look like you've been engaged in stimulating conversation," Lowell says.

George remains silent, his eyes vacant but no hint of anger brushing his mouth.

"George, I am leading an investigation of the BSO robbery, bombing, and related bodies. I am not accusing anyone. Do you understand?"

George sits silently. He looks away and nods.

"Can you please help me?"

"You're holding me illegally, no charges, no phone calls, no lawyer."

"You want a lawyer?"

George doesn't answer.

Lowell adopts a kinder tone. "Please tell me why you stand across from the stage door looking down St. Stephen Street."

Silence. Then he opens his mouth. "I stand there from time to time, but I don't know the first thing about the robbery."

"Were you shocked by it?"

"Of course."

"Then you would want to help me."

"If I knew one little thing, the slightest little thing that might be useful in the slightest possible way, I would tell you immediately. But I don't have the faintest idea."

"People often have information that they don't think could help, but information is linked to other information."

"I had nothing to do with the robbery, the bomb, or the dead people."

"I believe you. Why were you there this morning?"

George's jaw tightens, and he looks directly at his interrogator. "I passed by and stayed a couple of minutes, but I left well before the robbery."

"How did you know when the buses would be leaving Symphony Hall?"

George looks around, beginning to look cornered. "I don't remember how I found out."

"Did Melody tell you?"

George's cheek muscles spasm for a second before he composes himself. "Please leave her out of this."

"And you gave her a six thousand-dollar bow?"

"If you don't devote your life to playing an instrument, then it's your responsibility to support those who do."

"Did she tell you about the Brazil trip?"

"I haven't talked to her in a long time."

Lowell becomes sympathetic. "You came to see her, didn't you?"

George looks around nervously.

"You're in love with her."

George lets go, and tears fall down the sides of his nose. He wipes them with the back of his hand and then jerks his head to compose himself. Lowell looks up at the young cop standing uncomfortably.

"She's younger than my youngest daughter. I tried to stop this thing, but I can't. I have to see her." He wipes more tears. "I have to see her, that's all. She's soft and bright and . . . she has no idea that I think about her day and night. Some time ago, I saw her in front of Symphony Hall, and I collected my courage and asked her to join me for lunch, thinking that if I talked to her it would cure my obsession, but it only strengthened it. If my wife found out, if the people at work found out . . . they'd call me a pedophile."

"George, she's an adult. There's nothing to be ashamed of."

"Can you imagine if my daughters found out that I'm obsessed with someone younger than they are? They'd never speak to me again. I'd be ruined. I saw her a couple of times at receptions, and it was hard to keep my head straight. Sometimes, when I'm sitting in the audience, I think I might lose control, shout out to her or embarrass myself. I knew that I shouldn't get close to her again."

"She's not like a lot of pretty women who squash you when you're vulnerable."

Lowell sympathizes. He realizes that any man, including himself, could fall in love with Melody and not be able to stand upright again. Men do stupid things, but they imagine stupider.

George puts his head in his hands and sobs. "Me, a pathetic old man who satisfies himself looking at a girl and can't face reality. I never told anyone. I feared ending up like Bruckner, who tried to marry seventeen-year-old girls when he was sixty, then chased a fourteen-year-old when he was eighty. It's extraordinary that a guy who had such a painful, messed-up life, a country bumpkin bouncing around Vienna, could produce such powerful music."

"I'm sorry to put you through this. When you were standing on the corner, did you see anyone suspicious?"

"Never. I know when she comes, and I go there at that time. When Bruckner met Wagner, he fell to his knees in front of the master."

"Was anyone else there this morning?"

"Protesters, police. The musicians trickled in after 6:30. When Melody arrived at 6:45, she went to the loading area, and I left."

"The spotter must have known to arrive after 6:45.," Lowell muses out loud. He turns to George. "Have you ever sought help for this infatuation?"

"Perhaps it would be a good idea."

"It would also be a good idea if you didn't hang around here for a while."

George nods and puts his head back in his hands.

"You're free to go."

George looks up. "You won't tell anyone, will you?"

"You have my word. Melody said you were a nice man."

"She did?"

"She defended you in front of everybody."

George's eyes widen. Both men stand.

"I shouldn't thank you for what you put me through," George says. "I came to some realizations sitting here alone. A person doesn't sit silently anymore."

"I'm learning a lot, too, and it hasn't been about intestinal microflora."

Lowell extends his hand, which George shakes, head lowered.

"I researched her," George says. "She was hard to track because she changed her name and buried her past, but I discovered the tragedy in her life, which was compounded by her natural desire to blame someone for the misfortune. I believe that she wants to apologize and praise her father in front of the world. It must have taken a lot of courage for her to arrive at that point."

Lowell walks out of the room, ready to regroup.

Leitmotif: *A short melodic theme tagged to a character or event that is replayed whenever the character appears or the event occurs. Although not invented by Wagner, he was its master.*

Crescendo

Ninety-five minutes before Melody's arrest, Eduardo steps up to the podium again.

Time after time, he stands before halls full of fresh faces, some of the tens of thousands of people who attend BSO concerts regularly as well as people who have never been inside Symphony Hall before. For his 5:30 p.m. lecture, Eduardo talks about themes in music.

"How did compositions get names like 'Moonlight,' 'Pastoral,' or 'Passionate?' Instruments do not talk. How could you determine what the composer had in mind when he wrote the piece if it doesn't have words? Don't different listeners arrive at different interpretations? How can you possibly tell that music is about a lark, mountains, or the sea?

"This is not as big an uncertainty as it seems. We know how film music affects us—it tells us when to be optimistic, when to be afraid, who's the good guy, and who's the bad guy. When we see a large view of mountains, the music is expansive, while late at night in a dingy hotel room, the music is closed. We don't need announcers to tell us when danger lurks or two people are falling in love. Close your eyes, and the music guides you, right? People credit Korngold as the muse of movie music, but my vote goes to Massenet.

"Music is a language. People call it a universal language, but I don't think that's true. If we listen to traditional Chinese or Armenian musicians, we might not understand if their music is sad or happy. We don't understand their musical language.

"We even get tripped up on our own music. I remember a Zydeco band having the audience stomping their feet and prancing around the room to their happy sounds. Then I listened to the lyrics, the most dire, heart-wrenching stories about losing love and failing as a person to the point of contemplating suicide. How can such happy music incorporate such despair?

"We get messed up because our feelings are conflicted. A turbulent relationship may be what we want—it's certainly what we like to read about. We don't watch films about smiling vegetarians but about adversity and suffering. My grandmother, a devout Catholic, told people with pride and satisfaction how much she had suffered. Perhaps it's accented more in rural Brazil than here, but people find suffering and sacrifice alluring. The most beautiful music is sad, laments and requiems, because its sadness cures our own. Sorrow is a deep part of human experience."

Seventy-five minutes before her arrest, Melody meets the organizer of Art Unincorporated inside Whole Foods, located next to her apartment. She looks around for her cat but can't see him, probably scared off by the crowd noise. He has an uncanny sense of danger. The noise subsides as the store doors close behind her, replaced by soft rock music.

She understands right away that the organizer is a rational, intelligent man, not the radical militant that both FAS and Homeland Security described.

What is a militant anyway? Melody wonders. *Does it have something to do with military?*

Arnold Honegger, whom Homeland Security had

picked up from his Cambridge apartment, interrogated, and threw out onto the street, is a concerned, professorial type, no different from the musicians, a fellow who reads the *Boston Review* in rustic cafes and thumbs through used tomes at the antiquarian bookstore in Harvard Square.

"The feds accused me of robbing the BSO, bombing the hall, and dumping dead bodies," Honegger tells Melody as they walk through the pricy vegetable aisle. She recognizes a fluid *portamento* in his mid-range voice.

"They were really hostile, threatening to throw me into a prison where no one would know where I was. They called Art Unincorporated a violent group, when what we do is provide updates on laws and regulations affecting artists. You would think they would know by now that to get information, you have to treat people civilly."

"It's tempting for those in authority to use their power to get what they want," Melody says. "Especially if they're under pressure. You have to report them. Abusers thrive on disinterest, whether they're dictators or neighborhood bullies."

"If it means anything to you, my wife and I are BSO series subscribers."

"Thank you. It tells me that you want the best for the orchestra."

"The cops think that since we benefited from all the publicity about the heist, we instigated it."

They walk from the vitamin aisle to the triple crème cheeses.

"They've been checking us out all month," Honegger says. "I knew our meetings were observed, our names taken, our activities followed. That didn't bother me. It does bother me when the police try to take over a movement like they did with FAS. That's why we couldn't be in their coalition. They were compromised."

"I don't think the Boston Police had anything to do with that."

"My mistake, lumping all police together. That's like lumping all progressives together. I heard their mole was signaling the police whom to arrest outside Symphony Hall by shouting code words disguised as insults. The penetration we have to guard against comes from those who splinter the group, changing it to a detestable movement of malcontents. That was happening to FAS."

"If every group was being watched, the group that pulled this off would have needed to work in isolation."

"Homeland Security knew all about us. They should have told Lowell we couldn't have been involved. And who could have predicted that it would bring so much publicity? It's favorable publicity now, but if this drags out, or if the instruments are harmed, it could have repercussions."

They stop at the focaccia rack.

"The government had all the information on the baggage truck," Honegger says. "They had the logistics to pull this off—and the motive. In our group I doubt that you'd find one of our guys who knows how to drive that truck, let alone use guns."

"A woman truck driver," Melody says. "It's hard to believe anyone in government would risk this crime."

"You can't be a peaceful activist anymore. If fifty thousand people march down Tremont Street on Saturday, they get one inch on page fourteen in the *Globe*. If a half-dozen punks tussle with the cops, it makes page one. The media is slanted toward the violent few, so violence has become a tactic."

"Perhaps that explains the bodies."

"Borges has big stakes in this deal," Honegger says. "Literally, big 'steaks,' since he's been investing in Brazilian cattle futures. The vice president will turn a blind eye as a large swath of rain forest is turned into grazing land. They will be able to export more beef to the US. What do you think this deal is, a magnanimous and altruistic effort on the part of big business to benefit humanity?"

Melody thanks him and turns to leave.

"Who's your favorite composer?" Honegger asks.

"That's an oft-asked question, but why rate creativity? It's better just to appreciate."

China phones right after, telling her that she found out from the police that Gustav, the fellow who was stripped, beaten up, and left on Newbury Street, has a criminal record.

"Guess what for? Stealing cars."

"That must be the first solid clue. But what does it mean?"

"I don't know. They can't get a word out of his mouth."

At the same time in Symphony Hall, Eduardo is speaking passionately to his audience, "Music is ingrained in our lives. Just as we have an innate ability for language, so, too, is music innate. That does not mean that Smetana or Musorgski's music is natural any more than Portuguese or Swahili is innate, but language itself is. The five-note pentatonic scale, the seven-note diatonic scale, and the twelve-note chromatic scale are inventions, but music is part of being human. Every society has language, and every society makes music. Every society dances to music.

"American music, amalgamated from Europe and Africa and Native Americans, has conventions you and I understand, and it's influencing the world. Now there's Cambodian hip hop and Moroccan gangster rap. During the past few decades, our music has been influenced by Latin America. The influence is creeping in so subtly that we don't realize it, but the New World Compositions seeks to explore it.

"Composers follow trends. That's why when you listen to an unknown piece, you can usually date it—Baroque, Impressionism, 1960s oldies.

"We are bombarded constantly by sound. How often would the average person in the nineteenth century have heard music? Before recordings, people would sit around and sing and play. The Viennese could hear an orchestra or string quartet regularly. But most people were farmers, and it would be a rare and cherished event when they would be able to hear the latest tune, played by local amateurs, but they would listen more closely than we do.

"So, where do we get the idea that a composition is about the sea or God's kingdom if it doesn't have words? I'll leave that for us to reflect on. Last summer, when I was walking past the reflecting pool at the Christian Science Church, I realized that it's called that because it reflects our image as we stand above it. So when we reflect, we're looking at ourselves. Art allows us to see ourselves."

At the end of the talk, a tall trumpeter stands inside the lounge door downstairs and addresses the musicians with arms raised like an announcing angel.

"Have you heard the latest?" he declares *fortissimo*. "Maestro Borges was abducted by the radicals."

Melody hails a taxi from Whole Foods, forty-nine minutes before her arrest. A young man greets her at the Democracy Center.

"You're here to see our beloved super spy," he says. "He's fired up about an international conspiracy, and we're going along to calm him down. He's been dying to see you."

"Is he all right? How's he doing?"

"He's great. He wants to be the hero who saves the world. We took him to an apartment nearby. His mind turned it into a safe house for a movement that would overthrow the government or some such thing. Everyone likes him because he's genuine. I'll take you."

"I don't know how to thank you. I'll take care of him now. But I think that even though he had delusions, he may have been passing information."

The young man draws the wheezy breath of a smoker who quit years earlier. "Wow, you think under all that fluff and hype he knows something?"

"I think he may have been used."

"I'm sorry about your instruments. The BSO shouldn't be involved. Someone took a rope from a package and put it around his hands, as if to tie him up, and he liked that. It makes him feel important."

Guru's large eyes greet her with excitement. His hands are tied loosely behind his back. Three other people are sitting around a student-like den drinking sodas, eating burritos, and watching news of the heist on TV.

One of the fellows says to Guru, "I'll free you if you promise not to divulge secrets about us. You know how dangerous it could be."

As soon as he slips off the rope, Guru puts his index finger to his mouth to signify secrecy. Before Melody can ask him where he's been, he begins speaking rapidly.

"People from around the world came to Boston and pulled this off. The CIA and the Secret Service had it all planned out."

She puts up her hands to stop him. "Tell me everything, slowly and clearly."

"The FBI is involved, the CIA, Interpol—"

"Don't tell her too much," one of the fellows shouts jokingly.

"Start *da capo*," Melody says. "Who have you been talking to? Did you see anyone from the orchestra?"

"They confessed. The police don't know how big the network is, but Guru knows everything."

She stops him again and asks him to sit. "Have you seen your brother?"

He seems confused momentarily. His tone slows and drops a pitch. "They don't like him too much."

"When you told me his secret this morning—about making money—did he tell you why it's a secret?"

Guru looks away. "It takes money to build a school where I can teach soldiers and policemen, twice as much as he has. He's starting a secret organization for musicians. He works with Homeland Security. The bad people want to destroy liberty. He's bringing freedom to Brazil. Rossini said, 'Give me a laundry list, and I'll set it to music'."

"Were you giving him information?"

Guru shakes his head. "Gustav collected information."

"Gustav?"

"He's Secret Service. They found him on Newbury Street without any clothes. Isn't that funny?"

Melody takes a moment to think. If the mole knew about the heist, why didn't Homeland Security know?

"I told Malden Police Sergeant Alan Ostinato everything," Guru says. "If there's no art agreement, there won't be an orchestra."

"Do you know who Gustav was informing?"

"Secret Service. He was special ops."

"The police can't get a word out of him. Is your secret only with me?"

Guru nods.

"Good. Keep it that way. I know you're brave and don't care for your personal safety, but our secret can get dangerous for others. Right? You don't want to put innocent people in danger, do you? Now, we have to share our secret with one person you can trust. Is that all right?"

Guru nods.

"Good. No one else but us three. I'll make a phone call and arrange for you to debrief him. We'll talk with no one else, all right? You trust me, don't you?"

He nods again.

"I trust you, too. I'll find out more about this money so we can get you to train intelligence agents."

Presidential Liaison for the Arts Cage walks in the front door of Symphony Hall as Mayor Bond stands on the marble steps begging the press not to follow unfounded rumors. The mayor says he and the police have the situation under control. Cage enters somberly, standing behind the reporters near the ramp to the box office. When he understands that the reporters are asking Bond questions about Borges' abduction, Cage perks up.

"We have no direct word of any kidnapping," Bond says.

"Can you at least confirm that the conductor is not in the building?" a TV reporter asks.

"Let's not jump to extraneous conclusions," the mayor says. "As soon as we get confirmed information, I promise that you will be the first to know, but we have no new facts."

"Can you categorically deny that the conductor has been kidnapped?" the reporter asks.

"I can't deny that the Yankees will apologize to the Red Sox. I kind of doubt they will, but I don't spend time in denial."

A couple of reporters chuckle at Bond's inept analogy. They ask more questions until they understand that the mayor truly doesn't know anything. When the reporters disperse, Cage approaches Bond.

The mayor is surprised at himself for being genuinely happy to see the arts liaison. As they walk back through the doors, Cage tries to milk the mayor for information on the abduction, but he is as disappointed as the reporters.

"If this wasn't about serious music," Bond says, "It would be a fun day."

"The people out there seem to be having fun. It's dark,

and they're still out there."

Cage and Bond hustle up one of the backstage staircases to see Lowell.

"Let me guess," Lowell says the minute they enter. "You want to know how it's going."

Although Bond, Cage, and Walter wear dark suits, they dress differently. Bond's suit is well cut and stylish, Cage's is a staid government executive uniform, while Walter's is formally traditional. When Lowell has to give talks or attend official functions, he, too, wears a suit, but he doesn't eat with a tie, since he is convinced that a tie constricts the carotid artery. The body cannot afford constrictions after a meal, since thirty percent of the blood the heart pumps goes into the digestive process.

"What's this about Borges being abducted?" Cage asks.

"Sometimes you're right in front of the crapper door," Lowell says. "Sometimes there are three constipated guys in front of you. We got a call saying that he's gone to the other side and denounced American imperialism. I thought it was another crank, but we can't find him. New American Wave posted his picture on their website."

"What did they say they wanted?" Cage asks.

"They didn't say anything," Walter says. "I took the call. They hung up after that sentence."

"Wasn't Borges here with everyone else?"

Lowell notices Cage's cool attitude has vanished. He seems as flustered by Borges' abduction as by the second body, while the heist didn't disturb him.

"He disappeared when he discovered I was looking for his brother. His brother has been talking about a prank," Lowell says. "He was at the loading area and the bomb room this morning."

"Maestro Borges was the reason the BSO became involved," Cage says.

Lowell looks up. "Maestro Borges?"

"He proposed the ceremony concert."

"I heard it the other way around. Why was he so keen on the deal?"

"He found the way to merge money with music." Cage's tone is sarcastic.

"I'm not prepared to accept that he's been kidnapped," Lowell says. "Still less that he's deserted."

Special Agent Dufay comes into the office and greets Cage with a formal handshake, his face devoid of expression. "We're tracing the source for their latest stunt, which the media is broadcasting as fact. Borges was going from one militant group to another, and crazed." Dufay hands around a photo printed off the web. "The photo seems genuine—he looks pretty bad—and we had an independent report that he was in a building of lofts used by radical artists. When we raided the place, all we found was abstract etchings."

"The radicals are all out front of this building," Cage says.

"Either he's been abducted, or he's taken off with fourteen point five million dollars of instruments," Lowell says.

"Why would the maestro, who believes in this deal and organized the concert, abandon ship?" Walter asks.

"Maybe the instruments are worth more than he's getting off the ceremony."

Dufay steps forward. "FAS wants to make sure we never get the orchestra to Rio."

"They'd never risk kidnapping," Lowell says. "They're rational people, ladies and gentlemen who leave the truck in front of a police station, ignite firecrackers, and play with dead bodies. Kidnapping falls into a completely different category. They would know the consequences."

"Then where should we begin looking for him?" Walter asks.

"I think we should sit tight and work on the robbery. That's the central act. If he doesn't turn up, the kidnappers will give us information about him, or he'll send us a postcard of bare-breasted babes on a beach with violins under their chins."

"You'll have a better chance if you investigate the New Hampshire body and the bomb," Cage says again.

"We've rounded up a bunch more anti-agreement radicals, and we're busting butt," Dufay says. "The faster we act and the mightier our force, the better chance we have."

"Why haven't any of them yielded information?" Lowell asks.

"You have to warm them up."

Lowell holds his stomach. "My gastric juices are telling me that things have gone haywire."

Melody texts Felix, asking him to meet her and Guru at her apartment. Just then, she receives an incomprehensible text from Wisteria about the patron saint of music. She phones Tito.

"I know where she must be," Tito says.

He and China rush to St. Cecilia Church—named after that patron—around the corner from the Berklee College of Music. They find Wisteria sitting on the steps under a streetlight in the early evening darkness.

"I heard Borges got abducted by space aliens," she says, slurring her words.

"Artists," China corrects.

Wisteria laughs. "What's the difference?"

China looks at the bagged bottle at her feet and sees that Wisteria, an elegant lady who sipped a glass of fine wine with dinner, had downed most of a bottle of gin straight.

"Another of Borges' money-making stunts," Tito says cynically.

"We don't need Borges or any macho man conductor,"

Wisteria says. "Damn their hierarchy. We don't need some autocrat like Toscanini screwing women and then lecturing his orchestra."

Tito tries to humor and distract her. "Borges is positioning himself to be the next Toscanini or von Karajan, the world's great musical director."

Wisteria takes another swig and laughs. "Conductors love to attack Beethoven and Wagner with an authoritative baton even though those two guys flipped their finger at authority."

China and Tito pick Wisteria up by both arms and walk her the three long blocks to Melody's apartment. Melody and Felix are in the kitchen. Guru sits on the floor throwing little balls at Raja, which he returns like a dog.

Mel is shocked to see Wisteria, who usually moves as graciously as a Bellini aria, so reduced.

"I was just thinking," Mel says to the others, "perhaps one of us gave the hijackers information without realizing it."

"Who else would not want the orchestra to go except those who opposed the arts agreement?" Felix asks.

"Borges is a classical music evangelist," Melody says. "He's overly concerned about money, just like an evangelist."

"He should fast for forty days or smoke a performance-enhancing drug," Wisteria says.

"Dream on," Felix says.

Melody hears an E major scale, the key of heaven.

"Dreams have been wiped out by our industrialized world. It's rationality or faith," Tito replies in a crisp tempo. "Our wars are between reason and religion."

"On which side would you put music?" China asks.

"Music is reason, mathematics, even if it's religious music," Tito answers emphatically. "You don't play or compose by inspiration. You study, experiment, practice."

"The audience still prefers myth," China says, "like that nonsense of Bizet dying of a broken heart over *Carmen* or *The*

Rite of Spring causing a riot."

"Get a grip," Melody says. "We have only a few hours to find our instruments." She whispers to herself, "A few hours before I kiss my one-year career goodbye."

They assign themselves tasks. Tito will continue contacting every anti-agreement activist he knows. Felix will stay with Guru. China will remain in touch with the police. Each will text the other. Wisteria, hardly able to stand straight, will enjoy her first liberated evening any way she wants.

At 6:15 p.m., Rodrigo and Lowell accompany Amy through the loading area to avoid the crowd outside. They pass Milton, sitting in the basement with his arm around a crying female string player. The two cops walk around the corner to the lobby of the YMCA, the first YMCA in the country, built over a Red Sox field.

"Dad, I'd like to introduce you to Dukas," Amy says, using her ceremonial voice.

Both men extend hands. Lowell senses an affable man, clean-cut but not fastidious, who wears a light blue turtleneck and dark slacks, someone with whom he won't mind seeing his daughter walk down the street. Anything is better than her ex, a couch potato whose thrill in life was yelling at ballplayers on TV. They walk from the handsome wooded lobby to a side room, passing students working in a roomful of computers.

"You're a contra dancer," Lowell says to Dukas, forcing himself to make pleasantries.

"I began five years ago, and I love it."

"He's our point man. Whenever people get messed up, everyone looks to him." Amy continues nonchalant: "Dukas is chief researcher at Beth Israel Deaconess for a new treatment for diabetes."

The statement makes the right impression on Lowell, who raises his eyebrows and nods with delight. "The pancreas, a racemose gland. What ancini do you study?"

Dukas can't mask his amazement. "Beta cells."

"Of course," Lowell says with delight. "I've been fascinated by the pancreas' parasympathetic innervation, which can cause methane in the large intestine. The gas then—"

"Dad knows all about the digestive system," Amy interrupts, giving her father a stern look. She stands, ready to jump in and silence him.

Lowell adopts his good behavior pose. Here is a man with whom he can talk about intestinal flora without flinching. The way Amy looks at Dukas makes Lowell realize that she wants free time to have fun with him during that magical few months when love scintillates. It's supposed to happen to everyone, but Lowell doesn't recall experiencing it himself.

"I understand that you're also a FAS leader."

"We make a point of not having a hierarchy. I'm on the steering committee. When Amy asked me to see you, I called everyone, but no one knows about this. I can tell you categorically that this robbery did not come from anyone in our coalition."

Lowell feels that Dukas is speaking sincerely. "But you're, shall we say, established. What about the fringe elements?"

"People know people who know people. No one could even think of anyone who could have pulled this off. It's a mystery to all of us."

"Who's 'all of us'?"

"News reports said that several people were involved, meaning an organization. Isn't that right? It's difficult to keep a politically active organization hidden. We would know something third-hand."

"Unless the group kept a high code of secrecy," Lowell says.

"The FAS community is smaller than you imagine. It's hard to believe that a group of radicals came from Vermont and pulled this off without us knowing. Groups don't operate in a vacuum, and they don't do only one action."

"So we're dealing with a group way outside the mainstream."

"Have you considered the possibility of the government wanting to discredit us? They have a reputation of false flag operations."

"Other people have suggested that," Lowell says, "but what would be in it for them? They would draw attention to the agreement's shortcomings, which is happening now."

"They're beholden to big business, who want to discredit us. Politicians rely on handouts as much as the symphony does."

Amy, standing nervously next to her father in case something unusual comes out of his mouth, nudges Dukas. "We should be going. My father's very busy."

Lowell knows he has to make conversation with the man in front of him, who might be on track to become an in-law. He does not want to make the mistake of putting forth his intestinal theories like he did with the first husband, though he racks his brain at night wondering what she saw in such a dud.

"The average American eats a thousand pounds of food a year," Lowell says.

Amy drags Dukas to the door. Lowell has no choice but to extend his hand and shut his mouth.

When Dukas and Amy leave the lobby, Lowell turns to Rodrigo. "Let's get a couple of extra large French fries with lots of ketchup."

Lowell had read the first study about lycopene, a chemical found in tomatoes, helping protect the prostate. He increased his intake of ketchup immediately—for health reasons, of course.

Half an hour before Melody's arrest, Eduardo takes the Symphony Hall stage again and introduces a composer named Chadwick. "The St. Louis Symphony is premièring his piece next season on the theme of Manifest Destiny, a composition that is part of the New World Compositions. But we have pried a secret from him—he has also written a string quartet which, although originally not part of the cycle, would fit right in. We've convinced him and three other musicians to come and play it during this extraordinary day."

Chadwick garners a nice applause. Eduardo explains that he is a distant relative of George Chadwick, a Boston composer at the turn of the nineteenth century. Along with Parker, Foote, MacDowell, Paine, and Amy Beach—a rare female composer of the time—the "Boston Six" molded the American musical style that influenced American composers for the rest of the century.

"Before you introduce the piece, I know that you work with troubled kids," Eduardo says. "Can you tell us what you do?"

"We have an excellent program twice a week in a Brighton church basement where a bunch of special ed kids come for music education," Chadwick says. "Their social interaction is, to use the common expression, 'challenged,' but some have no inhibitions around music. They pick up an instrument or start dancing around the room, spontaneously making or responding to music."

"Can you share one or two observations?"

"I know you talk about music being innate, and if you spend time with these kids, you'll realize that's true. Certainly not all the kids are musical. Some you have to gently but firmly restrain physically. The musical kids go into an almost reflexive motion, playing one-finger tunes on the piano after a few minutes. They can't do society, but they might do music."

"Tell us about your composition."

"It's about Mexicans in Los Angeles. I thought about the theme while studying at UCLA. I saw the profound impact Mexicans are making on California, which was part of Mexico until 1846. California cities still have Mexican names. I tried to get a sense of a migrant's life by working with a family as a farm laborer, getting up at four and squeezing into the back of an old truck, then working the fields until sunset. After a few days, I was spent.

"The piece I wrote has a three-movement structure with Mexican themes. The upbeat first movement will be recognized by anyone who's been in a *barrio* during a Mexican holiday. The slow, thoughtful second movement is about migrant workers struggling under the oppressive heat of California's valleys, where hardship, hostility, and injustice reign. The quick final movement shows the emergence of a Mexican-American identity full of industry and pride."

Once again, music resonates from Symphony Hall on Sunday. TV executives had phoned the Latino radio and TV networks and offered them a feed of the performance, which they bought immediately. The media trucks outside beam the fifteen-minute piece into space and back to dishes around the US so that Chadwick's piece and news of the symphony heist receives the attention of the forty million Latinos in the United States.

After the performance, Eduardo, acting as host, talks about the development of opera in the 1600s, which, he claims, gave rise to the orchestra as we know it.

At 6:55 p.m., Dufay returns to Walter's office and hands Lowell a note.

After reading it, Lowell looks up. "Are you sure about this?"

The special agent gives a military nod. "Our informant told us. We hadn't paid attention before, but there's no doubt about it."

He leaves the room.

Lowell turns to Walter. "Did you know this?"

Walter reads the note. "Homeland Security spies. I don't."

"You know everything about your people. You must have at least suspected. It's a secret cell."

"Don't be melodramatic."

Lowell paces around the room with his hands behind his back. "Bring her here."

"There isn't any reason to pursue this."

"Bring her here," Lowell demands.

Reluctantly, Walter steps out and talks to Mrs. Schutz. A few minutes later, Melody appears in the room to confront a stern-faced Lowell. He points a commanding finger at the chair. After examining the faces of the two men, Melody sits.

Lowell stares directly into her eyes. "Tiffany Rogers."

Melody turns red. Every sound in her head stops.

"Why was Tiffany Rogers at the Saturday meeting?"

"I don't know anything about the robbery," Melody says.

"Start at the beginning. Where did Tiffany Rogers come from?"

"I just happened to be in that room with the bomb."

"Tiffany Rogers."

"It was an Internet name. I went to last night's meeting, because I wanted closure so that I wouldn't have anything blocking me from playing."

He places his hands on the arms of the chair and looks down at her. "Here you are, practicing constantly, all that pressure on your head, a make-or-break solo, and you drop in on a meeting that was trying to stop the orchestra from going."

"I had to be totally clear within myself. I was trying to

make peace with everything that would stop me from performing the solo."

"And a secret meeting with the leader." Lowell's voice is loud and dense.

"Just a talk. Tasa has been a mentor."

"You gave me the impression that you hadn't been active for a while. Why Tiffany Rodgers?"

"I used it on the sign-up sheet to stay anonymous. In the past month, a whole slew of new people became involved in FAS. Only the more seasoned people know that I'm in the orchestra. When you write your name, Raymond phones you, asks you to come to meetings and demonstrations. Everyone has email addresses under different names."

"Why didn't you tell me before?"

"I didn't do anything. Everyone there was arguing. Guru was there, too."

"You could have given the leaders information about the truck and the transport manager traveling to New Hampshire. And what are you doing running around talking to chief suspects? Are you trying to stop me from finding the robbers?"

"We don't let our private opinions overtake our professional lives," Walter intones, louder than Lowell.

Lowell ignores him, eyes fixed on Melody. "Who else in the orchestra besides Tito and that drummer Art Verra attended the Saturday meeting?"

Walter moves to stand between Melody and Lowell. "You're bringing back the McCarthy era."

Lowell looks at Walter with sudden clarity. "You knew about it, didn't you?"

"There isn't anything to know."

"You know everything they do, but you didn't tell me."

"I know that they have opinions," Walter says, still using his loud voice. "I also know that they would never betray the orchestra. Their politics have nothing to do with their performance. Even when they hate a piece, even when they completely disagree with the conductor's interpretation, even when they have to play fluff, they still carry out their professional service with depth and determination."

"You can't separate music from personal life. That's what the musicians told me." Lowell looks straight at Walter and repeats his question. "Why didn't you tell me?"

"Why should I introduce extraneous elements? Melody is a good girl. She's nourished by a different god than our generation, but she's absolutely dedicated to artistic music. No one practices as much as Melody, especially now when her confidence is on the floor. Do you know what it's like to play the same six notes over and over until you've sucked every possible mood out of them? She is our future. There's no reason to question her."

"Everyone is telling me how to run the investigation."

"You don't understand." Walter raises his arms, his figure dominating the room, his face red, his palms sweaty, his voice charged. "The thread is so thin. Before, people handed down music generation to generation, each generation adding and growing and enhancing it, but we've kept most young people musically isolated. We . . . we did this to them."

Walter gestures to Lowell with outstretched hands. "That's what happened to the Greeks and their music—zealous Christians stopped the steady evolution of art so that the world had to start all over again in the Renaissance. We're breaking that cycle again, but it isn't being stopped by a bunch of narrow-minded, repressive old men who seized control of the Church and strangled art and creativity. It doesn't have anything to do with repression. It's the cheapening, the dilution of music that heralds the cheapening of our lives. A man isn't worth anything anymore. We've robbed all value from him."

Walter stares at Lowell, his hands almost pleading. "We've been developing Western music for six hundred years, each age adding to the richness, changing, creating. How many hundreds of years will we have to wait this time while the world wallows in mediocrity, while men and women know a miserly image of culture through a narrow, miserly lens? Maybe, just maybe, we might manage to keep a small thread alive and pass on this art."

Walter points at Melody. "Young women like her are our key. Perhaps future generations will know Beethoven, but who will know the composers of Bel Canto or Sibelius and Dvorak?"

Dufay and his assistant walk in, drawn by Walter's voice, which penetrates the hallways. Walter interrupts his rant and turns to the federal agents. "You, young men, can either of you name the Austrian masters of the twelve-tone scale?"

The two agents look at each other.

"That would be Arnold Schoenberg and his students Berg, Wellesz, and Webern," Dufay says. "They didn't want to be hemmed in by the diatonic scale."

Walter is taken aback. "Sir, you must be the exception."

"The Bel Canto composers, Rossini, Donizetti, and Bellini, had no influence on Beethoven, though they lived at the same time," Dufay says. "And how can you speak of Sibelius and Dvorak in the same breath? Dvorak was a reticent fellow who was barely literate, while Sibelius was a sophisticated man of the world."

Walter looks at him proudly. "There's a bright young man. Sir, where did you get your musical education?"

Dufay drops his stern face and gives a childish smile. "I played violin as a kid."

Lowell scratches his head, trying to imagine the grim, muscular guy with a violin tucked under his chin.

"I played in the high school orchestra," Dufay says. "But the school turned the orchestra room into a computer lab. When kids aren't required to practice, they give up real soon and can't play another note."

Lowell shakes himself back to the present. "What's your point?"

"People today don't value musicians," Walter says. "Instead of respect, they steal our instruments."

"You're blind to how musicians were treated in past generations," Dufay says. "They were servants with no rights."

Walter cools down and sits. "Melody, take charge. Stand up for our orchestra. Stand up and start your solo."

Melody hears her four notes, four elements, four dimensions, four basic emotions. The federal agents are standing in the background like percussionists.

She stands and faces Lowell, her eyes open and focused, an impassioned expression, a confident voice. "We must save our art," she says, as if Walter has passed her the baton of righteousness. "Our movement to liberate art is growing because people are fed up with greed."

"That's it, Melody!" Walter shouts joyfully. "Throw out that childish minor etude and speak *espressivo*."

"How about speaking truth for a change?" Lowell says. "Did you talk to anyone about the baggage truck?"

"No. I was concentrating on removing any possible obstacles to my playing. I will not allow you to accuse an innocent person."

"Why did you meet Tasa privately?"

"She's been a great help. When this deal was tied to the trip, I told her about my conflict. At first she suggested that I cancel, but then we wouldn't inaugurate the New World Compositions. No one else could tackle the difficult parts of that solo. I have to play for someone special, someone I wronged. Last night she told me to go and play my best, and I felt liberated."

"What else happened?"

"Tito and I couldn't stay, because we had to be back at seven-thirty for the concert. Raymond and Gustav were obstructing the discussion."

"Did Tito also have private meetings?"

She hears B, E, E-flat, D-flat, all interconnected notes. She thinks about the guy who got beat up, Gustav. He wasn't informing Dufay; Raymond was doing that. Then who was he informing?

"Tito has never made a secret about his politics," she says. "I'm sure he told you himself."

"Did he keep them informed about the instruments?"

"Ask him." Melody holds her chest high, her shoulders open. "I don't want to be part of a generation that values only commodities."

"That's my girl," Walter shouts. "You've graduated from the largo to the allegro."

"How close were you to the leaders?" Lowell asks.

"No one is the leader, yet we're all leaders." Melody's tone remains self-assured.

Walter applauds and howls like Fred Flintstone, "Yabba dabba doo!"

Lowell backs off. "It must have been hard to take a trip you were dead against."

"It wasn't difficult." Her dark pupils are as dilated as a singer before a pivotal aria, her speech radically different from when Lowell first interviewed her. "I know the political aspect of the trip is wrong, but the New World Compositions and musical exchange with Brazil take precedence. Governments come and go, and so does money, but music is eternal."

More applause and a merry yodel from Walter.

"I suspected that you would react eventually," Lowell says about her sudden transformation.

"No you didn't. People in authority are always surprised when others claim their own power. I abandoned my passion for classical music a few weeks ago, but it's come back to me. I forgot that music is a healer. How can you possibly think I'm involved in the robbery? I need to go to Rio and play. I've done nothing this past month but practice. I trained my fingers to play the piece while I read the newspaper. Why would I have anything to do with such a plot? And against Eduardo?"

"Don't shout at me," Lowell says. "When a woman upsets a man, it inflames the front part of his prostate and constrains the urethra, making it hard to pee. I have to get up in the middle of the night, and then my wife gets mad at me. She says it's because I drink liquids at night, but I know that the high, angry voice of a woman hits the nerve fibers in a man's inner ear and shoots straight down to his prostate, strangling the urinary tract. That's why the singing fat lady is so powerful—she excites a man's most vulnerable part."

Walter makes a face at Melody that says she should let Lowell talk. She and Walter stand deadpan.

"I'm not allowed to drink anything after nine at night," Lowell complains. "It gets really hard to tinkle when you're standing at a urinal with a line of guys behind you. You just stand there, and it's downright impossible to get it started, all because a woman upsets a man's prostate."

"Save your prostate. We want our instruments back. Why are you blaming us?"

"If you withhold information, you rob me of time to follow another track."

Maybe that's what the bomb and the bodies are about, Melody thinks, *robbing Lowell of time.*

Before she can mention this possibility, Rodrigo walks in.

"Electric atmosphere. Speaking of which, I've got news about the electricians. The New York Philharmonic has their names as subscribers, the first time they subscribed."

"What's suspicious about going to concerts?" Melody says.

"Contractors?" Dufay's assistant says.

"Yes, contractors. This music is written for them."

"Enough," Lowell says. "Melody, I don't want you nosing around anymore."

"I'm just starting to get it."

"Give me your handbag."

"What?"

"Are you refusing to cooperate with the police?"

"You'll have to arrest me."

"Fine. You're arrested. The charge is obstinacy."

"I won't have you blame me without evidence. You know nothing about the case. Zero. So stop accusing innocent people."

"I'm not accusing anyone. I want to conduct the investigation without obstacles. You're an obstacle."

He snatches her handbag and takes out her phone. He tells Rodrigo to put her in a room where she won't cause any more trouble.

"You can't do that," Walter says. "It's totally illegal."

"I'm tired of everyone telling me what I can't do," Lowell says. "Take her away."

"'Stone walls do not a prison make, nor iron bars a cage'," Melody says, quoting Richard Lovelace. "I've shaken my fear. My spirit shall never again be confined." She remains straight and forthright, her slump and repression discarded.

Rodrigo takes her around the corner to the broadcast booth, an ex-broom closet that overlooks stage right. He asks her politely to step inside.

"I'll tell China that you're here."

"Everyone will know right away."

"I see that. News travels like a bugle call inside these walls."

"All the clues are there," Melody says. "We have to reason it out."

"You've turned into a different person," Rodrigo says.

"My fingers are free. Finally, they're free."

As Rodrigo closes the door, Sergeant Ostinato enters the building with Maestro Borges.

Harmony: A pleasant mixture of pitches played together, often not part of the melodic line. Too much harmony is boring.

Fourth Movement
Vivace

An hour and fifty minutes before Borges' arrest, Lowell storms down to the basement, shadowed by Walter, singling out Tito and just about grabbing him by the collar.

"Do you think it was right to feed FAS inside information about the organization you work for?"

"I did no such thing."

Other musicians form a circle around the two men.

"You were at last night's meeting. You were their point man, weren't you?"

"Absolutely not. I'm part of FAS, and I did go to last night's meeting, but more importantly, I'm part of the orchestra."

Walter listens mutely to Lowell's interrogation.

"How do you describe what you did for them?"

"There isn't *them*, it's *us*, and we discussed how to stop the BSO's involvement in this terrible deal. I already told you and everyone here that I'm against it."

"Someone passed up-to-date information to the

robbers. If it wasn't Melody, it must have been you."

"I gave no secrets. Last night's meeting was useless."

"At the same time trying to steer me away from FAS so I'd waste my time looking elsewhere."

"I never violated my loyalty to the orchestra," Tito says to Walter. "I would never put politics above music."

"Did you tell them about the truck?" Lowell asks.

Everyone in the room is intent on every word.

"Lieutenant, if I discover that my closest friend wants to bring the slightest harm to the orchestra, I would report him to Walter right away."

"Someone gave information, and it didn't go to the feds."

"I swear twice over that I didn't. I didn't even think of the truck."

"You spent last summer in Venezuela at a camp for political activism."

"Are you reduced to that?"

"And you just happened to be late this morning."

"Holy shit," Tito says.

It is the second time Lowell hears that phrase in Symphony Hall. Lowell holds "shit" in high regard and feels uneasy about mixing it with anything holy.

"Felix and I ran straight to the buses." Tito turns to Walter. "I never compromised my work with the orchestra."

"At times we are called to answer to our conscience." Walter taps him on the back and quotes Socrates' defense at his trial: "'To a good man, nothing is evil'."

"Nothing is evil," Lowell repeats.

"Where to now?" Lowell asks Rodrigo.

Rodrigo leads Lowell, Walter always at his side, into the large basement room where the Tanglewood Chorus rehearses.

The eminent chorus is all volunteer, not even receiving ticket discounts for spouses.

Sergeant Ostinato is standing with an angry Maestro Borges near the three tiers of risers the orchestra uses.

"Conductor Borges, why didn't you tell me that it was *you* who concocted the Rio ceremony?" Lowell inquires instead of asking the maestro where he has been and if he is okay.

Borges' upper lip twitches. Walter moves a chair, eyeing him suspiciously, motioning for him to sit facing Lowell. Borges sits and crosses his legs. Ostinato stands at attention behind him.

"I didn't have much to do with it."

"You arranged for the BSO to play the Rio ceremony."

"It was other people's idea. I just agreed."

"You connected the BSO's scheduled concert with the arts agreement. Why did you lie to me?"

Borges exhales deeply. "I knew people in Boston would be against the agreement." His posture and expression remain fixed. "I didn't want to make a lot of noise about it and create a division among the orchestra. In the end, only one malcontent refused to go."

"And how is it that you disappeared?"

"I didn't disappear. I was trying to find my brother, Guru."

"Were you successful?"

"This exceptional policeman helped." He turns and points to Ostinato.

Ostinato gives a statuesque military salute. "The chief designated me to recover the instruments." He looks earnestly at the void ahead.

"You know the problem?" Borges says. "That girl agitated my brother. She doesn't care about his handicap." He points at Lowell's chest. "Neither do you. She told an autistic person that she wanted him to break an international conspiracy. She teased him, but he took it sincerely and went into a frenzy."

"What kind of frenzy?"

"Because of her prodding, he took off to all those militant groups like Art Unincorporated. He takes people at their word. I followed him into the lion's den."

"That explains the rumor of your being abducted."

"That girl. Who would have the audacity to give themselves the name 'Melody Cavatina'? She goaded my simple brother to help the terrorists. They contaminated and used him."

"Art Unincorporated used Guru?"

"I was desperate to find him. I had to track down the terrorists themselves first. You can't look them up in the Yellow Pages. Fortunately, Sergeant Ostinato, with no regard for himself, was also searching for clues about the instruments, and he found me looking desperately for my brother. He had already met Guru in a dingy basement where they play modern music on out-of-tune instruments, but then we remained one step behind him. This good sergeant said that she excited him into some international conspiracy. I became frantic. He's my brother, but you don't care. You're going around destroying our lives when you should be getting us to Rio to broadcast the concert. You even refuse to return our luggage."

"Let me run this by you again," Lowell says. "Guru was entangled with the anti-agreement activists, and since you were searching among them, people assumed you were abducted."

"The only thing the press does well is report rumors."

Borges stands and stomps around the cavernous room.

Lowell asks Ostinato how he located the groups outside FAS. Ostinato replies that spending three solid hours on the Internet will make you an expert on anything.

"If only we had more policemen like this sergeant," Borges says.

Ostinato raises another salute.

"He led me from one meeting place to the next."

"You met them?"

"Sergeant Ostinato discovered that Guru is being used covertly by that terrorist cellist. You see, she's guilty, but you're not taking action against her. You'd think no one could be as brazen as that girl, even when surrounded by police. I'm ready to wring her neck. When she defiled such a beautiful composition during rehearsal, I was angry. I had heard that she was gifted but couldn't reconcile that with how she played."

Borges' mouth is near foaming. "Maybe you're against our going, too. Maybe you're wasting time so the deadline can pass. We have four and a half hours."

"Everyone is telling me how I should conduct the investigation. Then again, you are the conductor."

Lowell steps outside, talks briefly to Sergeant Rodrigo, and then reenters. "Guru is with Felix. Melody found him and phoned Rodrigo. They're calming him down so he can talk to me."

"I don't believe it." Borges takes a whole measure rest. "I demand to be in the room while you interview him."

"I'm afraid not. You have not been straight with me." Lowell turns to Ostinato. "What's your conclusion about the anti-agreement groups?"

"In my opinion, they were not involved in the robbery."

Eduardo is finishing his latest lecture and thanking the audience when China comes to the backstage door and tells him that Melody is being detained in the broadcast booth. Eduardo runs upstairs, but the cop guarding her won't let him in.

"Ask the lieutenant," Eduardo says. "Tell him I'll convince her to give any information she has."

The cop returns with Lowell's permission.

"You think she knows more than she's saying?" the cop asks Eduardo.

"I feel bad, because I encouraged her to help find the hijackers. What was I thinking? I guess I was desperate for her to play. It's been a traumatic day."

"The lieutenant doesn't want her confusing things, that's all."

Eduardo enters the booth, putting his lecture notes on the bench. Melody is glad to see him. Giving lectures makes him vibrant and active, and she loves him in that state.

"I've been giving talk after talk," he says. "I'm sorry I didn't pay attention to you."

"Lowell is mad at me."

"It's my fault. I didn't allow myself to feel how much the robbery affected me. I shouldn't have talked you into playing cop. I'm sorry. Let's stop this and leave it to the police."

"I'm just making headway."

"You know more about the heist than anyone else, but the police are the ones who really know. I'm sorry I encouraged you to do this. We shouldn't try to be detectives any more than we should ask the detectives to be musicians."

"I'm not doing any harm," Melody says.

"Lowell thinks you are. Call it off now."

"Why are you so adamant?"

"You can't do anything here, imprisoned in the broadcast booth."

"I have been doing something important. I've been thinking. Everything that happened was done by thoughtful people who wanted to stop us from leaving town. We just have to look at each action and work its logic backwards."

"Mel, stop it. Leave it to the police."

"We have only a few possible suspects. If we track each event for each suspect—"

"You've been taken over by this—"

"Borges and his money fit in somehow."

"When I finished writing your solo, I realized that you had inspired the music. You were my muse from the beginning, ever since I wrote that first quartet. I've written my best for you."

"It hurt me not being able to play the concerto the way I heard it. The more I agonized about it, the worse it sounded. Then the heist and the bomb this morning, Wisteria and—it got me thinking."

"Don't think too much, or you'll end up like me."

Melody makes a face to stop herself from laughing.

"Last week Walter phoned me about your playing," Eduardo says, "and I came and heard you in the Mussorgsky. I was beside myself that your talent had been corrupted. Maestro Borges squashed you further, as if he unconsciously wanted his big project to fail, as if he felt guilty about success."

"Borges has a focused agenda."

Eduardo takes three folded sheets from his jacket pocket. "I'm working on a string trio for you. I wanted to give it to you on our anniversary."

She unfolds the score. She is touched.

"This is the opening section," he explains. "I have to rework it."

"No instrument can express like the voice."

"Only the most experienced can write for voice. Notes on a page mean nothing. They can be played proud or circumspect."

"Will you always write the score?"

"That's how it is. I write, you interpret. I never once told you how you should play. I gave you a lifeless sheet of paper. Your playing gives it breath. That's what inspiration means, to breathe."

"Perfect duet. Is that what you're aiming for?"

"Perfect never works, not musically."

In his speech she hears sounds from her solo, intermingled with other voices she has been hearing all day. Can she use those sounds to determine who is lying?

"Borges hates me because I'm against the arts agreement."

"When you play, don't look at him. Just watch his right hand beating out the tempo and his left hand bringing you in."

"Where does he get money?" she asks rhetorically. "By doing their bidding."

"Mel, stop it."

"And what's the best way to send the money without anyone noticing?"

"Enough."

"'Cash is king', Guru says. She stands straight and projects her voice, leaving a dead silence in its wake. "Eduardo, you need to get me out of here."

Eduardo stares at her in confusion. "What are you talking about?"

"Get me out of this booth." Her every sound is clear. Her music remains in the middle strings.

"That's like running from the police."

"I need to confront Borges."

"You're already in a lot of trouble. I helped you get into that state."

"Ask China. She'll find a way to get me out of here."

Melody can see that he won't do it. She looks out the small window at the interior of the concert hall and sees a new audience entering.

"You have to go for another lecture," she says. "Tell China to get me out of here."

"Stop this entire thing. You've become another person."

She snatches his phone from his pocket before he has time to react. He lunges to grab it back, but she turns and holds it in the corner, her back to him to protect her grip. Eduardo takes her shoulders to pull her away, but she holds fast and texts two words to China: "Spring me."

She returns the phone to Eduardo. He makes awkward, inept movements.

"No, I'm not stopping. Go downstairs and talk about music, your favorite activity. I need to get to Rio and dedicate the concert to someone I betrayed who has only been good to me. He's landing in Rio now."

He pauses, looks at her, grapples for words, and then opens the door to go downstairs. Melody hands him his lecture notes. She shuts the door and leans against it, relieved, breathing heavily, *fortissimo* music in her head.

Why does he have lecture notes?

Sixty-five minutes before Maestro Borges' arrest, Felix suggests to Sergeant Rodrigo that they meet Guru at the café on Gainsborough Street.

"He's calmed down," Felix says. "The lieutenant could say that he's debriefing Guru like spies do in movies. He'll be off on something else tomorrow."

Rodrigo arrives at Melody's house with Sergeant Ostinato, and they take Guru to the funky café, which is full of students chatting over their devices. Lowell joins them, noticing in Guru a short, awkward guy with a genial upbeat manner, so different from his stiff brother. He shakes his hand and welcomes him to a small, round table in the corner, alternative music filling the café, the students oblivious to the commotion around Symphony Hall.

"Too bad you don't have your bagpipe," Lowell says to Ostinato. "You could have marched the crowd up and down Mass. Ave. Do you take requests?"

"Anything but 'Amazing Grace'." He salutes and stands behind Lowell.

"When Melody told me that you needed my help,"

Guru says, a broad smile across his smooth face, "I had to do my duty. I taught policemen how to interrogate criminals."

"Guru. How did you get that name?"

"Because I know what other people don't. Guru knows everything."

"I bet you don't know who pulled off the heist."

"I bet I do."

Lowell leans in close to him. "Just between us. We're all law enforcement."

"It was a prank," Guru whispers.

"A prank?"

"Eric Satie was always pulling pranks. My brother will conduct the orchestra in front of millions."

"Who was in on the prank?"

"Gustav. He ended up naked on Newbury Street."

"That sounds like a prank."

"Only I know that he's Secret Service."

"Did you tell Gustav about the prank, or did he tell you?

"The information is top secret."

"You don't have to use low-level language with me. We all know it's called intelligence, not information. Tell me, who did Gustav contact? What exact words did you and he use?"

Guru looks left and right. "They operate outside borders."

"But you know their names."

"They all use aliases."

"Did he tell you who he was giving this intelligence to?" Lowell asks and re-asks this question from every angle, but by the way Guru answers, or doesn't answer, Lowell concludes that Guru doesn't know to whom Gustav, a convicted car thief, was giving information.

"What intelligence is Gustav collecting?"

Guru's face becomes confused.

"You can tell me," Lowell says. "That way I'll learn your method."

Again, Guru makes *non sequiturs*.

"Was Gustav part of the April Fools' joke?" Lowell says.

"That was my idea." Guru straightens his shoulders with pride. "I got it from a Brazilian movie about a father who wanted to have Christmas dinner in the summer. What a crazy idea, Christmas in summer."

He laughs, and Lowell laughs with him, one hand on his stomach. It is Lowell's first laugh of the day.

"You're a great guy," Lowell says, and he means it. "Christmas in summer," and he laughs more.

"My brother spends all his time playing piano and studying sheets of music. He hears music just by looking at sheets of paper. I can read music, too. Can you?"

"I played in my high school marching band. It was the only way I could get on the football field."

"My brother says this trip will make enough money to start the secret organization. Sky Horizon doesn't know about it."

"A lot of money?"

Lowell doesn't realize that Sky Horizon is a person.

"To buy a house where I can teach soldiers and policemen. Mahler was a patient of Freud. I know all about Cage, but Melody said that I have to keep that top secret."

At the same hour, down the coast in Greenwich, Connecticut, three police cars pull up to a large brick house sitting behind a substantial but unkempt garden off Maple Avenue. As the officers approach, they hear the sound of a circular saw.

A guy covered in construction dust, a carpenter's pencil behind his ear, opens the door when they knock. Classical music echoes from a radio in the empty hall. Looking puzzled, he faces the police while his brother, who is taping drywall in the adjacent room, stops and looks at the front door.

"You guys the Giordani Brothers, the Boston electricians?"

They nod.

"When did you guys move here?" a second cop asks.

"We grew up here," one brother says.

"Our mom died last month," the other adds, and the cops express their sympathy.

"We're fixing up the house and putting it on the market."

"Did you hear about the Boston Pops heist?"

"You mean the symphony? We've been hearing about it all day. We had our last job there this week."

"They're asking if you guys saw anyone suspicious."

The two brothers look at each other, look around the room.

"I don't know who was supposed to be there and who wasn't," one says.

"We bid low on the job because we like being around music," his brother adds. "Our dad taught French horn at the Longy School in Cambridge. We had a couple of long talks with Maestro Borges. He's famous."

"Uptight guy," the first brother says, "but he's spreading music around the world."

"They must be hard up if they're asking us," the other says. "You don't think they suspect us, do you?"

"It's like going to the hospital and getting a dozen useless tests—they've got to do them all or they're being negligent," a cop replies.

"What do you expect to get for the house?" the third cop, quiet until then, asks.

"This is our retirement. Our parents bought the place in fifty-nine for thirty-six grand. We expect to get it on the market asking two point seven five mill, all tax free, thanks to the Republicans. You guys Republicans?"

"Cops are usually Democrats who work for Republicans."

"We're visiting relatives in Colombia. We might buy a winter home there."

"Borges wanted to know exactly how we would get money down there to buy property," the other brother says. "I told him that cash is king. It's a dangerous world. Everybody has to protect himself. When you have hundred dollar bills in your knuckles, people bend over backwards to make you comfortable."

"You're not supposed to walk around with that kind of cash," one of the cops says.

"There's a lot you're not supposed to do here that you do in South America."

"What's that on the boom box?"

"The Sibelius *Violin Concerto*," the first brother says. "Sibelius and Mendelssohn wrote the two knock-out concertos for violinists."

The police leave the house and phone Lowell, reporting that they double checked that the electricians' mother had died and left them the house.

Within minutes, the Everett electrical inspector phones Lowell. "You getting a musical education sitting in Symphony Hall?"

"A viola is bigger than a violin," Lowell says. "Unlike other people who are the best in their fields, these musicians aren't arrogant."

"You haven't met soloists. Who's getting rich off the Rio deal?"

"The same people who get rich on all these deals. I wonder who's getting rich on the robbery."

"FAS—their cause is all over the news. Now the whole world hates that arts agreement."

"One by one they've told us they're clean."

"I got hold of the guy who worked with the electricians." The inspector says. "He confirmed that the brothers inherited a mansion. They gave him a more generous severance than you and I will get. If you've got cash in front of you, you wouldn't be busting your buns on three-way light switches. Ever think the robbery isn't a local thing? Music is international."

"It would be too much work to come from a distant city, set up shop, collect information, get to know the city and its burbs. You can't run that type of operation away from home. Outsiders get lost in Boston. The British lost the war because they couldn't find their way."

"Maybe your theory about the robbers having an inside connection is off the mark."

"The feds activated an entire floor in the Hoover Building and are tracking down every group and every person who has ever spoken against the deal. I don't know that they'll do anything but rustle up a new series of charges from the ACLU, and their methods are, understatement, unhelpful."

"Deliberate?"

"Or they're trying too hard because they screwed up."

"Where does that leave you?"

"Four pancakes short of a stack," Lowell says, "with an empty syrup jar right in front of us."

After she reads Melody's text to spring her, forty minutes before Maestro Borges's arrest, China whips into action. She tells Felix and Tito. Felix expresses concern about doing something illegal.

"It was illegal of Lowell to detain her to start with," Tito says.

China claims, erroneously, that the most Lowell will do is get mad at them.

They concoct a hasty scheme to sneak Melody out of the second floor broadcast booth without Lowell knowing. The plan involves China pulling away the cop guarding Melody, saying that she wants to tell him something about Melody in private. Then Tito will arrive and distract the cop even more by buttonholing him with a litany of government dirty tricks actions. Both musicians will keep the cop out of the line of sight of the broadcast booth so that Felix can slip Mel across a technician's crawlway around the back of the stage, then down an unlit ladder.

The plan goes pretty much on track, even though they underestimate the cop's reluctance to leave his post. They have to make a big blowout to get him around the corner. He does not see that Felix has snatched Melody away, but it doesn't take long for him to discover that the broadcast booth is empty.

The conspiring musicians have no plan after that. Felix and Melody work their way across the crawlway and down the ladder. using the light of Felix's phone. They end up behind a short, thin door in the stage left corridor across from the green room for visiting soloists. Felix and Melody realize they're trapped. Where can Mel go now that everyone knows she has run away from Lowell?

Ordinarily, people are not in the corridor when the orchestra is not playing, but because eighty musicians are hanging out backstage, Melody has no place to go. Felix texts their quandary to China and Tito. They come around and find Melody and Felix in the dark cubicle. Even Mel can't figure a way through the hall without being seen—until everyone hears Mayor Bond walking down the corridor, waving and bestowing good wishes in all directions.

Everyone in the hallway turns toward his magnetism. China puts her arm through his and walks with him a few paces, drawing everyone's attention away from the door behind which Felix and Melody are trapped.

"We have a proposal," China says to the mayor. "It's

about music education."

When everyone's attention is turned, Felix pops into the corridor. The others are making so much noise around the mayor that no one sees Melody lunge behind Felix and cross the corridor into the green room.

"We shouldn't have done that," Felix says when they are both inside. "Now you're in even more trouble."

"I have two choices—either I solve the puzzle or I'm fired. Being fired would be a lot more trouble."

"What can you do? You're in a different prison now. You can't step out of this room or someone will see you."

China brings the mayor back to the green room, unaware that Mel has made it her refuge.

Melody stands behind the door, inviting Bond in as if she lives there. The mayor is obviously struck by having two pretty women next to him. Tito enters and stands next to Felix. China joyfully pushes the mayor inside, then closes the door.

"We wonder if you'd like to come to our concerts," China says.

"I'm an ardent supporter of music," he says, wearing his best politician's smile.

"Do you know classical music?" Felix asks.

"I love all music," Bond says as if warming up for a speech.

The mayor sits in the armchair while the others take chairs facing him. Melody sits on the bench behind the piano. It is a room where performers wash up, tune up, give interviews, and get ready for concerts. After concerts, it is where performers meet admirers.

"Tell us what you think of classical music," China says.

Bond is about to speak, but China stops him with a slight movement of her eyes. "Not that," she says. "What do you *really* think?"

Bond looks around and speaks as if in secret. "I'm a scientist. Honestly, I don't know much about your music."

"It's music for uptight white people, right?" Tito says.

"We want to talk about education," Felix says. "Actually, study after study proves that playing an instrument increases children's overall abilities, but it hasn't filtered into the school curriculum."

"The way to improve students' reading and math is to teach them music," China says, speaking triple time and not waiting for a response. "There are enough unemployed musicians who can teach. The city's public schools have either no music education or almost none."

"Here's our proposal," Tito continues. "Spend twenty-five million dollars a year on music education as a five-year pilot program to see if it improves students' academic scores."

"Twenty-five million is nothing for Boston," Felix says. "You spend that on salt when there's a heavy snow."

The musicians are exhilarated by their audacity, firing comment after comment. Melody remains half hidden behind the piano.

"You can get most of that money underwritten by state and federal grants," Tito says. "Select a committee of music teachers to decide how the money should be spent."

They stop and wait for Bond to reply.

"Eighty-five percent of our public school students are minorities," Bond says. "Look at you and your orchestra. How many people of color do you have? How easy is it for a nine-year-old kid who lives in a rough neighborhood to start playing fiddle? Would you join a black church, be the only white face there, singing, 'Were You There When They Crucified My Lord?' Or is it that you want them to be white like you, acting in blackface?"

"That's what we want to change," Tito says. "We want the classical community to understand that segregation is unacceptable. We feel comfortable in a black jazz club, but we haven't made African-Americans comfortable in Symphony Hall. The fault lies here."

"Why don't you come back to me when you get some color in this hall?"

"Why don't you help us make that happen?"

Bond leans back in his chair as if he is on a porch of a country house. "Guys in the inner city know how to make a beat, but you look down your noses at that, say that your music is better."

"We don't say it's —"

Bond cuts him off. "Yes you do. Kids get extra credit for listening to your music. They know the music they like, not what you say they should like. It comes naturally, makes you dance."

"A lot of what we play is dance music," Felix says. "We have studies that say—"

"You have studies, I don't doubt that. You have studies that say your music is superior to jungle music, but your music doesn't sell itself. If black people thought it was groovy, they would come. If your Mozart was so good, why didn't he write music kids like? A scientist asks, what's the best way to obtain change? I wrote models of the future climate. Do you have models? What do you classical music guys want?"

When Melody hears the door open, she makes herself into a ball and hides behind the piano. A cop sticks his head into the room. China jumps up and stands in front of him.

"Sorry to disturb you," the cop says. "We're looking for that young brunette."

Bond is about to point to Melody when he sees her ducking her head.

"We were talking about uptight white people," Tito says. He turns to Bond. "Black people are cool."

Bond takes the hint and winks at Melody. The cop tries to look around the room, but China, Tito, and Felix keep standing in front of him.

"We're having a serious conversation about serious music," the mayor says.

The cop excuses himself and leaves.

Mel stands. "Mayor, you're a wonderful man." She gives him a hug. "You're one of the wisest people in government, and we appreciate your intellect and judgment. We're trying to solve the crime, working from a different perspective than Lowell."

"It would mean a lot to me if you succeed in finding the instruments."

"Don't dismiss us because classical music is different from rock," Mel says. "Give us a chance. When children learn music, it stays with them forever. If they're exposed to only one kind of music, it limits their world."

"Such a program would be watched by voters across the country," Tito says. "Look outside at how many voters are standing there."

"I'll talk to my advisers," Bond promises.

"Announce it when the police solve the case," China says. "It will make a big hit."

"And we want to offer you a season ticket," Felix says.

When Bond leaves the room with good wishes, Melody asks China to bring Borges.

At 8:20 p.m., following one of Eduardo's lectures, Lowell finds Cage in the hallway.

"This is a real boost for music," the arts liaison says.

They walk to a room past the room used as a kitchen during Pops concerts and a mini clinic during the regular season.

"When I was a kid, I fantasized about going into politics," Lowell says, "standing in front of crowds and making rousing speeches."

"For your information, I'm a diplomat, not a politician."

"Does that mean you represent politicians?"

Cage relaxes and leans against the cupboard. "I represent the arts."

"How did that come about?"

"Every country but ours has a ministry to promote culture. The electronic media forced us to have an international treaty on royalties. That's when my position began."

"You've been spying on FAS and the other groups, right?"

Cage makes noises of denial, but Lowell cuts him off. "You had a dossier on everyone in these groups. Special Agent Dufay showed me some of them. You know who attends meetings, and you have their email lists. You also had at least one mole in a coordinating position."

"That's Dufay's doing."

Lowell blows off the comment with a snap of his wrist. "You knew what these groups were up to, yet you were blaming them. I didn't have to investigate—you knew all about them. And you must have known they weren't involved in the heist. "

"We're not as all-knowing as you think."

"Let's concentrate on FAS. You know their members, those who turn out for demonstrations and write letters to their congressmen."

"That is mostly true."

"I want to know if we're digging in the same cesspool. You knew that the people we interviewed had nothing to do with the robbery. Isn't that true?"

Cage shifts his legs. "You're missing something."

He walks around. Lowell notices that he has dropped his Washington attitude.

"People assume that government is efficient, has omniscient knowledge and global reach, that it has a policy, even. Yes, Special Agent Dufay kept track of the various organizations and had penetrations, but he didn't understand. If you look at the government's record, it misses more than it catches. The government can spy but paradoxically remain ignorant, because it understands in a government way. Look how long it took to discover that Melody attended that meeting, only because she signed her name with an alias."

"Let me ask you directly—did the government have any hand in the robbery?"

Cage continues pacing. "I knew from your questions that you suspected this. That's not a yes or no question."

Lowell senses that Cage is still speaking genuinely.

"The government is this big conglomerate, a multi-trillion-dollar organization employing millions: Republicans, Democrats, technocrats who don't care, throw in an extremist or two, people with agendas. It doesn't have one policy but different policies, including policies opposed to the party line. One branch often works against another. Many in government oppose the arts agreement, while on the other side are zealots bent on discrediting FAS. Having them portrayed as robbers and bombers could be a good way to deflate their balloon, especially if their balloon is flying high."

"Everyone's poop smells different. You wondered about the government's involvement, and what did you conclude?"

Cage gestures with his arms. "The last thing they wanted was this robbery. You already understood that. It would make no sense for the government to have any involvement. FAS was a pain, but it had no real power."

"You say it's not the government, FAS say it's not them, and Walter says it's not the musicians."

"The vice president was generous with the BSO," Cage says. "He promised a two point five million-dollar arts grant for renovating this historic building." Cage frowns at Lowell's surprised face. "Didn't Walter tell you?"

China can see on the backstage video monitor near the green room that Eduardo is in the midst of another lecture. Next to the monitor is a magnetic board that shows the seating positions for musicians for each piece during a concert. Seating arrangements change, depending on the conductor's taste, the size of the orchestra, and the logistics of having soloists or a chorus.

China brings Borges down the hall past the concertmaster's room without telling him that Melody wants to confront him.

When China opens the door, Borges sees Mel sitting on the piano stool. "Why don't you leave us together," he says.

China shakes her head.

Borges looks at Melody. "You don't want me to tell Lowell where you're hiding, do you?"

Melody nods at China, and China leaves reluctantly, closing the door behind her, but she remains in the corridor.

"If you tell me who stole the instruments, I'll make sure you stay with the BSO."

Borges sounds conciliatory, but his pitch, stress, and juncture do not fool Melody. She looks at his insincere face and moves to stand in front of him.

"I figured out where you're hiding your money. That's why you wanted your luggage back."

"You sniveling little busybody."

His anger does not affect her.

"It's only part of the money, isn't it? The major part comes—"

She sees Borges raise his arm to strike her. She puts her arms together and deflects the blow. In one steady, automatic move, just as she had been taught and re-taught by the sect, she swivels and attacks his eyes with her index fingers. As he reels, disoriented, Melody kicks the back of his knee. He goes down. China bursts in the door, stunned to see Borges groaning on the floor, Melody pinning his neck with her knee.

"Call Lowell," Melody says. "I'm not sure how this relates, but it solves part of the puzzle."

When Lowell arrives with Walter, Rodrigo, and Alan Ostinato behind, Melody releases Borges.

Lowell grabs her shoulder. "What do you think you're doing?"

"I have—"

"I don't care what you have. I'm through with you."

He pushes her to Rodrigo. "Take her away."

"She's dangerous," Borges says. "She just attacked me without the slightest provocation."

"Put her in handcuffs," Lowell shouts.

"Why don't you listen to what she has to say first?" Rodrigo asks, standing next to her.

"Do you want to go to prison?" Lowell shouts at Melody. "Why are you so set to get in my way and impede my work?"

"She's a lying terrorist!" Borges says. He stands and dusts off his clothes.

"She's a good girl," Walter shouts. "She's trying to get our instruments back."

"There's nothing wrong with my hearing," Lowell yells. "Everyone quiet down."

Ostinato takes Melody's side, saying in a reasonable tone that they should listen to her, since she called them.

"All right, Melody. You have one minute, but if you tell me one more half-truth, I'll throw you in the deepest darkest dungeon," Lowell says.

She points at Borges. "He has a suitcase full of money in the crate for Rio."

Lowell recalls that the maestro was the only one interested in getting his baggage back.

"It's the best way to send cash," Melody says, "in a crate separate from the instruments. No one would touch our baggage. It's the money he extorted from the entertainment companies to get us involved in the ceremony."

"She's violent and needs to be put away," Borges says.

Walter is already dialing Milton, telling the transport officer to find Borges' suitcase among the crates and bring it. Borges continues making illogical threats.

When Milton arrives with the suitcase, Borges protests. "You have absolutely no right to touch my belongings. I will not be treated like a criminal."

"Then you open it," Lowell says.

Milton places the black suitcase on a chair in front of Borges.

"Open it," Lowell directs.

Borges doesn't budge.

"We'll stay here until you do."

Borges still doesn't move.

Walter bursts forward, grabs a blunt weight used for propping open a door, and hits the small lock until he smashes it. As predicted, the case contains neat bundles of bills.

"As subtle as a samba dancer wiggling her bare hips in front of a line of Bulgarian Orthodox monks," Milton says.

"It's all legal." Borges holds his back even stiffer, his voice rising as he addresses Lowell. "Do you work for a pat on the back? I don't work for free either. You think that because I'm in the arts I should be donating my time for stale bread and cheap cigarettes? A CEO who makes millions gets his picture in *Forbes*, but a musician who makes a fraction of that is called corrupt."

"Did you also buy Brazilian beef futures?" Lowell asks.

Borges' face becomes aggressive. "Did Cage tell you that? I never trusted that man. Do you know what I'm doing with this honorarium that several companies gave me, legally? I'm building an orchestra and championing young musicians. Do you have any idea how much it costs to run an orchestra?

Do you? You have to become a businessman more than a musician. Already I sponsor a competition for young string players and support a music school in Brazil. The more money I make, the better for music. We have the lush melodies of *Cavalleria Rusticana* because someone sponsored a competition that Mascagni won."

"How much are you making off the ceremony?" Lowell asks.

"This performance will initiate a new way of paying artists. You have to fight for every cent. I refuse to be treated marginally by the music industry. I refuse to beg. Massachusetts makes more in sales tax on my recordings than I make in royalties. Most people download music for free. The trifling we make doesn't compare to other professions. Even rock musicians get a scant portion compared to record companies, producers, and Internet distributors. Do you know what it costs to record a disk?"

Lowell remains silent.

"The Bach *B-Minor* I produced last year cost $140,000. We'll consider it a major success if it breaks even. You can't record classical music in America or Western Europe, because it's too expensive. You can't record in a studio. And how much do we get?"

Again, Lowell lets Borges answer his own question.

"The best-paid classical conductor gets a piddling couple of million a year, even though he has recorded thirty albums. That's the top of the top. Everyone else struggles. Although eighty million Americans attended a classical concert last year, classical sales are only two percent of the market, mostly played by second-rate orchestras or mediocre disks sold to young lovers for candlelight dinners. I need money to record Brazilian composers. Yes, I'm being compensated for taking the BSO to Rio."

"You made a deal to use the BSO for the ceremony in exchange for a suitcase full of hundred-dollar bills," Lowell says.

"Then wouldn't it be really stupid of me to have any part in a plot to destroy the deal? It might be better to ask you, lieutenant, if you fabricate crime in order to keep your job."

"And if the concert doesn't happen, will you be compensated?"

"Only this," Borges says, shaking his hand at the briefcase to minimize the answer. "Cage made sure there's no kill fee."

"That's why the money had to come with us," Melody says. "It also shows that the robbers didn't know this or they would have kept the money when they hijacked the truck."

"It's good to keep people on edge," Lowell says. "Confident people hold their gluteal muscles too tight. Makes it hard to go number two."

"We'll make quality recordings in Brazil without the overhead," Borges says. "And who benefits? Musicians and composers. Are you going to throw us all in jail?"

"Was your brother providing information about FAS?"

"You believe his illusions. Dufay had his own informant." Borges inhales, his face enraged. "Do you have any other questions?"

Lowell shakes his head. Borges pivots on his heel to leave but is stopped by Sergeant Ostinato's arm.

"You got it all wrong," Milton says. "Music isn't money. It's love. It opens with quick lust, then transforms to slow, gentle strokes, whipping up into climax. You close your eyes in satisfaction, and you don't have to deal with a wet blob in the middle of the bed."

"What else do you know?" Lowell asks Melody.

"The heist was the last thing Borges wanted. His goal is to build a musical organization that rivals Boston. He wants to spread music, and he has the misguided notion that money can do that."

"You know something about Guru as well?"

"Someone used the poor fellow via Gustav, but for what end?" Melody scrunched her face. "We've been going on the assumption that the robbers were also the body snatchers and the bombers. That's probably not true."

"The bombing and body snatching, like the heist, had to have been planned beforehand," Lowell says.

Melody pauses, as if putting her bow on her lap. She hears slow, uniform beats. "The first body in New Hampshire was planned. They knew you would discover it wasn't Milton, which would make us think that someone knew about someone else's plot."

"Enter the mole," Lowell says.

"But Dufay's mole didn't know anything," Melody says. "Dufay was so ignorant he left town. The New Hampshire body was a delay tactic, a body thrown in the middle of nowhere. They only had to delay for a day, so a two-hour ruse helps. The bomb was the same—a delay tactic, a hoax. The robbers didn't have delay in mind—they left the truck in front of a police station."

Sergeant Ostinato ignores his high school friendship with Lowell again. "Sir, besides concluding that FAS was not involved in the robbery, we have to conclude that neither was the conductor."

"You're doing a wonderful job, Al," Lowell says. "I already told your chief. If we get a tip, I'll make sure you're on the team that picks up the instruments."

Ostinato stands at attention next to Rodrigo.

Lowell turns to Borges. "Taking this much money out of the country without declaring it is illegal. The bribe you got is underhanded. You'll have to sort this out with a judge."

He directs Rodrigo to send the maestro to the police station. Then he turns to Melody. "You're pretty handy in battle."

"It was easy. Borges was off balance and out of control."

Lowell looks at Walter. "Tell me what you got out of the government."

"They were ready to pay the bills."

"Is that all?"

"More or less." Walter's shoulders are as evasive as his words.

"What about remodeling the hall?"

Walter takes a moment to collect his thoughts. "We were under pressure to cancel the trip. The vice president was paranoid that we would cave in. His party would lose massive financial support if this deal didn't go through. I saw that we were in a strong position and bargained. The more pressure we got, the more generous his budget. I could have gotten more out of them, but Louis, the big boss, told me to quit."

"At two and a half million?"

"We wrote up a National Endowment for the Arts grant, which I was sure we'd get."

"Did his generosity had something to do with your decision to go?"

"No one had to give us money," Walter says. "The trustees were set on the trip, but it was a nice perk."

"So you get a grant, and no one knows it's a bribe. Why didn't you tell me before?" Lowell asks. "Let me guess: It wasn't relevant."

"What's relevant is that we were robbed. We didn't get anywhere near what Borges got."

"Would you get the grant if you didn't go?"

"You think a politician would help us if we crossed him? Two and a half million is a handsome sum, but in our overall budget, it wouldn't make us do something we didn't want."

Deceptive Cadence: A series of chords that anticipates resolution on the tonic chord, but the tonic never comes, and resolution remains elusive.

Finale

Lowell and Melody stroll up and down the silent hallways of Symphony Hall, Lowell's hands behind his back. Despite the cold and the hour, clusters of supporters remain on the street.

At 9:30 p.m., Mrs. Schutz instructs the baby-faced police sergeant to let in the last audience. The hallways become crowded with people scrambling to find a good seat, even though there will be little to see. Lowell and Melody watch them pour in, and then they flow with the crowd, walking up to the third floor. They enter a door leading to one of Symphony Hall's two curved balconies that run along the sides of the hall, each side containing three rows of seats.

The only remaining seats are located in the cramped third row. Lowell has to keep his legs in the aisle in front of the leather-upholstered door. He wonders if the musicians play better during galas when seats cost several hundred dollars. What is the financial value of a concert? Do money and music mix? How much does Melody—or other musicians—care about the money coming in the door?

Eduardo faces the audience from the middle of the stage, where the conductor stands. He talks about music composition, a lecture that is at times practical, at times incorporating the General Theory of Relativity. The audience follows enthusiastically, laughing at all the right moments.

"Composers like to talk about music," Melody whispers

to Lowell, "while conductors just get up and perform."

Lowell finds himself being interested in the lecture—not the lecture exactly but rather the excitement in the hall. Eduardo falls into his favorite topic, music united with the cosmos, then talks about how composers take two- or three-measure themes and create variations. He plays brief examples on the piano from the Berlioz *Symphony Fantastique,* whose remarkable last movement, "Dream of the Witches' Sabbath," is studied by composition students, a lecture that the lieutenant follows easily.

Lowell notices the gilded proscenium stage, one solitary name dominating the top: Beethoven. At the back of the stage stands an array of gold pipes of the 4,200-pipe organ, some pipes the size of a pen, others as high as a three-story building, all powered by a compressor in the basement. The organ's console can be placed anywhere and plugged in as easily as plugging a printer into a laptop.

He looks at the Greco-Roman statues positioned around the top of the hall, copies of marble statues from antiquity that share a connection with music or art. The hall contains little pomp and circumstance. He glances around the large, open auditorium and tries to imagine sounds bouncing from wall to wall, which creates the resonance for which the hall is famous. Is that what it's all about, satisfying the sense of hearing? Is it all about sound?

"Sound can't exist in a vacuum," Eduardo says. "Only in a few tiny corners of the universe, like our planet, can sound travel through our atmosphere and into our souls, but the entire universe is afire with vibration, rhythm, harmony."

Melody focuses on Eduardo and thinks about their relationship. She hears the solo in her head, variations on four notes, beginning without a rhythm, her fingers moving rapidly up and down the neck, her bow jumping strings, and then comes the underlying tempo—quick-quick, slow-slow.

Her four notes have simplified.

When the half-hour talk ends and the audience applauds, people pick up their coats and leave, going back out into the cold darkness. Melody and Lowell work their way down to the ground floor, walking together as if they are old friends. Several people remain standing at the foot of the stage talking up to Eduardo. One by one, they, too, leave, and the hall becomes silent except for Eduardo putting away the sound cart he used for giving talks.

Lowell, standing in the middle of the hall, calls to him. "It's remarkable that you gave such a speech with only a couple of pages of notes. You must really know your stuff."

Eduardo looks out at him. "I've given eight talks and participated in three performances. Music should never be an elective."

"May I ask you something?" Lowell says. "What's the difference between music and noise?"

"A question that every man has to answer for himself."

"Very Zen. Walter has definite ideas about this."

Melody leans on the back door, her fingers playing on her wrist.

"Ask if there's any difference between music and silence," Eduardo says.

"I need a new set of ears to listen to silence."

"It's not ears. Deaf people like Beethoven and Fauré were sensitive to music. Music is moving, vibrating, being alive. It encompasses much more than our ears. Look how emotional people get about a song and a singer."

"My guess is that music goes straight up to the hippocampus and makes the liver produce cortisol. Nothing affects the soul without also affecting the gut."

"Most composers write for people. They compose a flute sonata for a certain flutist or write an aria for a particular soprano. Composers dedicate a piece to a loved one, a patron, a soldier killed in war. Music is associated with human experience. Leoncavallo's father was a judge on a case of a jealous actor killing an unfaithful wife, which became the inspiration for the opera *Pagliacci*. Shakespeare inspired two thousand compositions."

Lowell walks upstairs to Walter's office, which, during the past fourteen hours, has become his home. He opens the door and stands in the doorway, seeing Walter sitting thoughtfully, a tape of a concert playing quietly on a sound system.

"How much did Beethoven pay?" Lowell asks.

Walter stares at him blankly.

"To have his name on the plaque in the middle of the stage? It's the only name up there. Must have cost a fortune."

"Yes, he gave a lot," Walter says. "The money others give pales in comparison."

"You could have called this Beethoven Hall."

"Beats the hell out of Disney Hall."

Despite the emotional exhaustion and failure to solve the case, the two men talk in a comfortable tone, so different from when they first met.

"Is it true what China said, that most musicians don't know much about the world outside music?" Lowell asks.

"Musicians aren't any different than other people. Some don't vote or know about the outside world, while others are political activists. Some collect trains or dolls while others are football fanatics. Some sing in church; others are atheists. There's no such thing as a typical musician."

"You can usually find trends," Lowell says. "What kind of people become classical musicians?"

"When the BSO started, most musicians came from Europe. The first conductors and principals were French. A hundred years ago, the music schools had mostly German or Italian students. Fifty years ago they were heavily Jewish. The fact that Jews are dedicated to music is a reason they're so successful. Now the music schools are more Asian, and it doesn't take much imagination to see Asians as our future leaders."

Walter relaxes his shoulders and continues. "We're all mixed up. Christian melodies are based on Turks and other heathens. White Americans use black gospel tunes. Proper music is founded in earthy folk songs of almost every country, and half our instruments originated in the Middle East. Max Bruch, who wrote *Kol Nidrei* and other Jewish songs, was Protestant, while the popular Christian spiritual 'Spirit in the Sky' was written by the Jew Norman Greenbaum."

"Musicians die young?"

"Toscanini conducted the première performances of *Pagliacci* in 1892 and *La Bohème* in 1896, and people my age remember him leading the NBC Orchestra in the fifties. Pablo Casals played his cello in the White House for William McKinley and Teddy Roosevelt, and then he came back and played for JFK."

Lowell walks around the small office. The taped concert ends, and the audience applauds.

"Women weren't allowed in orchestras," Walter says. "except for the harp. Even gay guys don't play the harp. In 1960 the BSO had three female musicians. Now a majority of conservatory students are female."

Lowell points to the tape player. "When was this recorded?"

Walter responds with an enthusiasm that Lowell has not observed in him thus far. "It was a fantastic concert featuring the Poulenc *Stabat Mater*. Our music director conducted, and everyone was in top form, a magical night." Walter's face is bright, even on the verge of happiness. "I remember it perfectly, but I've never listened to it again. I went down to the archives and dug it out. We have one of the largest music libraries and archives in the world."

"It's not been a bad thing," Lowell says, as if thinking out loud.

"What's that?"

"The heist. The bodies. The bomb." He walks around

the room. "It hasn't been a bad thing."

Walter raises his eyebrows.

"It's been wonderful all around," Lowell says. "Profitable, to use an economist's language."

"What are you talking about?"

"Art and music have become the talk of the town—and the country."

"The instruments—"

"The robbers practically assured us that the instruments are safe. You said they can't do anything with them."

"They'll want a ransom," Walter says.

"If they took a suitcase of hundred dollar bills, they wouldn't be able to spend it without us eventually tracking them down. I don't think they'll ask for a wire transfer."

"What are you getting at? We're missing the Rio engagement."

"So far you've missed a concert that you said wasn't important. The majority of players wouldn't mind if the government's deal was scrapped, as long as they get their instruments back."

"FAS got all this good publicity. Even if they go ahead with the ceremony, the government's deal is already compromised."

"Exactly," Lowell says. "FAS is the big winner, since their case got world attention, but the government also wins in a roundabout way, since it strengthens the opposition. Governments run better when they have to account for their actions. A strong opposition creates a strong government."

Walter stands. "But FAS robbed us."

"Maybe, but if they don't return the instruments soon, people will turn against them. Let's say they need to show their power. If they return the instruments unharmed, they'll be heroes, gentlemanly bandits, romantic idols."

"So, why haven't we been able to track them down? Why does no one know them?"

"Yes, FAS has made a big hit, but you're conveniently forgetting another factor—classical music has also received a boost, concerts streaming over the web and onto national television. Look around, it's been wonderful for classical music. And for the BSO, well, you couldn't buy this kind of publicity, could you, Walter?"

The strain of the day shows on Walter's face and in his walk. After returning from the airport in the morning, he hasn't seen the light of day. He ambles down the stairs and into the tuning room, his manner distracted, his face as absent as those who finish the Boston Marathon.

Several musicians in the room stand when he enters. Walter touches a couple of people on the shoulder, then walks slowly to the center of the room. Concertmaster Goldberg stands, and Walter takes her hand in both of his.

"It's ten fifteen," Walter says to the room. "I never knew how exhausting it is to sit around and wait. Let's go home now. There's nothing any of us can do. The police will work through the night, so let's get some sleep and see what tomorrow has in store for us."

The musicians react slowly, many with downcast faces and slumped shoulders.

"How's the investigation going?" one man asks.

Walter is about to say, "We're following several clues," but he stops himself. "Honestly, we're not doing too well. Every road we follow comes to a dead end. We've come to a double bar. We're now at the mercy of the Master Composer." He glances around the room. "I'm sorry, I let you down. But we're all in this together, and you know that I'll stay with it until we get a break in the case. I'm sorry. Your Moses has failed you."

"Most of us were dead against being used," someone

says. "Now we only want our instruments back."

No one moves for a moment. Then Tito steps forward. "I, too, am sorry if I committed any impropriety by talking with FAS about the BSO. I never put politics above the orchestra or compromised us, but on reflection I should have kept my strong feelings out of this and abstained."

The other musicians nod acceptance. Concertmaster Goldberg works her way to the door, and one by one, the others follow her.

Melody and her friends decide to return to her apartment. She says she'll follow them, but first she seeks out Guru and tells him that he has done an excellent job and should go home.

"That guy they beat up and left on Newbury Street—he was the boyfriend of that American Indian who played here today," Guru says.

"Sky Horizon?"

"I know who gave the robbers information."

"So do I," Melody says. "I did."

Melody runs around Symphony Hall, finding Cage backstage. She takes him into one of the insulated basement practice rooms and closes the door.

"Guru talked to you via that loafer informant Gustav who was beat up," she says. "Neither of them talked to Homeland Security."

"How much information could those two have?"

"Guru waited for us to come back from the airport. I told him about Milton and our baggage, because I was turning in my cello this morning. Gustav stole cars for the hijackers. He also became your mole. The robbers eventually discovered that he had betrayed them, so they punished him."

"Sounds like you have it all wrapped up."

"You couldn't involve yourself directly," Melody says.

"If Lowell's investigation uncovered that a government agency had a hand in the robbery, the press would have no mercy on them."

"Yes, you had no part in the robbery, and neither did FAS. You discovered that the truck would be hijacked, so you switched your position, unexpectedly speaking favorably for the arts agreement that you knew wouldn't happen."

"Why are you berating me?" Cage says, an aggressive edge to his voice. "I'm on your side. I want art and music to flourish, and so do you. We don't want to be bulldozed by cheap commercialism."

"We don't have to deceive people."

"Get real. The problem with musicians is that they still think they're the underclass, paid to entertain the upper class. Were you ready to sit aside and allow this catastrophe? Would you have the première of the New World Compositions turned into a soda commercial? Many in government announced they would resign if that agreement was adopted. I would, too. This is where we drew the line. A bunch of CEOs bribed and forced their way on the BSO, and we're supposed to be deaf, dumb, and mute? I did everything I could to stop this deal by words, but it wasn't enough."

"The bomb and the first body were your invention to slow down the investigation, the body thrown in New Hampshire to waste as much time as possible," Melody says. "You must have planted the bomb during this morning's activity. I happened to tell Guru that Milton would drive to New Hampshire after loading the instruments. Guru told Gustav, and Gustav told you. Gustav must have unscrewed the radio antenna so Milton couldn't hear the news. You arranged for a body to look like his."

"Big bearded guy, easy to mistake for a homeless vet."

"All you wanted was extra time, a ruse to distract the

police. You also encouraged Special Agent Dufay to concentrate on FAS and the other groups, not the baggage truck.
You made sure they didn't know about the plot. Neither did
anyone in FAS."

"We beat them at their own game. Now we can put
together a real treaty for artists."

"Anyone who ever talked to Walter would know that he
would never allow the orchestra to go to Rio without us having
our instruments. So, who did it? Who stole the instruments?"

"Open your eyes, Melody. We won a major victory by
stopping this deal. You'll see how fast the president raises the
position of Liaison for the Arts to a cabinet post. Then we'll
have some real funding for the arts."

When Mel enters her apartment, she finds her friends sitting
around her kitchen table. Their chatter is the deep penetrating
tempo of a *ciacona*.

Melody tells everyone about her conversation with
Cage. "He hitchhiked on someone's plan to steal our instruments by delaying the investigation. His plan worked, but he
won't tell me who robbed us." She looks at Tito. "I don't agree
with your theory that Walter had a hand in it."

"Me neither," China says. "Walter would never lift a
finger to hurt anyone, certainly not the BSO."

"That's right," Melody says. She sits, and Raja jumps on
her lap. "He opens himself much more to China and me than
to you guys. He's an autocrat, and maybe a Freudian would have
fun dissecting him. But you saw what he looked like back there.
He felt miserable about letting us down. He covers for all of us.
If we were going into battle, he would stand in front with his
arms outstretched to protect us. We're his life. I don't know
what he'll do when people don't need him anymore."

"Okay, I did imply that Walter had a hand in this," Tito

says. "I'm leery of the domineering type. Beethoven's dominance drove his nephew to attempt suicide."

"Beethoven was crazy," China says. "Walter is not."

"Maybe I unconsciously wanted Walter to do something big during his last season," Tito says. "But I knew it wasn't FAS, and I wasn't sure who else it could be."

"I also can't believe your idea that the government pulled off the robbery," Mel says. "It would be too risky for them. They've become more and more cunning. They manipulate the news and make black seem white. They might have done it if they were absolutely sure they could get away with it, but there would be too many people involved—people to plan the heist, supervise, carry it out. They would have had all their propaganda ready for the press. But they weren't ready. The feds left town thinking everything was fine. This came as a total shock to them."

"Dufay was a musician," China adds. "You never lose your reverence for instruments."

"It's also true that the government intended to humiliate FAS," Tito says. "Homeland Security's been all over them and hasn't found anything. Who could it be?"

"Lowell eliminated George as a suspect," Melody says.

"And Borges and the electricians and Milton," Felix says. "Who's left?"

"Let's make a pact," Tito suggests. Melody hears a *cabaletta,* a simple aria with a repeating rhythm. "No more guessing about the robbery. Let's save our energy for what we can work on and leave the cops to obsess over the rest."

Everyone agrees.

"We'll stay here and abuse Mel's hospitality," Felix says. He turns to Melody. "I promise I'll fill your fridge for all that we've eaten and drunk tonight."

"I haven't done this since college," China says, "sit around a kitchen table drinking wine and talking."

"If we had instruments, we'd whip them out and play

together," Felix says. "Actually, people across the country who don't know the difference between a cello and French horn have now seen an orchestra."

Melody looks up. "You know something?" The others look at her. "I'm completely ready to play."

Everyone bursts into applause, and Melody beams.

"I've heard you play *vivaci assai*," Tito says, "but this is the first time in a month I've heard you speak it."

China puts her arm around Melody, and even Eduardo breaks his policy about public affection and puts his arm around her as well.

"I found my voice," Mel says. "The sad music has left me, and my fingers are free." She holds up her hands and wiggles her fingers. "I don't know if it was the robbery or standing up to Borges. Maybe it doesn't matter if we don't go. Maybe it doesn't matter if I stay with the BSO. I can decide what to do. I wanted to dedicate the solo to my father so the world would see he is a good man. Maybe I'll have to do it quietly and directly."

Everyone offers their congratulations.

"I feel sorry for Guru," China says. "No one had to involve that innocent."

"It was the most exciting day of his life," Felix says. "He had a terrific time involved in the grand conspiracy. How often does anyone get to be in the center of a real police case? Actually, we'll never hear the end of it."

"We'll also have to see if the mayor agrees to fund music education," China says. "That would be a major victory."

Tito goes to Melody's vinyl collection. "Listen to this," he says, putting on the Otis Redding song "I've Been Loving You Too Long."

"You know what this is?" He pauses to let them listen. "Wagner. Chromatic progression in a crescendo. It's sex straight up."

Others take out their devices and put on examples of

musical associations, such as the link between African-American and European music.

"What's the most performed piece of any genre, rock, jazz, classical?" China asks. "*Messiah*. Why? People understand the words. If it wasn't for *Messiah* and *Nutcracker*, we'd have many more unemployed musicians and dancers."

"Can you imagine the royalties?" Tito says. "How many cell phones play 'Ode to Joy' or the 'Toreador' song from *Carmen*?"

Wisteria, who had been snoozing on the couch, enters the kitchen rubbing her eyes. Tito brings a chair for her.

"Before today," she says, "I thought classical music was a dying form. Perhaps another couple of generations, just like you see the Catholic Church imploding. Who attends Mass? The same people who attend classical concerts: old, middle-class white people. When this generation dies out, I thought, we'll start cutting the number of concerts, and the whole thing goes downhill from there."

"We're in a transition phase," Eduardo says. "We don't know the genre for our age. Opera is on the rise, and we have a tremendous number of trained composers and musicians. We see jazz, rock, and musicals incorporated into artistic music, and musical influences from other countries. It might be that the repertoire twenty years from now will be different, but popular music can't swallow us up. There will always be a desire for art."

Wisteria turns to Eduardo. "You know what? You're full of crap."

Eduardo starts to laugh, then Wisteria laughs, then the whole table shakes with laughter.

"Why do we listen to you?" Wisteria says.

"Don't tell my students," Eduardo says. "They're forced to listen to as much babble as I dish out."

"What you say seems interesting," Wisteria says, "but you can't put it into practice, so you're constantly letting yourself down."

"Being full of crap is one of the things I am," Eduardo says, "like Felix sweats solos."

China turns to Tito. "Dance?" Tito is not only a precise bassist but also an excellent dancer.

"We shouldn't," Melody says. "Not today."

After a moment to acknowledge Melody's reluctance, everyone stands spontaneously. Tito finds ballroom music on his phone and puts it through Melody's stereo. Eduardo puts away the dishes while Felix and China fold the table and move the chairs to create an open floor.

China closes her eyes, and he leads her around the kitchen step by step, Tito decisive and China willing and positive.

"Tito, everyone knows you're no good for a woman," Felix says, "but you're good with women."

When the music ends, China nods at Eduardo. "Why don't you dance with Mel?"

Eduardo stands. Melody wavers with a mixture of reluctance and modesty.

"When have you ever hesitated to dance?" China asks. "Put on a tango," she directs Tito. "Alexander Borodin died dancing."

Eduardo stands and takes Melody's hand to bring her to a standing position. China and Tito let them have the small floor.

"Your turn to tell us how to take a woman," Felix says to Eduardo.

The couple faces each other, Mel examining their two-year relationship.

Eduardo puts his arm around her. "The man takes control and makes the music live inside us. Music is expressed in choiceless movement, like the curvature of space-time. Every object goes into its designated motion."

"No intellect," Wisteria says. "Dance without sin, love without heartbreak."

"You guys move like you're oiled," Tito says. "I don't understand how a heady guy can move like that."

Eduardo smiles at Melody. "You're more sensitive to my lead now."

"Doesn't it seem wrong that we're here having a good time after being robbed of what we value most?" Melody asks.

The doorbell rings. The friends look at each other. Melody goes to answer, the others following her with their eyes. A police officer stands looking in.

"Are you Melody Cavatina?"

"Yes," she says, surprised.

"Lieutenant Lowell would like to see you. If you don't mind putting on your coat and coming with me."

"You just can't take her away," Tito declares.

"I didn't do anything," Melody says. She turns to look at the other musicians. "Really," she says with outstretched arms and an alarmed voice, "I didn't do anything."

"We'll all go with you," Eduardo says.

"No," Mel replies. "I'll go alone."

Fifteen hours and fifty minutes after the heist, Melody stands at Walter's office door. Lowell is alone inside, soda cups and fast-food containers scattered on the desk. He gestures her into the room.

Raja enters, too.

"How'd you get here so fast?" Mel asks the cat. "And in the building?"

He sniffs Lowell.

Lowell points her to the chair. Then he pulls another chair and sits opposite her so that his knees are outside hers, almost touching.

"Tell me about your relationship with Eduardo."

"We're often blind about our own relationships."

"I'm coming to that conclusion myself. Our eyes see outward. We can't see ourselves."

"Eduardo and I were together for a year and a half."

"Were you going to get married?"

The question shocks her slightly, but the late hour and her sorrow make her want to give a direct answer. "We never made plans. Sometimes he went into one of his 'creative periods.' That's what he called them, although he didn't put out a lot of work during those times."

"During his creative periods, he can be unsocial?"

"He would go off and think. I learned to live with it, I guess. He said that if you're in company, you have to talk, but if you're alone, you have to create."

"You're not seeing each other now, is that true?"

Melody hesitates. She shifts her knees back and forth, but Lowell has given her no room to cross her legs. "We're going through a period of reassessment."

"Who controls the relationship?"

"He does." The words roll off her tongue without thought. "I mean, well, I'm his inspiration."

"Does he hang out with revolutionary types?"

Melody keeps thinking about the last question. *Does he control the relationship?*

"Well, does he?"

She laughs nervously. "He only hangs out with revolutionary musicians."

"Revolutionary musicians?"

"It's how Eduardo's group thinks about music, pushing the edge, creating something new. Some of them played here today."

"How do they revolutionize?"

Talking about their relationship makes her nervous. "They get together and talk music, play music."

"Who are they? How many?"

"The composers and musicologists who initiated the New World Compositions. Some are also performers with day jobs. Some teach around here. Why don't you ask him?"

"We never interviewed him because he wasn't on the bus to the airport. He's not part of the BSO. Would it be right to call his group rebels?"

"You can say that about many artists." She moves her eyes from side to side to avoid saying something she'll regret later. "They care about their work and listen closely. You should hear them when we're listening to a new piece. Phrase by phrase, they'll pick out themes and shout out—that's Ravel, that's Grieg, that's *Traviata.*"

"What did you talk about after last night's concert?"

"What does that have to do with anything?"

"Mel, I'm on your side, working to get you to Rio so you can play for your father."

She looks up sharply at him.

Lowell nods. "Yes, I know about your father. He landed in Rio two hours ago with his friend the sheriff. Please, Mel, between you and me, what did you and Eduardo talk about?"

"Well, I told him that my solo was his best music. Everyone in the orchestra was wowed by it, and we were looking forward to the New World Compositions."

"What did he say?"

"That it would take time for the work to sink in."

Lowell raises his eyebrows. "Time to sink in? Is that how he said it?"

"Yeah, I guess. He handed me the score a month ago. Sometimes it takes a few listenings to understand a piece, but it was way outside what we think of as music."

Lowell leans close to her. His warm breath comes in gusts, touching her face. "You're playing his finest work, and it wouldn't be understood right away."

Melody feels worried. "You don't have to take my word

for it. Ask Walter. Eduardo and I spent time teaching under-privileged kids." She wiggles in her chair. "I don't understand your interest in us. We love music. The person who stole the instruments hates music."

"Hates the music deal."

"You're wrong," Melody says in a louder voice than she has been using. "Music is our life." Her face is flushed.

"Mel, I'm privileged to know about your mother."

Mel's face is both alarmed and sad. "I'll stand in front of the world and dedicate my solo to him and her. I needed someone to blame after my mother's death, and I concocted this wild story about him to avoid blaming myself. My mother never lit candles before. We didn't have candles in our church, only bright lights. I couldn't accept that it was my fault, so I blamed him. I've been freaked about playing solo ever since. That competition was the only time I played solo, and look what happened. He helped many others stop drinking, and he preached kindness and forgiveness."

Lowell puts his hand on her shoulder. "Go home and get some rest."

She stands. Lowell has shaken something loose about her relationship with Eduardo, another truth she is fighting against. Perhaps she reminds him of his own daughter.

"Don't you see?" she says. "You can't love music and hate life. You can't love life and hate music. They're insep-arable."

"Go home," Lowell says softly, "or you'll send my gastric acid down into my intestine and up into my esophagus."

"Between Eduardo and me, we can play a dozen instruments. We care for instruments."

She is about to say more, but the phone rings. They glance at the clock—11:30 p.m. They both turn to the desk and watch the apparatus ring again. Lowell strolls over and presses the speaker phone.

A computer-like voice speaks two sentences.

Melody and Lowell listen to the voice in two different ways. He listens to the words and writes three or four of them in the margin of his notebook while she listens to the tone. Even though it is a disguised voice passed through a voice distortion app, she recognizes the rhythm, tessitura, and syllabication. Where has she heard those qualities before?

"What?" he asks, studying her.

She doesn't answer.

"You'll face Jesus on the mountain in Rio," he says.

"You know what that statue is called? Christ the Redeemer."

Lowell looks down at Raja, who has taken a serious interest in Lowell's shoes. "You and I make a good pair. You're a cat person, and I'm a dog."

He goes to the door and shouts Walter's name with an exclamation mark. Walter's footsteps sound down the hallway, and he appears in the doorway.

"The robbers phoned again," Lowell says, an uncanny calmness in his voice. "They left the instruments in a vegetable warehouse in South Boston. They said they made their point."

Walter's cheek muscles go into spasm. His hands move in agitated excitement. He yells left and right, his roar filling the hall a second later.

"Mrs. Schutz! Mrs. Schutz!"

She darts into the hallway.

"Call all the musicians," Walter says. "Re-book that charter. Call our maestro and tell him that he has to sub for Borges to initiate the New World Compositions but not be part of that ceremony nonsense. He can study the score on the plane and have a rehearsal before the concert. Tell Milton to reload the truck."

He turns as if seeing Melody for the first time. "We'll be on our way to Brazil in the morning at 7:00 a.m. sharp. Everything will go as it was planned for today."

She is still trying to place that voice. She runs through

the voices of her friends, orchestra members, people in FAS. It isn't it. It's the voice of a quark.

"The guy disguised his voice and probably used a dropped cell phone," Lowell says. "We'll never trace him."

Like a flock of sparrows congregating on a single spruce in spring, within a half-hour, the musicians converge on Symphony Hall, scrambling for their instruments as fast as Milton can distribute them. They hug them, take them out of their cases and kiss them, hoisting them triumphantly in the air. Several women cry with relief. Milton cries with them.

"Would you like to come to my apartment?" Melody asks Eduardo.

He winks and slips his arm around her. "Time for the coda. Saturn is high in the sky again."

Despite the cold that once again covers the city, Melody walks home with her wool hat in her hand and her gloves in her pocket, a waxing gibbous moon in a clear sky guiding the way, Eduardo walking silently next to her, Raja following behind. She hears Eduardo breathing, hears the hiss of the street lights, the quiet introversion of the Sunday night city.

They enter her apartment and hear Wisteria in a deep snore on Melody's bed. Eduardo turns on WBUR radio news.

Melody stands in the middle of the living room watching him. Raja jumps up to his high perch and looks down on them.

"You have to fly with us tomorrow. There isn't a later flight."

Eduardo nods. She stands a few feet from him. She takes off her black sweater and throws it aside. She takes off her cotton blouse and throws that, too.

She turns to her side and gives him the profile of her

breasts. He steps forward and cups his hands on her bra.

"It's been a long time," he says. He takes off his shirt.

She lays him down on the couch, the same burgundy couch on which they made love on their first date. She climbs on top of him, her hands pressing down on his shoulders.

"It was you, wasn't it? You and your group."

He remains silent. She stays straddling him with her hands pressing his shoulders.

"I should have figured it out when I saw your panicked face as we heard about Milton's supposed murder. You were aloof before that, but when you heard murder, you knew that someone butted into your plot, but you didn't know who. Then the bomb shocked you senseless. Your careful plan went terribly wrong. You, who used toy guns, now had a murder and a bomb. That's why you wanted *me* to investigate. You wanted to find out who knew about your plot."

He smiles. "How did you come to that conclusion?"

"I recognized the voice of Chadwick, the musician who played here, when he phoned Lowell."

"He believed that a children's center shouldn't have toy guns. He also knew how to subdue disturbed people without hurting them, a useful skill for handling the truck drivers."

"You found out that they didn't want to frame you— they wanted to impede the investigation. Who would want to do that? Someone who didn't want the arts agreement."

"We planned it months ago as a prank, guerrilla theater, a publicity stunt for the New World Compositions, a replay of robbing the Indians. Reporters got it right away. When the government turned our concert into this anti-art event, we got serious. We won't allow ourselves and the BSO to be used like that."

"There was an informant in your midst—Sky's boyfriend."

"Sky got him to steal cars. When she learned that he double crossed us, she got her friends to take care of him."

Eduardo wiggles to get up, but Melody remains solidly on top of him.

"I told Guru about Milton and the baggage truck. He told Sky's boyfriend, who, in turn, told Cage. Cute. You used me, didn't you? I was also your informant by answering innocent-sounding emails. You came last night to see if there was a change in plan."

"I came to talk to you."

"You also figured that Walter would want you to speak to people. You had lecture notes ready."

"I thought I was being helpful," he says, a *capricious andante*.

"Sky was ready with her piece. So were Chadwick and the others. Isn't that right? Did she drive the truck?"

"The main job of a beekeeper is driving truckloads of hives from farm to farm."

"You engineered your group to play before a nationwide audience. You're a bunch of revolutionaries."

"That's the highest compliment you can give any composer." Eduardo's tone is serious *ma non troppo*.

"I've been thinking about our relationship all day. I'm only a stepping stone for you. Do you know what I've gone through?"

"Yes, I do." He tries again to move but she keeps his shoulders pinned. "You've changed from an insecure cellist to a confident woman. Now you're speaking without an instrument. Every critic is waiting to see you play with the power and delicacy that you're capable of."

"So, instead of slapping you, I should congratulate you?"

"Congratulate yourself. Had you gone to Rio this morning, you would have blown it, sure as Venus in the night sky."

"Don't be so cocky. I can turn you in."

Melody and Eduardo turn toward the radio, where

Mayor Bond's victorious voice begins a press conference.

"I am elated to inform you that we've cracked the case," he says, followed by a wave of cheers and applause.

Shouts of jubilation from outside bring their attention toward the window facing the street. Then they look back at each other, Melody still holding him firm.

"I figure you were the one with the dark coat who signaled when the baggage truck left. If a policeman asked what you were doing, you could say you were making sure everything was going fine. Did you see me board the bus?"

Eduardo doesn't respond.

They both listen as Mayor Bond says he's taking the opportunity to invest twenty-five million in music education.

"Mayor Bond comes across as a lightweight, but he's a wise man," Mel says.

Eduardo puts his hand on hers. "Are you going to turn me in?"

"If I turn you in, you'll become a celebrity. No jury would send you to jail. Directors will beg you for movie rights. Maybe John Adams will write an opera of the episode. Besides, Lowell already figured it out. He knew you'd phone."

Melody gets off him and stands. "I knew I couldn't trust you, because I couldn't confide in you. Eduardo, I can't we with you anymore. Love is trust."

Eduardo doesn't move. "You want to end a relationship with me?"

"Yes, Eduardo. You must leave. I've been thinking about it all day. We have a terrific musical relationship. Period. You need to go out and get to the edge of despair. Shout, scream, feel. Go out and learn to love."

"We've done so much together."

"I gave myself to you, but now I found myself. You have yet to do that. Now I must fly."

Eduardo still doesn't move.

"You'll have your career, and I'll have mine. I will

always love and respect you, but we can't be a couple because we can never be equal or trusting." She opens the front door and stands by it. "I have a plane to catch early in the morning and a concerto to play, and I want to eat Jell-O before I go to bed."

She watches him dress. He doesn't look at her. He puts on his coat and walks to the door. She takes off her necklace with Eduardo's ring and gives it to him. They look at each other.

"Thank you for the beautiful solo," she says. "I'll play it in front of the world and show what a creative composer you are. And I'll atone for a decade of blame."

She watches him leave, then shuts the door with her foot and leans back against it, thinking of Lowell and laughing. He told her that he has to get up early to look after his grandson. He has found someone who will listen to his theory about the chemical interaction between the pancreas and the spleen.

She glances up at Raja. "Let the world listen to my Carletti. I know it will be grand."

On the radio Mayor Bond says, "Classical music is reborn in Boston, and I'll be there."

Melody hears in her head the triumphal end of Beethoven's *Ninth*:

> *Joy, Daughter of Elysium,*
> *Joy, Beautiful Spark of Divinity.*